Boxed In

Before we reached the landing, Holmes had one of my arms in his steely grasp, and his lips were close to my ear.

"Get your hand gun, old fellow, and tiptoe back down this way. Position yourself by the door and watch that box like a hawk. There's something in there, Watson, something alive. I'll duck round by the front stairs to the entrance door, which is not locked. When you spot it opening, you'll know I'm in place and we'll have whatever is in that Trojan horse bottled up."

Like a dark shadow Holmes was gone, and my heart was pounding as I made all speed to secure the Webley from my bedroom and inch my way back down the stairs to my station. I was in a bit of a blue funk when I took position by the half-opened door and peered into our sitting room. Somehow the thought of a great Anaconda snake slithering out of the strange box kept coming to my mind . . .

Also by Frank Thomas:

Sherlock Holmes and the Golden Bird

SHERLOCK HOLMES

AND
THE SACRED SWORD

by Frank Thomas

Adapted from
the memoirs of
John H. Watson, M.D.

PINNACLE BOOKS   LOS ANGELES

SHERLOCK HOLMES AND THE SACRED SWORD

Copyright © 1980 by Frank Thomas

An original Pinnacle Books edition, published for the first time anywhere.

First printing, September 1980

ISBN: 0-523-41013-1

Cover illustration by Jacques Devaud

Printed in the United States of America

PINNACLE BOOKS, INC.
2029 Century Park East
Los Angeles, California 90067

Contents

Preface

That Sherlock Holmes was sans peer as regards the fine art of deduction is uncontested. That his exploits sparked the halcyon days of the late-Victorian period with wonder and excitement is universally accepted. But where, pray tell, would readers be were it not for that staunch and loyal man of medicine John H. Watson, M.D.? It was his eye for detail and his facile pen that gave us the adventures of that most unusual individual, Sherlock Holmes. Without Watson, Holmes would be but a dim legend, if indeed that.

The Doctor's passing severed that final living link with those fascinating years during which his friend reigned supreme and criminals cringed at the mention of his name. But Watson left his words, thank heaven.

Here's a toast to that gentle and patient man who so enriched his generation of readers and all those that followed: To Watson, noble benefactor of both the science of criminology throughout the world, and fascinated readers everywhere.

And one last note: I am grateful to have been on the spot that harrowing night during the London Blitz when Cox & Company, banking firm of Charing Cross, was bombed out of existence. For it was then that the famous dispatch box containing the priceless unpublished cases came into my hands.

Now . . . back to the days of derring-do and deduction too.

Back to the mists and moonlight where it is always 1895.

—Frank Thomas
Los Angeles, 1980

Acknowledgments

In transferring Doctor Watson's word to the printed page, the author benefited from the assistance and encouragement of that foremost Holmes scholar and lecturer, John Bennett Shaw of Santa Fe, New Mexico. And Professor L. L. Aaronson, Institute of Romance Languages, checked the language of the period.

Elsie Probasco provided superior research, and Mona and Frank proofed copy and made workable suggestions. Thank you Mother and Dad.

Sherlock Holmes
and the Sacred Sword

Chapter One

The Dying Man

It was the evening of one of those rare days when there was an aura of peace at 221B Baker Street. Sherlock Holmes, with no case of importance at the moment, was seated at the desk, pipe in mouth, affixing clippings in one of his great file volumes. The precipitation that had manifested itself with pugnacious persistence during the afternoon showed no signs of abating. Globules of moisture were marching earthward in endless, serried ranks to be whisked from their vertical descent by gusts of north wind and fired against our windows like tiny pellets from a massed battery of celestial air guns.

Holmes, like all true artists, was highly susceptible to moods and influenced by his surroundings. I anticipated that the inclemency would foster one of his dark periods, but his manner had been singularly cheerful during dinner. True, he had remarked somewhat peevishly that the criminal classes had displayed a deplorable lack of invention of late, but this was a familiar complaint uttered more from habit than conviction. To believe him would be to consider that crime was on the wane, an obviously false contention when one considered the two casebooks already filled with Holmes's exploits of the past twelve months.

I was occupied with the recording of certain of Holmes's doings—before, as he once said, "they become churned by the undertow of time." I had just realized that some notes I required were in my bedstand upstairs when I heard the sound that my subconscious had been waiting for. The paste-pot was shoved aside, the file volume was closed, and Holmes was on his feet. Restless, of course. His footsteps crossed the room and there was the tap of his pipe against the mantel dislodging dottle from its bowl.

As I rose and crossed to the back stairs, I made a silent wager that within two minutes he would begin his nervous pacing of our quarters, his brain yearning for facts as other men hungered for food. He would become testy, resentful of the fact that the finest mind in England was without a puzzle in which to insert the probe of specialized knowledge. But then, I thought as I entered my bedchamber, we have been through this before. The wheels due to spin for genius seldom remain dormant for long. Events proved me right.

There was the ring of the ground-floor door and when I descended to our sitting room, Holmes was on the landing gazing down the seventeen steps leading to our first-floor chambers.

"Come up, man, by all means," he called down the stairwell. "Billy," he continued in a softer voice, "not a word of this to Mrs. Hudson."

I found this remark puzzling until a huge form appeared at our door. That in itself was not surprising since visitors to Baker Street came in all sizes, but this one was carrying another man in his arms. As he crossed to deposit his burden on our couch, I instinctively headed for my medical bag beside the cane rack. Billy, the page boy, was on the landing and he gave Holmes a look of understanding as he closed the door.

When the large man retreated from the couch to allow me to inspect the body on it, Holmes muttered, "Watson, this is Burlington Bertie, an acquaintance of mine."

I nodded in acknowledgment—and then my breath was dragged into my lungs, an involuntary reaction to a grimy shirt soaked with blood. Wound around the middle of the body was a white silk scarf, which I cut loose. There were three vicious knife wounds in the man's abdomen and chest. My stethoscope revealed that his heartbeat was so faint I had trouble finding it. I looked up at a grim-faced Holmes and the huge man beside him with that, alas, frequent complaint of my profession.

2

"The man is dying, and there is nothing I can do."

"Aye," mouthed Burlington Bertie. " 'Twas me thought 'e'd about had it."

As though to disprove my diagnosis, the body on the couch twitched slightly and from slack lips came a sound like an exhalation.

"Holmes . . ."

My friend was beside the body in a trice.

"Yes," he said, his steely eyes intent on the prostrate figure.

"They . . . they found it."

The words were barely audible and there was a froth of blood in the corners of his mouth. "Chu . . . it's Chu. . . ."

The colorless lips, stark against an ebony black face, tried to form more words, but the effort was too much. Suddenly the face fell to one side and the features sagged. His eyes had been closed tight as though screwed against pain, but now they opened as a final signal that the end had come.

My hands moved automatically, returning instruments to my valise. Then I gently closed those staring eyes, as inanimate now as two agate marbles.

In deference to a departed soul, there was a lengthy silence broken only by the somewhat stentorian breathing of Bertie standing alongside the whipcord body of my friend. I used pieces of the long silk sash to clean up the blood around the wounds in the corpse and then rose to my feet with a sigh.

" 'E went out like a man," said Burlington Bertie to no one in particular.

"Best tell us about it."

Holmes's eyes found mine, and after depositing the blood-stained silk in our wastebasket, I made for the tantalus and gasogene.

" 'Ow 'bout 'im?" A grimy thumb indicated the body.

"He's not going anywhere." Holmes crossed to the mantel and extracted shag from the toe of the famous Persian slipper. "Where did it happen?"

"East Hindian Docks, Guv. I was amblin' along mindin' me business loik always, but I ain't never been deaf.

3

There's this rumpus and some shouts and then, through the rine, I sees this cove battlin' with three boyos 'oo is definitely tryin' to do 'im in. The odds looks a little rum and while I'm tellin' meself to keep outa trouble, this 'un 'ere, the Negro, fetches one rascal a sharp crack and 'e comes stumblin' back agin me. 'E turns, 'e does, and I sees a flash of metal, so I coshed 'im alongside the ear and 'e staggers back off the end of the dock and there's a splash. Another one of these 'ere blokes turns on me and some'ow me foot gets tangled up wiv 'is and 'e goes down. I figgers 'e best stay there and I gives 'im a clip wiv me boot and 'e's quiet like. Well, by now I'm kinda gettin' me steam up but the Negro, 'e swings the third boyo in a sorta arm lock and then lets go of 'im and 'e flies across the dock and goes off the side. But there's no splash, just a kinda soggy sound like a glob of suet bein' thrown against a wall. 'E got mixed up with the pilings, you see, so it's not to worry 'bout 'im. But this 'ere Negro, 'e ain't in such good shape as I can readily see, so I pulls off my nuck——"

"Nuck?" I regretted my involuntary question as I handed Bertie a large glass. He did not choose to answer but thanked me with a wide smile that disclosed perfectly formed teeth, startlingly white against his grimy, stubbled skin. As he drained half the tumbler, Holmes filled the conversational void.

"The silk scarf around the man's body was Bertie's, my good Watson. A tool of the trade, one might say."

"Now, Mr. 'Olmes, yew knows I've been straight since you give me that break a mite back."

"We'll not argue the point now," replied the sleuth. Despite the situation of the moment, there was a fleeting spark of humor in his clear, piercing eyes. "What happened then?"

Holmes accepted a glass from me, and with a look at the body on the couch, we all drank a toast. Out of common courtesy I was forced to retrieve Burlington Bertie's glass for a refill, listening intently as I did so.

"Well, Guv, 'e was sore 'urt but 'e manages to say your nyme . . . *Olmes* 'e said loik it's the most important fing in the bleedin' world. So I says I knows yer and 'e slips me a five-pound note and says there's another one iffen I take 'im to yer. Well, I figgers I gotta do sumpin' wiv 'im and 'sides, maybe Doctor Watson 'ere can patch 'im up. So I gets 'im to an 'ansom and 'ere we is."

"He said nothing else on the trip here?"

Burlington Bertie shook his head. " 'Twas all 'e could do to breathe, Guv. Coupla times I figgers I'd be deliverin' a bleedin' cawpse! I didn't miss by much, at that."

Holmes thought for a moment, then his features sharpened with decision. "All right, Bertie, I'm interested in the men on the dock. The assailants. One went into the water, you say."

"We can forget 'bout 'im, is me thinkin'. 'E'll surface in the Thames estuary iffen I reads the currents right. The other ain't no better. They'll 'ave to pry 'im off that pilin' and that's a fack."

"Then it is the third man." Holmes crossed to the desk, opening the cash drawer and extracting a bill. "Here is the other fiver you were promised. Now get back to the docks. The last of the assailants may still be there, and I want to know who he is and, especially, who he works for. It's worth—"

"Never mind, Mr. 'Olmes," Bertie's bull neck swiveled and he looked for a long moment towards the couch. "Whoever that cove was, 'e put up a good fight. I figgers I owes 'im somethin'. I'll try and snare that third bird for yer, and hits on the 'ouse."

The burly man made as though to depart but was arrested by a gesture from Holmes. The sleuth took a piece of the newspaper from the end table and wrapped it around the remnants of the silk scarf, which he retrieved from the wastebasket.

"Take this with you, Bertie, and dump it somewhere. For all concerned, I think it is best that you forget this incident. What about the hansom driver?"

" 'E's waitin', Guv. 'Tis me sister's fella, and 'e owes me. Mum's the word."

The stairs creaked in protest at the weight of Burlington Bertie as he descended. Another of those unusual types that I encountered through my association with the world's only consulting detective. As Holmes crossed towards the

5

couch, I heard the front door being shut and bolts going home as Billy secured our outer portal.

My friend was hunched down by the body, his eyes surveying the kinky hair, the ebony skin, and the tall and muscular body.

"Who is it, Holmes?" I inquired.

"Haven't the faintest idea."

"But he asked for you by name."

Holmes shook his head. His thin fingers extracted a seaman's wallet from the inside pocket of the man's coat with the gentle touch of a pickpocket. Opening it, he studied a passport for a brief moment and then replaced the wallet where he had found it.

"The name means nothing to me, Watson. However, the papers could be forged. There's a lot of that going on now."

Holmes's eyes seemed to attack the dead face like twin scalpels, searching for some indication, some identity clue perhaps.

"A Nubian, I would say. Possibly a Wahhabi, but I don't think so. From the Sudan, no doubt."

His fingers touched the head gently and then inspected the hairline, which was low on the forehead.

"Now this is interesting," he stated almost to himself.

Suddenly he seized the man's hands, holding them palms down, staring intently at the nails. He rose, crossed to the mantel, and seized the clasp knife that was thrust through unanswered correspondence. Allowing letters to spill on the floor, he returned to the corpse and, it seemed to me, began to scrape at the nail of one finger. I was momentarily horrified, but then that lean face turned towards me and there was the half-smile of triumph on his lips.

"I knew all was not as it seemed," he said.

Flinging the knife to the floor, Holmes crossed to the door, which he opened as I watched in silent amazement. Before he could call, our loyal page boy appeared.

"Billy," said Holmes in his clipped manner, always so evident when he was hot on the scent, "I want you to secure a carriage and go immediately to the Diogenes Club. Tell Mr. Mycroft Holmes to come immediately. Speak only to him. If he is not there, do not leave a message.

6

Then hasten to Scotland Yard and find Inspector Alec MacDonald. He is an habitually late worker and will probably still be there. Impress upon him the importance of coming back here with you." He slipped the lad some coins. "You understand?"

Billy's impish face was aglow. "Right on, sir." Then he was gone.

Holmes closed our door with satisfaction. He regarded the body on the couch for a brief moment and then surveyed me with his slow smile.

"A bit puzzled, ol' chap?"

"To say the least. What has your brother to do with this?"

"Everything. Burlington Bertie acted in good faith. The man said 'Holmes,' and he brought him here. The corpse is but recently from Egypt. His passport told me that, and in appearance he is of the Sudan. You see, Bertie brought him to the wrong Holmes. The dead man wanted Mycroft all along."

Chapter Two

The Revelations of Mycroft

My mouth was agape, not strange for anyone associated with the great detective, and I tried to sort out some sense from the events that had descended upon us and the partial revelations to which I was now privy. Standing like a block of wood and feeling the dullard indeed, it was frustrating to view my friend, whose movements were like quicksilver. The languid theorist of Baker Street was no more; in his stead was the man of action, his splendid mind churning with possibilities, with fascinating questions that teased and provoked his completely unique talents for answers. He disappeared up the back stairs and before I could frame a question as to what was going on, he was with me again, a bed sheet in hand.

"Here, Watson, we'd best cover the inanimate object that was so recently a man. A visitor is not beyond the realm of possibility, and an unknown corpse on our couch would excite inquiry from even the ultrasophisticated."

As I aided him in arranging the starched and pristine white over the dark body, it crossed my mind that the sheet, like a tent half-raised, would provoke speculation as well. However, Holmes had developed misdirection and half-truths to a fine art. Nevertheless, I ventured a thought if only to make my presence felt.

"Could we not remove the body to a bedroom?"

" 'Twould induce a shock in Inspector Alec MacDonald from which he might never recover. The corpse breathed its last right here, and here it must remain until the ponderous sinews of the law assume lugubrious movement." Holmes paused to cock an eye at me. "A correction, ol' chap. The presence of my brother could well be a signal for a departure from the norm. Mycroft positively exudes an aura of dark and mysterious doings."

"I still don't see how he—"

"Nor do I. Though I have spotted a glimmer of light. If Billy is sufficiently persuasive, my brother should arrive in advance of our friend from Scotland Yard, which may be of aid in resolving the mechanics of this matter."

This went completely over my head, but there was one point I could comment on, and a long overdue thought at that.

"Really, Holmes, your use of that child Billy borders on the shameful. His apparent innocence could wheedle a haunch of venison from a hungry lion, whereas in truth he is more knowledgeable of the world and its foibles than one twice his age."

"And a good thing. There is an adage among circus people relative to that: 'Catch them young and break them in early.' It is the Billys of this world that are our salvation, Watson. We cannot last forever."

My response was a snort of disapproval, but I could find no rebuttal. Holmes was, above all, a pragmatist, and pragmatism is a philosophy that tends to defy argument. Our devoted page boy was a working cog in the machine that Holmes had constructed. To argue with success is a high-hurdle effort at best.

A glance of reproach at my friend found his back as a target, for he was now at the desk scrawling rapidly on foolscap.

"As soon as Billy rejoins us, these cables must go out," he commented. "The latest activities of our old adversary are now of the utmost interest."

"Our old who—?" Never had I sounded more like a Greek chorus.

Holmes's eyes were torn from his writing by astonishment.

"Sure you heard the dead man's last words?"

"About someone finding something?"

"After that. He distinctly said that it was Chu. That can mean but one thing, Watson."

"Good Lord!" I berated myself for being so obtuse. "Chu San Fu, of course. Why, the blighter actually had me kidnapped. I've good cause to remember him."

Holmes's pen was moving again when another reasonable thought insinuated itself into my mind.

"But see here, Holmes. You smashed the Oriental crime czar following that Golden Bird matter."

"Severed his tentacles is more to the point," he said, not looking up. "His opium dens, fan-tan games, houses of ill repute, and smuggling operations were closed down, one by one, through the offices of MacDonald's Limehouse Squad. But the wily Oriental is still at large, and who knows what schemes are brewing in his inscrutable mind?"

This did give me pause, and I sat by the fire to muse on the matter. If the Chinese criminal had resumed his old tricks, I would be well advised to keep a sharp eye out. Chu San Fu had lost much face through the activities of Baker Street's most illustrious resident, and the fires of revenge had to be burning fiercely within his concave chest. I sensed that the recent peaceful atmosphere of our abode was with us no more.

My friend concluded his writings with a flourish and stacked the cable messages in preparation for the page boy. With so many things as yet unexplained, my mind stubbornly settled on a matter of little consequence.

"I say, that silk sash around the deceased's body. What was it you called it?"

"A nuck. Part of Burlington Bertie's equipment. He's a smash-and-grabber, you see. Wears the sash around his middle but can remove it to cushion his fist prior to smashing a shop window to extricate what is within."

"Such a strange name."

"And I don't know the origin," admitted Holmes. "The jargon of the underworld springs from obscure genes indeed."

He was standing by the window again, his eyes intent on the street below.

"Ah, another hansom and I deduce that it is Mycroft.

Billy made fast tracks. In his absence, do be a good fellow and unlock the outer door."

I was already headed for the landing when I paused.

"How do you know it is your brother?"

"For one thing, the hansom is so inconspicuous, so completely ordinary that it shrieks of Mycroft, who shuns attention. Then the driver is a prototype of everyman, devoid of expression. And, finally, the hansom is at our door and my brother's portly form is alighting with some difficulty."

Descending to the street door I felt it small wonder that my deductive powers were limited since half the time Holmes was twitting me.

Mycroft Holmes's hand was at the knocker when I opened the door. As he entered, I noted by the flickering gas jet of the neighboring street lamp that his hansom was as Holmes had described it. The driver was indeed one of those faceless types, commonplace and stolid, but Mycroft's agents all shared a considerable breadth of shoulder and a fit look. The older Holmes was shaking moisture from his hat and regarding me with his impassive gray eyes.

"Surely, my good Watson, you are the most patient of men."

"How so?" I asked, following him towards the stairs to our first-floor chambers.

"You have put up with my brother's eccentricities for lo these many years with apparently no ill effects, though I would guess that the strain must be considerable at times."

"You jest," I replied automatically.

Mycroft Holmes's seemingly reluctant acceptance of my friend's activities and style of life were an old tune that did not grate through repetition.

"I do trust Sherlock has good reason for summoning me," he continued. His progress up the stairs was slow of necessity because of his corpulence and underscored by a series of puffing sounds interspersed with grunts of protest. "I almost refused his invitation, a difficult task when facing a sober and sincere lad with the light of the Grail shining from his innocent eyes."

"Don't be deceived by that innocence," I cautioned with a chuckle.

12

"I'm not," replied the government man.

Gaining the landing, he smoothed his coat around his sizable paunch and, with a sigh and shake of his head, entered our chambers.

I noted that Holmes had retrieved the clasp knife from the floor and that along with the unanswered correspondence, it was now back on the mantelpiece. He was never overly neat but seemed to take pains to tidy up on those rare occasions when Mycroft Holmes visited our quarters.

Removing his topcoat, which I took along with his hat, Mycroft surveyed the room with his light, watery gray eyes that habitually mirrored an introspective look and missed nothing. Nodding towards his brother with that precise and somewhat formal manner they adopted with each other, the second most powerful man in England made promptly for our largest chair.

"I am greeted with a touch of melodrama, Sherlock. A Negroid body on the couch? What will Mrs. Hudson think?"

My mouth must have dropped, and even Sherlock Holmes looked slightly startled, a fact that did not escape his brother.

"Come, now, if you wish to cover the corpse, don't let part of a hand dangle from under the sheet. I assume the cadaver is why you sent for me. Now, really, I cannot explain away dead bodies in your establishment. There is a limit to my influence."

This gentle badinage seemed unusual for the intelligence expert, habitually so noncommittal. It was not until later that I realized his lightning-sharp faculties, on a par with my friend's, had seized on the situation, had projected it, and was furiously thinking as to what position he would take. In truth it was Mycroft who was caught off guard, but not one quiver in his massive face revealed it.

"We had a visitor," stated Sherlock Holmes. "A man attacked on the waterfront and fatally wounded who was intent on reaching 'Holmes.' But he was taken to the wrong one."

The sleuth crossed to the couch, gently removing the sheet part way to reveal the face of the dead man. Mycroft regarded the dark visage impassively though I noted that his lips pursed several times.

"How much do you know?" he queried.

"Very little."

"No message? No final word?"

"Yes. But before we go into that, what is the background of this matter? I have, by chance I will admit, become involved, and curiosity is the hallmark of our family."

Mycroft's mouth had a stubborn look about it.

"It's a touchy matter, Sherlock."

"Oh come now, the cat's out in any case. When I noted that the man's hair might have been artificially treated to produce that kinky look, it took me but a moment to realize that the dark skin could well be the result of a dye. Jolly good job, that. I'd like to know the formula. With my suspicions aroused I made a test, and your supposed Nubian didn't pass."

Mycroft Holmes for the first time allowed the shadow of surprise to touch him.

"Cruthers was one of my top men. His native disguise has fooled the best for years."

"But not the very best," replied Holmes, who never ranked modesty as a virtue. "The moons on his fingernails are white. If he were Negroid, they would be blue. Not a fatal oversight," he added. "I doubt if anyone else would have thought of that."

"You relieve me," said Mycroft drily, but I sensed his words were sincere. "This whole affair may reflect rather badly on my department. I had a hunch and risked one of the best of my people in the Egyptian-Sudan theatre to check it out. Losing Cruthers makes that a costly decision."

Sherlock Holmes viewed his brother's large and sober features for a long moment, then replaced the sheet over the dead man with a shrug.

"Your agent didn't die in vain. Here's the whole story." He paused for a moment to thumb shag into the briar that he favored on occasion. A wooden match ignited the pipe, and he continued through clouds of smoke. "One of my people discovered your agent under attack on the East India docks. Two of the assailants came to a bad end."

Mycroft made as though to speak but was forestalled by a gesture from his brother.

"I've dispatched a man to check on the third. Cruthers could barely utter the name of 'Holmes' and was brought here. He just made it, but before death, he left a singular message. The exact words were: 'They . . . they found it. Chu : . . it was Chu.' "

"So," said Mycroft after a considerable pause. "I was right. At least partially. By Chu, Cruthers must have meant Chu San Fu, your arch-enemy."

"And England's," responded the sleuth grimly. Placing his pipe on the mantel, he returned to the body on the couch. "Your agent brought some tangible evidence, or my fingers play me false." Taking one of the corpse's arms, he reached up the coat sleeve. "When I first became aware of this Watson and I were not alone, so I thought it was a matter we could wait upon."

Securing a gleaming object that must have been fastened to the dead man's forearm, Holmes crossed to display it to the seated Mycroft. Standing alongside the sleuth, I surveyed the object eagerly.

"By George, it's beautiful!"

No one disagreed with me. It was a dagger in a sheath of gleaming gold. Gently, Holmes extracted the ornamental blade, undamaged, pure in design, and seemingly produced that very day by the loving hands of a master craftsman. Yet I knew instinctively that it came from a time so ancient as to be shrouded in the mists of the past.

"Egyptian, of course," murmured Mycroft Holmes.

"Without a doubt. Note the sheath festooned with the jackal's-head design. God of the dead," Holmes added, sensing my puzzlement. "The blade is of hardened gold, and see the handle with the familiar cloisonné work of glass and semiprecious stones. At the end is a lapis lazuli scarab."

"I did not know you fancied Egyptology," said his brother.

"Do recall that I once had rooms in Montague Street,

just around the corner from the British Museum, with much more time on my hands than now."

"What does the dagger suggest to you?"

"Ancient, indeed, and valuable. Originally, the possession of royalty. There is a thriving trade in Egyptian antiquities, though something as valuable as this would have been gobbled up by a museum or wealthy collector long ago."

"Deduction?" persisted Mycroft.

"There are flash floods in Egypt that sometimes reveal undiscovered tombs to local graverobbers. I seem to recall a whole village whose inhabitants have been robbing the dead for over three thousand years."

"Kurna."

"Surely a record for the trade of thievery, would you not say, Watson?" Holmes had made note of my expression of complete amazement. "Of course," he continued, "a tomb not rifled by graverobbers might have been found, though none has been to this date."

Holmes retrieved his pipe from the mantel and sat in the easy chair by the desk. "So much for deductions and our brief encounter with your man Cruthers. It is now your turn."

"I'm glad I don't have to explain this to the Cabinet," was Mycroft's surprisingly frank response. "In the field of geopolitics, I find that anticipation is of inestimable value. Gentlemen, there is a spirit of unrest in that potential cauldron that is the Middle East. My agents can't pin it down but it is there, and the spectre of Mohammed Ahmed Ibn Seyyid Abdullah will not permit my ignoring it."

"Mohammed who?" I exclaimed.

"The Mahdi, ol' chap," answered Holmes. "As I recall, China Gordon was one of your heroes."

"General Gordon was but one of our great losses," said Mycroft.

"Then it is a holy war you fear."

"Considering the locale, it is more in the realm of the probable than the possible. The results of the last one were staggering. It was but in '83 that the Mahdi wiped out a ten-thousand-man Egyptian army under Billy Hicks. He took Khartoum, and his followers killed Gordon. If the Sudanese prophet hadn't died in '85, we might be still mired in that mess."

Holmes was regarding his brother with that sharpness of expression so evident when his mind was engrossed.

"There's more to it than that, I'll wager."

"What alerted you?" responded Mycroft quickly.

"History will no doubt brand us for colonialism, but the thin red line of the British Army has prevented periodic outbursts of bloodletting and will again. A responsibility of the Empire. There has to be more."

Mycroft Holmes surveyed both of us for a long moment. Then he sighed.

"General Kitchener is preparing for the reconquest of the Sudan."

I stifled an exclamation. So it was to be war. The death of Gordon, a boil under the saddle blanket of Britain, was to be avenged.

Holmes was eagerly leaning forward in his chair. "Of course. With Kitchener headed south, an outbreak of religious violence on his flanks and rear would be fatal. Bismarck was right. Never fight a war on two fronts."

A discussion between the offspring of the family Holmes could prove most frustrating to the listener. Their statements were clear enough, but each seemed capable of anticipating the other's meaning, at least in part, without words. It was as though there was another channel of communication open only to those two minds.

Holmes sprang to his feet with that nervous energy that indicated he was prepared to cross the Rubicon.

"Something has intrigued you about ancient Egypt," he said, indicating the ornate dagger resting on the desk.

"Call it a sensitivity," admitted his brother. "I picture some mystical pronouncement from the past couched in the general terms used so effectively by the Greek oracle of Delphi. Something that a zealot could twist to serve his purpose. Then it would be like a fire in a wheat field. Conflagration first, with devastation as the aftermath."

Mycroft Holmes had been talking to the ceiling, but now his dreamy eyes fastened on both of us.

"Recently some unusual antika objects have appeared, and there has been talk of a strange expedition in the Valley of the Kings. I sent Cruthers to try to hire out as a digger and evidently he succeeded. Note the dagger, Sherlock. Why did he bring it back? Where did it come from? Who found it? Until now I suspected international politics, but the mention of Chu San Fu in connection with the matter sheds a different light. What interest would he have in Egyptian antiquities other than the fact that he is renowned as a collector?"

"He *was* a collector," was Sherlock Holmes's response. "I happen to know that his great horde of art objects has found its way to the market and has been disposed of. Which makes the rascal very solvent at the moment. Also, I consider the Chinaman to be a megalomaniac, and in my experience a zealot and a man with a deranged mind have a great deal in common. Yes, faint outlines of a pattern begin to emerge. If you do not object, I shall look into this matter."

Mycroft's ponderous shoulders registered an expressive shrug.

"Knowing you, Sherlock, you will do so whether I object or not. However, I need assistance regarding this and must conceal the activities of my own organization. The P.M. would but laugh at me. Government believes in crossing bridges only when they come to them. If you and Watson and that ragtag army at your command will give a hand, do be my guest."

"That ragtag army can be very effective at times," responded Holmes somewhat haughtily.

"Agreed," was his brother's answer. "But please, Sherlock, no practical jokes. Lord Cantlemere has not yet recovered from your outré sense of humor regarding the Mazarin Stone affair."

Mycroft Holmes's words were delivered lightly, but I sensed that he hoped his plea would be heeded. The intelligence expert was the calmest and most secure of men, as unruffled and serene as the fortress of Gibraltar, yet I felt that dealing with his mercurial brother produced a certain feeling of unrest even in him.

The older Holmes, with the air of one who has done all he can, began to rise from his chair.

"Cruthers will have to be disposed of," he stated, "and the less fuss, the better."

His considerable form moved across the room with the peculiar grace so often exhibited by those of his size. At the window he flashed some signal towards his hansom below, then turned to me with an expressive glance, which I was able to interpret. By the time I reached our ground-floor door, his driver was on the stoop carrying a large lap robe. When I indicated the stairs, he mounted them quickly and silently. By the time I reentered our chambers, the driver had the dead body swathed in the lap robe and was lifting it effortlessly from the couch.

"I'll be right down," stated Mycroft, and of a sudden the driver and his burden were gone. Helping Mycroft into his greatcoat, I attempted to brighten the somewhat grim atmosphere.

"Your driver doesn't surprise easily."

"Men who *do* have slow reflexes," he muttered. Before turning towards the door, he shot a keen glance at his brother. "You fell in with my Egypt theory with uncommon ease, Sherlock. Could it be that you possess information that I am not privy to?"

Holmes deflected this verbal lunge with a perfunctory parry. "Whatever I come upon will be revealed in due time."

As Mycroft grunted, I made to open the door. Hearing footfalls on the stairs, I wondered if the silent driver was returning, but it was Billy on the landing and at his heels was the dour face of Inspector MacDonald. As I stood aside, the policeman caught sight of Mycroft Holmes.

"Good evening, sir," he stammered in surprise. Then his natural instincts took over. "Would that be your hansom at the curb, sir?"

A nod was his answer.

"Well, your driver is placing a most peculiar object within, and—"

"I must leave," interrupted Mycroft Holmes, "since I'm due in Whitehall now. Possibly the Inspector would like a drink, Watson, it being brisk without."

"Thank you, no," said MacDonald, a puzzled expression on his long face. "Not while I'm on duty, sir."

19

"My point exactly," said the intelligence expert. "Do enjoy a libation, MacDonald."

Understanding forced itself onto the Scot's face as Mycroft Holmes, with a nod to his brother and myself, made his exit.

"Well, if that's the way it is, I wouldn't mind a wee drap, Doctor."

He removed his hat and coat as I crossed to the sideboard.

"I was catching up with some paperwork, Mr. Holmes, but your lad stayed right there till I came with him. 'Tis glad I am that I'll never have to question him officially, for I could nae get a word from him."

Holmes's thin face brightened. He took great pride in Billy.

"I gather there be a spot of trouble, Mr. Holmes," persisted the Inspector, accepting a glass from me with a look of gratitude.

"Potentially," replied the great sleuth, "though there are fewer official complexities than I had anticipated."

There was a wise look in MacDonald's eyes, and instinctively his gaze strayed to the door through which the elder Holmes had disappeared.

"It's our old acquaintance, Chu San Fu, Mr. Mac. He might be throwing his hat in the ring again."

MacDonald's tumbler came down on the end table forcibly enough to make me wince.

"Not that again. 'Twas hard enough to chop the beggar down the last time. Though it did get simpler towards the end."

There was a look of satisfaction about Holmes. "I wondered about that. Do fill me in."

"Well, sir, the Limehouse Squad just happened to get a complete list of the Chinaman's business outlets, associates—a blueprint of his organization. But you know all about that." The Aberdeenian underlined the "you," a tinge of irony in his voice and a rare trace of humor in his expression. "So we closed him down, bit by bit. He'll nae set up shop in England again and that's a fact."

"You mentioned the climax of this extensive project," prompted Holmes.

20

"Chu San Fu seemed irrational. Had his followers resisting arrest. Twice there were shooting scrapes. 'Twas like he was making it easy for us."

Holmes's eyes shifted to mine. "An interesting pattern for a doctor, Watson?"

"Not unusual," I replied. "A megalomaniac, his grandiose delusions shattered, totters on the brink."

"If you mean he was barmy, I'll go for that," said MacDonald. "We never could convict him personally. He was too well covered. But we put him out of business, for sure."

"At least for the time," commented Holmes, and there was a chilling note to his words. "How are your sources on art objects, Inspector?"

"Safes and Lofts keeps an eye out. We've got a pretty good line on the lenders' shops that pick up the under-the-table stuff, along with the active fences."

"I had in mind the legal trade. Word reaches me that Chu San Fu's treasure trove has been sold. The market is positively glutted, for he had one of the great collections of the world."

" 'Twas above board, Mr. Holmes. We could do nothing about that."

"Indeed, no. But it is my thought that, despite the fact that you have dried up all his sources of income, he must be well supplied with coin of the realm."

"From the sale of his collection." There was a wary look about the Inspector. "It's your feeling that he's getting ready for something new?"

"It does seem possible. I assume the Oriental is still in London?"

"Aye, sir. We may have written him off as a has-been on our books at the Yard, but we haven't forgotten him."

"Excellent," said Holmes, rising to his feet. He must have rung the buzzer to our downstairs landing, for there was a gentle tap on the door. "I'm activating some of my sources, and it might be well, Mr. Mac, if we give the Chinaman a long, hard, second look."

As I secured the Inspector's hat and coat, he evidenced an expression of disappointment. "Would there be anything else you'd like to suggest, Mr. Holmes?"

The sleuth chose to be frank. "I could din your ears with

conjecture, but it's hard evidence you're needing, is it not?"

MacDonald shrugged as Holmes opened the door.

"We all have our ways," he said, and on this philosophical note he departed.

"A moment, Bill," exclaimed Holmes crossing to the desk to secure the pages of foolscap he had written on earlier. "After you show the Inspector out, do see that these get off, will you?"

Passing the boy some coins, Holmes closed the door and began to rub his hands together in a satisfied manner.

"My dear Watson, we have had a fullsome evening, have we not?"

I had to agree with him there.

In truth, there was a feeling of familiar comfort in that the mood of our establishment was again normal. The wheels were spinning and at a rapid rate.

Chapter Three

Another Puzzle

The following morning I rose quite early for me, my mind churning with the possibility of another outbreak of violence similar to the one that had claimed the heroic General Gordon.

Holmes and I breakfasted together but he was preoccupied, and experience cautioned me that it was useless to try to rouse him from his thoughts. The rain was still with us, and since I had no medical calls on my calendar, *The Lancet* claimed my attention for a time. I noted that my friend spent some time inspecting the golden dagger that had come our way the night before and then, wearying of it, had crossed to the window to gaze at the dreary scene outside.

The sheaf of cables that had been sent the previous evening meant that Holmes had initiated certain inquiries and now, while awaiting responses, he was going over the matter of the departed agent, Cruthers, the dagger, and the fears expressed by his brother. I rather hoped that he had plenty to think about since, as readers of my words know, he was not of a patient nature.

As my head rose to survey the silhouette of the great detective, it was immediately obvious that matters had taken an unexpected turn. His eyes, which had been viewing the outside scene in a moody manner, were now fastened on an area immediately below his vantage point, and his whipcord frame leaned forward slightly. On occasion, he did bear a remarkable resemblance to a predatory bird about to swoop.

"Ah ha, Watson! What have we here? A carriage at the curb. A gentleman descending from it, for his clothes are of Saville Row. Eureka! He is hastening to our very door. Considering the state of the weather and the resultant lack of traffic, I would say this indicates a matter requiring the attention of certain unique talents. That is the way you put it in those stories you write, is it not?"

I was prompted to remind him that those stories, which he oft-times accused me of foisting on a patient reading public, were but recountings, devoid of form or content without his actions. But Holmes's eyes were sparkling and he was rubbing his hands together like a gleeful money lender. I did not wish to intrude on his happy anticipation, but my native practicality took hold.

"See here, Holmes, you do have that Mid East matter to consider."

"Not until more information comes our way. Meanwhile we have a man who has come through the rain on this wearisome day, and we cannot deny him an audience."

Here we go again, I thought. Holmes, self-appointed protector of all in need on three continents, because he hated a wasted moment and his ego could not let him pass a puzzle by.

While Billy announced our visitor and Holmes signified that he should be shown up, it occurred to me that my smug attitude would get a justified comeuppance if the man turned out to be a solicitor for church funds but such was not the case.

Mr. Clyde Deets of Mayswood, as he was announced, was well turned out indeed, from his lucent top hat and black frock-coat with white waistcoat down to his patent-leather shoes. I noted, as he deposited his hat and gloves on our occasional table while greeting Holmes, that his hair was thinning. The flesh on his face was pale, even after braving the wind outside, but firm. He had a small moustache somewhat military in its cut. As he seated himself in the basket chair indicated by Holmes, he brushed some droplets of moisture from his black satin cravat. The word "foppish" came to my mind, but the square cut of his shoulders with the suggestion of bunched muscles caused me to amend it to "meticulous." I liked to have such little observations at hand should Holmes ask my opinion, an infrequent occurrence.

"There are cigars in the coal scuttle," said the consulting detective with a gesture of his hand.

Deets suppressed surprise at the eccentric arrangements in our quarters. I hoped Holmes would not secure shag from the Persian slipper.

"Thank you, no, Mr. Holmes." He seemed ill at ease. "I feel most fortunate in finding you in your lodgings," he added lamely as his eyes questioningly swiveled towards me.

"This is my associate, Doctor Watson. His discretion is beyond question, and he is quite indispensable to my investigations."

While Holmes had used these words, or similar ones, many times through the years, they always prompted a glow of pride, though I had my own ideas as regards their truth. Suddenly, a thought surprised me. Did Holmes really believe this?

It was not apparent to me whether Deets resented my presence or not. "We had a bit of unpleasantness at the family home last night. Mayswood, you know."

I didn't. Holmes gave no indication as to whether he shared my ignorance or not. There was an awkward pause, then Deets continued:

"Felt some professional help was required, so I dashed over here first thing. Came right to the best, you see."

I noted Holmes's eyebrows escalating slightly, and there was an air of mild amusement about him.

"Not immediately to our door, Mr. Deets. There is a smudge of dusty ash on your topper that is indigenous to our railway system, and surely I note a return ticket in your waistcoat pocket. Then there is some mud on your shoes, inevitable considering the weather, and judging by the color of the soil, I would venture the guess that you went from the railway station to an address in the Hyde Park vicinity."

Deets's eyes had widened and there was that look, half

amazement and half apprehension, that I had seen so many times before.

"Mayswood is down Surrey way, Mr. Holmes, and I did toddle over to the home of my solicitor before coming here. I say, you are a bit of a crackerjack, are you not? Lawyer Simpson lives in Hyde Park for a fact. Old fellow thought I should contact the police, but the idea of a squad of constables descending on the ménage didn't fill me with enthusiasm. Felt if you might be persuaded to lend a hand, things would be more discreet."

"Let us consider what this unpleasantness involves."

I shuddered in my mind at what Holmes's reaction might be to a tale of domestic strife, but Deets did better than that.

"Fact is, Mr. Holmes, we got burgled, or jolly well would have but for happy chance."

Once started, our visitor swung into his tale with commendable alacrity, and he presented it with a minimum of extraneous verbiage, a fact that I knew weighed well with Holmes.

"Wife's up country visiting her sister. Just me in the house along with the staff. Had planned on running over to the Turf Club for dinner and whist. A short distance from Mayswood the carriage horse threw a shoe, so we came back, you see, to hitch up another. Found I'd left my cigarettes, and while Alfred was changing horses, went back inside to locate my case. Rather fancy it. Lucky, you see. Turned a bullet once and saved my life, but that's another story. Anyway, I went upstairs with Dooley, the butler, on my heels. Old fellow brushed against a shield on the wall, and it fell with a fearful clatter. Then we heard another sound above and rushed up. We have an upstairs sitting room. Used to be a sort of art gallery. Father was keen on oils. In any case, found the French windows wide open. Rain blowing in. Someone had been there all right, but not a sign of the beggar."

Deets paused for a breath and his delivery slowed down. It was then I gave him credit for more sense than I had previously.

"Now, I wouldn't be calling on Mr. Sherlock Holmes if

26

that was the whole story. Fact is, can't figure how the would-be robber got there. Considering the time between my leaving Mayswood and my return, the blighter couldn't have been in the house more than five minutes. A spot sooner and Dooley and I might have seen him. Now, there's a balcony outside the gallery. French windows open onto it. But it's thirty feet from the ground if it's an inch. Flat marble walls, Mr. Holmes. No handholds and no convenient ivy. No tree close by, either."

At the beginning of Deets's story, Holmes's mood had been one of concealed boredom, but his attention was caught now and he regarded our visitor with that keen glance that indicated the gears of his mind were meshed and moving.

"You assume the uninvited visitor gained access to the balcony?"

Deets had evidently anticipated this line of thought. "There was no other way for him to enter the room. All of the downstairs windows at Mayswood are barred. Doors were all locked and bolted. Dooley had checked them on my departure. If you would view the premises I think you would agree with me that entry from the ground floor was impossible. You're the detective, but from where I sit, the thief had to gain access to the house via the balcony. For the life of me, I can't see how. He didn't use a ladder, for Dooley and I rushed right out and there was no sign of anything like that. Actually," he continued after a thoughtful moment, "how he got away so fast is as mystifying as how he entered! No sign of anyone, and yet we'd jolly well heard him while we were on the stairs. Chap just vanished!"

"Well," said Holmes, and there was relish in his manner, "you have presented an intriguing problem. A viewing of the scene is called for, naturally. But first, some questions that might cast light on the matter. Your burglar, if that is what he was, is evidently skilled. Premature assumptions are subject to error, but this does not seem like a common smash-and-grabber after the family plate. About the staff, how many in residence?"

"Dooley, of course. We have a male cook, Frenchman;

two inside maids. They all live in the main house. The gardener and grooms live by the stables in quarters. Alfred, our coachman, lives outside as well."

Holmes rose and selected the straight pipe he sometimes fancied. With it, he crossed to the Persian slipper containing his shag.

"You mentioned flat marble walls."

Our client's round and quite youthful face creased in a grin and he fingered his moustache.

"Fact is, Mayswood's a bit of a fortress. Not by intent. Just sort of happened that way. White marble all round, which is rather the style down our way. We've considerable grounds, but no trees close to the house. On a bright moonlit night, place looks a bit like a Greek temple. Father—gone now—was something of an art fancier. He had the lower windows barred. Not that his collection was a famous one. Just an idea he had, you see."

Holmes, puffing out clouds of smoke, had an almost benign expression on his hawklike face. The more our visitor made the entry of the burglar seem impossible, the better he liked the whole matter. At that moment I would have wagered five against one that he was thinking: "Ah ha! This may turn into a two-pipe problem after all."

My friend leaned one arm against the mantel, peering down at Deets, his eyes alight.

"Your very words lead us to what may be the key question. What was this elusive burglar after?"

Both of Deets's hands turned palms up as though disclaiming any knowledge whatsoever. "There's the rub, Mr. Holmes. Oh, there're some pieces of value. One does collect things. But the wife's jewels, what she didn't take with her, are safely in the box at the County and Suburban. I keep a spot of currency on hand but it's no great thing. Any articles of value he may have fancied would not have been easy to leave with. Furniture, tapestries, and such. There is the family plate, but it's rather heavy stuff and a man would have some trouble lugging enough to make it worth his while."

"No papers? Documents? Bonds?" queried Holmes.

"Some deeds, but nothing that is convertible." Deets had another thought. "Then there is this, Mr. Holmes: How's this chap going to get away with anything at all? He couldn't dump objects off the balcony. A bit noisy, to say the least. If he tried to get out via the ground floor, he could unbolt the doors all right, but it still takes a key to open them."

"That would present no problem to an accomplished swag man," replied Holmes. "However, with four persons on the premises, to say nothing of the outside help, I agree that it would be a risky matter."

"I'm sorry to be the squirrel with such a hard nut, Mr. Holmes," said our visitor apologetically.

A faint smile teased the corners of Holmes's mouth. "If the solution was simple, you would have no need of me."

Surprise infiltrated Deets's eyes, to be replaced by the imp of humor. It crossed my mind that this outgoing type might well have a perspicacity that he took pains to conceal.

"For a fact," he replied agreeably. Then came a sudden thought. "You don't suppose the rascal—you don't think he came to the wrong house?"

"A possibility, though I choose to ignore it. For no concrete reason. Just mark it down to my feeling for such things."

There was a considerable pause as Holmes, and Deets as well, mused on the matter.

"What would you have me do?" queried the sleuth finally. "I assume, from your immediacy on the scene, that nothing was taken."

A negative shake of the head was his answer.

"Then the tracing of stolen goods is ruled out. What we have is a burglar, assumed, whose plan is frustrated by your opportune return to the scene. Means of entry and, indeed, exit, are unknown." My friend turned towards Deets suddenly and employed a little trick I had seen him use before. "You realize, of course, that if he does not try again there is little chance of ferreting him out."

Our client, for I considered him as such now, nodded, and there was a seriousness about him.

"I'm rather intrigued by puzzles myself. I want to know how this chap got in and got out so I can make sure it doesn't happen again. I'm willing to pay and pay well for that information." Possibly he didn't feel this explanation was in sufficient detail, though it made sense to me. In any case, after a short pause he continued. "I did mention the fortress aspects of Mayswood. I guess I never considered it before, but it does provide a certain peace of mind."

"Temporarily dispelled by last night's occurrence," said Holmes. "Your problem is intriguing enough for Watson and myself to come down to Surrey and look round. I assume it is raining as hard there as here, so our visit need not be made immediately. Any clues on the outside of the house have certainly been washed away."

"Dooley and I took a turn around the grounds with lamps last night, Mr. Holmes. Not with your expertise, of course. It was a quagmire. I fancy the fellow could have worn hob-nail boots and no marks would have remained."

Deets's businesslike approach to the matter seemed to please Holmes. He returned to his favorite armchair and sat, his hands crossed in his lap, gazing at the man. There was another pause.

"I wish," said Holmes rather grudgingly, "that there was some motive for your nocturnal visitor."

"So do I, Mr. Holmes," Deets said frankly, meeting the sleuth's intense eyes squarely.

Holmes finally seemed satisfied. "All right, Mr. Deets, we'll come down tomorrow. If the weather continues foul, no matter. Watson and I will be there."

"For lunch, perhaps?"

"Agreed. In the interim, I assume your household is on the alert?"

Deets's smile had an infectious quality. "When I left, Gaston, our chef, was busy sharpening a rather alarming carving knife. The butler, Dooley, is an old Crimean man and rather intrigued by the prospect of action. I noted several pokers were missing, so I suspect the housemaids are prepared as well. Mayswood is a bit of an armed camp."

"So much the better," commented Holmes casually. "But let's not have a poor delivery man set upon by mistake."

On this lighter note, Clyde Deets made his departure.

I waited, with some difficulty, until his footfalls faded on the stairs.

"Now see here, Holmes," I exploded, "I know this presents an enticing pattern. Mysterious intruder with an obscure motive who seemingly materializes and then promptly vanishes. All the elements that you love so well. But there is that matter that Mycroft brought to your attention."

"And fate. Burlington Bertie bringing the dying man here was what really got us involved."

"You're splitting hairs. The fact is that the Empire could be in difficulties."

"True," he admitted. "Well, this case of the mysterious intruder seems a minor one that we may be able to dispose of in short order."

This had to satisfy, and I turned to the word-squares of the day. Those beguiling combinations had long ago presented a most nagging challenge until I realized that I possessed a secret weapon. After a lengthy passage of time, Holmes broke in on my concentration.

"You know, ol' fellow, relative to the Surrey matter, I cannot rid myself of the feeling that all has not been said. If the intruder made his entry and escape, a fact that we must assume or there is no case, we shall find out how. What intrigues me no end is the why."

"We certainly don't know that," I replied, my mind elsewhere.

"But I'm not sure that the same can be said for Mr. Deets."

"He seemed most cooperative."

"Unusually so. His recreation of the event was delightfully to the point. I could wish witnesses in court were as concise. But there is the question of his cigarette case."

I lowered my paper. "You've lost me, Holmes."

"He went upstairs at Mayswood for his cigarette case that had once turned a bullet and saved his life. Now I just wonder, Watson, who fired the bullet?"

Chapter Four

The Bizarre Intruder

It was shortly thereafter that Holmes departed the premises. He stated that there were some investigations regarding our adventure of the previous evening that he wanted to tend to and that he might even inquire into Mr. Clyde Deets. I made a move to accompany him but he would have none of it, stating that his efforts would be but contact work and did not require my always welcome assistance.

I turned my hand to my case history again but could make little progress. There was the guilty thought that my friend was braving the elements while I remained cozy and warm within. But I forced myself to brand this as fruitless castigation. The number of Holmes's available contacts, regarding all sorts of information, was enormous. It seemed reasonable that some of them would speak to him more freely without his biographer in attendance.

At loose ends, I returned to my word-squares.* Holmes returned in the late afternoon. As he shook moisture from his coat, I busied myself with the tantalus and gasogene and we sat before the fire and clinked glasses.

"A friend at the British Museum did not prove informative, ol' fellow, though when I described the gold dagger

---

* Also called "word blocks," they existed in England in the 19th century. In 1913 the first crossword puzzles appeared in publications and by 1920 achieved the immense popularity they enjoy today.

something struck him. I was able to draw for him that scroll-like design on its blade, and he identified it as a cartouche.

As my eyebrows elevated, Holmes continued. "A seal of a royal personage. Now, to Deets. With your frugal sense, Watson, you might be happy to learn that Clyde Deets of Surrey is solvent and runs a most respectable business. Moved to that area around five years ago. Father was a recluse and died shortly thereafter. But here's a puzzle: prior to their arrival at Mayswood, nothing is known of Deets, *père* or *fils*. Complete dead end as regards family history and origin. Rather singular, but then not all our clients date back to the Norman Conquest."

"In other words—" I began.

"In other words, I discovered very little and got rather wet doing it. Your expertise with the decanter is of medicinal assistance. Now tell me of your day."

"My dead end is a six-letter space in the word blocks," I said, reaching for the paper. "State of unrest—reversed."

As Holmes's eyes narrowed, I added: "Third letter might be 't'."

"Try 'citceh,' which is 'hectic' reversed."

I reached for my pencil with some excitement. "This might open up a number of things. Associate in ten letters, third letter 'c' if 'citceh' is right."

"Surely easy for you, Watson. 'Accomplice.'"

"It fits. Drainage in five, second letter being 'i'."

"Ditch. Err—Watson—"

I overrode him. "Discordant in nine. Third letter 'c'."

"Cacophony. My dear chap—"

"Uncanny in five. Second letter 'e'."

"Eerie."

"Holmes, you've done it. I believe I can—"

My voice dwindled away as I found my friend regarding me with a strange look, akin to wonderment.

"Watson, I've been trying to mention that there is an amazing quality about you. Intuitive, perhaps, or just the ability to say the right thing at the right time. You are a treasure, indeed!"

Since his remark struck me dumb, I could but regard him with a slack jaw. The wonderment faded from his eyes

34

to be replaced with that far-away look, a sure sign that his massive intellect was working in high gear.

" 'Hectic' was the word, but the instruction 'reverse' suggested a key. Our client's name is Deets. Not a common name but nothing unusual either. Uninteresting might be the best description. But reverse it and you have 'Steed,' which opens up fascinating possibilities."

Holmes was on his feet making a beeline for the bookcase, from which he extracted the 'S' file. There was a tight smile on his face as he leafed through pages. "Sansbey, the poisoner . . . interesting case, that. . . . Slagar, the Serbian strangler. Never convicted. Sloppy police work there. . . . Ah! Here we are! Maurice Steed-Spaulding, British Army, Retired. I'll try to dredge through the chaff . . . graduated Richmond—"

"Army, you say?" I burst out with a sudden remembrance. "Captain Spaulding, the African explorer!"

"Leading expert on Egypt. Hmmmm. . . ."

"Oh, was he an Egyptologist? Don't know why I associated the chap with Africa."

Holmes's face rose from the file briefly. "My dear Watson, Egypt is in Africa."

"Oh. So it is."

Momentarily nonplussed, I watched Holmes's eyes race through a page before turning to another.

"Wasn't mixed up with that Piazzi Smythe chap, was he? You recall the theory of the Pyramid Inch and the Great Pyramid."

"Piazzi Smyth was a pyramidologist, Watson, and the theory of the Pyramid Inch was disproved. Steed-Spaulding was a student of cultures and of religions as well. Wrote two books on the latter. *The Coptics of Egypt* and *Islam Comes to Egypt*. Both considered monumental, though the last one did receive adverse criticism. He traced the rise of Mohammedanism in Egypt beginning with the Arab invasion of 639 and laid emphasis on the tolerance of the Islamics towards Jews and Christians as opposed to the attitude of Christianity during that period."

His eyes rose from the book, sparkling with interest.

"It's becoming crystal clear, Watson. Spaulding took the

35

first half of his hyphenated name, reversed it, and used it on coming to Surrey."

"I say, Holmes, is this not wild conjecture?"

"Conjecture, yes, but not so wild. Spaulding was brought to my attention . . . let's see, I have a note on that."

He regarded the file again and then snapped it shut.

"It was June of '94. Sir Randolph Rapp expressed some puzzlement regarding the gentleman, and I did a little investigation for him. Spaulding's expedition to Abydos in Upper Egypt and his first expedition into the Sudan were considered the coups of his time. He was involved in a second trip to the Sudan that he abandoned half way, and he returned to England and took up the raising of dogs in Stoke Newington. There was, in '90, an attempted robbery of his estate. Matter was hushed up, but I'll wager that is when our client's cigarette case saved his life. Following the robbery, Spaulding sold out and dropped from sight. Five years back that was, and you will note that the Deets arrived in Surrey at that time."

"It fits. I'll give you that," I admitted. Another thought crossed my mind. "If Rapp brought up the matter of the explorer and author in '94, that must have been right after your visit to the Khalifa at Khartoum."

I had always been tantalized by the real reason for Holmes's journey to Mecca and then to the Sudan, but he brushed aside my bait quickly.

"Sir Randolph Rapp was very interested in Captain Spaulding, as I am right now. It's the matter of the Sacred Sword, you see."

I sighed. "Please, Holmes, can we run that last bit over again."

My friend smiled, replaced the "S" file in the bookshelf, and took his pipe from the mantel. "In the folklore of Arabia, it is said that the sword of the prophet Mohammed still exists, secreted away in some subterranean crypt in an unknown oasis. The unsheathing of the Sacred Sword is to signal the rising of the followers of the Crescent, who are then to drive the infidels into the sea."

"A holy war," I exclaimed, "in keeping with what Mycroft fears. But what has the late Captain Spaulding to do with that?"

"You know that Rapp, in his line of work, picks up a lot of rumors and is a great believer that myths and folktales have a basis in fact. Somehow he caught wind of the whisper that an Arabian chieftain feared that the Sacred Sword would be used as a device to lead his people to annihilation, a blood bath. He supposedly gave the sword to Captain Spaulding, considered a true friend of the Islamics, despite the fact that he was Christian. Spaulding was to remove the weapon to England until such time as it could be returned without being an instrument to incite and inflame."

I was shaking my head and should have known better.

"That sounds a bit far-fetched, Holmes."

"A moment. The attempted robbery at the Spauldings' dwelling in Stoke Newington may have been an attempt to secure the sword entrusted to the Captain. Whatever, it got their wind up and they changed their residence posthaste and their name as well."

Holmes puffed on his pipe furiously for a moment.

"We can dissect the matter piecemeal, ol' chap, but we're rather flogging a dead horse. The recent intruder at the Spauldings' home in Surrey was not a thief to my mind at all To use the language of the ha'penny dreadfuls, he was 'casing the joint.' "

"Attempting to find out where the sword was hidden," I said suddenly.

"Now you're on the track." Holmes's voice held a tone of approval. "Consider Deets's, née Spaulding's, reaction. He knew what the intruder was doing there. Though nothing was taken, he still enlisted our aid in hopes of finding out how to forestall a future attempt. He might well have called in the police, but I think the prospect of Scotland Yard on the scene rattled him. Suppose they located the hiding place of the sword?"

I was being drawn to Holmes's idea in spite of myself and tried to use the logic that he had made famous.

"All right, let us say that your brother's fear of an uprising is well-founded. We have proof, by virtue of the dead Cruthers, that a tomb could well play a part. The dagger he brought is tangible—I can see it, and his dying words certainly tie in Chu San Fu to the matter."

"Who else has the resources and the overbearing ego to involve himself in such a wild scheme?"

"But where does that leave this Sacred Sword idea?"

"We have been introduced to two situations, but do not place them in opposition to each other, ol' boy. They both face towards the Mid East, specifically Egypt. Let us consider them with an intellectual togetherness."

"You feel the Sword is part of Chu's plot?"

Holmes was knocking out his pipe on the stones of the fireplace.

"The wily old dog is a bit of a showman, you know. With the Sacred Sword, he might well set himself up as a latter-day prophet, a leader of Islamics throughout the world."

"But Holmes, it is just an inanimate object."

"What makes sense or follows the laws of logic is not always important, Watson. It is what people believe. I can see the idea of a horde of nomadic horsemen surging forth from the desert and elsewhere finds no fertile soil in your mind. But they came before, you know. Not just under the Mahdi. At one time they flooded into France."

"The Battle of Tours?"

"More recently, the history of Europe for a half century was dictated by the alarming thought that the Grand Army of the Republic might rise again. The shadow of 'Le Petit Corporal' had our statesmen quivering even after Waterloo and his subsequent death on St. Helena. Presumably we live in an age of enlightenment, but should you turn up with a sword named 'Excalibur' and prove that it was the weapon of the great Arthur of legend, I imagine you could stir up quite an uprising. Certainly among the superstitious and clannish Cornish and others as well."

The thought of my waving a great two-handed blade and leading a horde to conquest and pillage had to introduce the dwarf of derision to my manner with the midget of mischievous merriment trodding on his heels. The latter increased in stature as the chuckle on my lips grew into a chortle and then blossomed to a full guffaw. It was so ridiculous, but then the truth of Holmes's words regarding the Corsican shouldered my laughter aside. As my face sobered and grim lines appeared, Holmes surveyed me with his wise eyes.

"Now I believe I shall ring for Mrs. Hudson and request two dinners. Tomorrow may be an important day in our lives."

I could but agree. Men can be stirred to the marrow when deep-seated loyalties or hostilities are aroused. Holmes had once discoursed at length on the matter of racial memory. I had not followed him at the time, but it was making more sense now.

It was during our evening repast that the first messages arrived. Holmes quite rightly assumed that they were in response to his cables of the night before and relegated them to the desk until we had enjoyed an after-dinner cigar together.

Then, with a sigh, he seated himself to go over the communications. The acquiring of information through the knowledge or efforts of others was onerous to Holmes. In the early days it was standard procedure for us to be on the scene of the crime in jig time and make our own conclusions. Or rather, have Holmes make his. But now the scope of the sleuth's activities had widened and it would have been impractical indeed not to take advantage of the far-flung web of contacts and sources that he had taken such pains to weave.

I was in the dark as to what progress, if any, was being made. Possibly the messages were confirmations of a time and meeting place with some associate, or perhaps an answer to a direct question posed by Holmes to a highly qualified source. I was mentally framing a query that might prompt a revealing remark from him when there was a gentle tap on the door.

"Come in, Billy," said Holmes.

The page boy did so but there was no cable or envelope in his hand.

"It's a box, Mr. 'Olmes. Two delivery men brung it. It's fer Mr. Mycroft 'Olmes, sir. Care of Mr. Sherlock 'Olmes, this address."

"Now that's strange. Mycroft made no mention of this, and surely he has any number of working addresses. Well, best we have a look at it."

"Rather big, sir."

"Oh," said Holmes, springing to his feet. "Come, Watson, and let us see what object comes to Mycroft via our dwelling."

Within the front door was a crate easily five feet long by three feet in width. I glanced at Holmes blankly and drew a responsive shrug. Holmes positioned himself at one end of the box, and with Billy's help I lifted the other end and we maneuvered it up the stairs and into our sitting room. Happily it was not of a great weight, and we had it lying adjacent to the fireplace in short order.

As Billy departed from the room, my friend was surveying the unexpected object with curiosity, which was heightened by the fact that one of the slats of the packing case was obviously loose.

For a moment Holmes waged an inner struggle and then lost it, crossing to secure the clasp knife, though this time he made sure his unanswered correspondence remained neatly stacked on the mantel.

"See here, the object is earmarked for your brother," I protested.

"Agreed, but Mycroft would not deny us a peek, ol' chap."

Holmes had the loose piece of wood pried up before I could muster another objection, and by then it was too late. The knife's stout blade was working out the thin nails that secured the crate and, I blush to admit, I was helping Holmes for I, too, had caught the flash of gold in the light of the fireplace.

What was revealed was certainly unusual. It was the size of a small steamer trunk but glistened with a color unknown to commercial luggage. It was rectangular and its sides were adorned with figures and objects that were strange to me. Finally, an obvious thought forced itself upon me.

"Holmes, if this is of gold, how did we lift it so easily?"

My friend tapped the top of the box with his knuckles.

"Made of wood, I'd say, Watson, and overlaid with sheet gold. A backing of plaster, perhaps."

He had his pocket glass in hand now.

40

"The ornamental work marks its origin. Egyptian without a doubt. Note the figures, male and female."

"The males seem to wear a kilt type of skirt."

"With the navels showing in each case," replied Holmes. "I believe that is a mark of a certain period in Egyptian art but don't recall which one. See the plethora of signs? Cobras, birds, and this one, resembling our infinity sign, is the life symbol of the Egyptians."

"Whatever do you suppose is inside?"

"That tantalizing thought must remain unanswered, ol' fellow, for we seem denied even a brief look-see."

The sleuth's index finger indicated silver bolts that slid through gold staples and were secured firmly by small and strange-looking locks. Evidently the top of this shiny box opened in the middle like a miniature double door. "The greater mystery is why this object is here. This is no error, for it is plainly addressed to 221B Baker Street."

Holmes stood by the mantel for a moment, his broad brow furrowed in thought, and then either he reached a decision or some new idea came to his superb mind.

"Well, I can draw no meaning from the ornamentation save that it reflects court scenes. Egypt must remain Mycroft's specialty until we learn more, and as to the contents, we can do naught but guess. Here, Watson, let's stretch this afghan over the container, for the hour grows late."

Automatically I helped Holmes cover the box, though his reason for doing this escaped me completely. Once the object was under the afghan that my friend took from our couch, a rapid gesture of warning put me on the alert. All was not as it seemed.

"Let's see," said Holmes calmly. "I'd best get these messages out of the way."

He was at the desk fiddling with papers but only with one hand. The other was signaling towards my medical bag by the cane rack and I made for it with alacrity, bringing it to Holmes at the desk. He kept up a desultory flow of conversation, like a man preparing to retire for the night, all the while removing my stethoscope.

"Stir up the fire, will you, good fellow?" he suggested, affixing the instrument to his head.

I had a poker in my hand in a moment and stirred up the logs, noting that Holmes tiptoed to the covered object and applied the stethoscope to its cover. I took pains at this point not to make undue noise and, after a moment, Holmes seemed satisfied and removed himself to the desk area where he restored my indispensable medical aid to its resting place.

"Well, Watson, shall we turn in?"

"I'm for it," I said rather loudly, and my accompanying yawn was authentic and not dumb show.

Without further ado Holmes extinguished the lights, but now I understood his suggestion regarding the fire since the flames still provided illumination in the room. Following Holmes's lead, I went towards the back stairs. My friend carefully left the door ajar and we progressed up the steps, making a bit more noise than necessary in doing so.

Before we reached the landing, Holmes had one of my arms in his steely grasp and his lips were close to my ear.

"Get your hand gun, old fellow, and tiptoe back down this way. Position yourself by the door and watch that box like a hawk. There's something in there, Watson, something alive. I'll duck round by the front stairs to the entrance door, which is not locked. When you spot it opening, you'll know I'm in place and we'll have whatever is in that Trojan horse bottled up."

Like a dark shadow Holmes was gone, and my heart was pounding as I made all speed to secure the Webley from my bedroom and inch my way back down the stairs to my station. Somehow the thought of a great Anaconda snake slithering out of the strange box kept coming to my mind and I was in a bit of a blue funk when I took position by the half-opened door and peered into our sitting room.

The box with its cover was plainly visible in the dancing light of the fireplace. I reasoned that the afghan was a device of Holmes's in case there was a peephole through which a human eye could have observed us. The thought of something human helped my nervous state until I began to wonder what form of mankind could be secreted in such a small area.

It was then I noted that our front door was silently opening. Its well-oiled hinges made no protest, for which I was grateful, and then its movement ceased. Now for the waiting.

Whatever had entered our quarters in such an outré manner must have been patient, for at least a half hour went by and my bones were aching, desirous of a change of position, which I was able to affect silently several times. Then there was a stir, and the afghan began to rise and then slide down, revealing the golden box. The entire top was rising, and I immediately realized that the bolts had been to create an illusion and that the top was actually secured from the inside. There was a lengthy pause, and then I could dimly discern two small, dark hands that lifted the top of the box. A figure rose from the interior and gently placed the lid on the floor. It was with difficulty that I suppressed an exclamation.

The black hair of this almost doll-like figure hung in two braids down the back of an oversized head that seemed wizened and not young at all as its size at first had suggested. He hopped out of the golden box agilely, landing silently with bare feet on our carpet. A flicker of the firelight revealed broad lips that were skinned back exposing small teeth, filed to a point. There was such an evil menace about the face that I shuddered. It looked like a coconut shell with features painted on it in the manner of primitive art among the aborigines of the South Pacific. But the filed teeth were shockingly real and lent a death's head quality to this bizarre apparition. A loin cloth and a child's-size rough shirt was its costume.

Standing on the floor, it seemed no more than four feet in height. Small eyes, which were flicked with yellow, searched the room, and I was careful to remain frozen at my vantage point. Finally the figure moved, or rather glided with the grace of a wild animal, and I was reminded of the quick but fluid motion of a weasel. The creature gave scant attention to the furnishings, once convinced that the room was empty, but surprised me by crossing to the bay window and, after some effort, succeeded in opening it.

I could not fathom what this strange form of humanity was up to and was further bemused when it returned to the center of the room, peering at the bookshelf with a nervous glance. Then it clambered onto the chair to survey the desk top and evidently found the object of its search. The ornamental dagger that Cruthers had brought with him was plainly visible, and a tiny hand scooped it up. I thought the figure would hop down from the chair, but primitive curiosity took over and the blade was drawn from the scabbard and tested on the tongue of the creature. Then the dagger was returned to its sheath and the figure did descend to the floor as the front door swung open and the beam of a bull's-eye lantern fixed the native in its light. There was a high-pitched, tinny sound from the small throat and, dropping the Egyptian dagger, the creature shot across the room and without pause dove through the bay window!

I was in the room myself now, and as I ignited one of the lamps I heard the sound of a horse suddenly in the outer darkness. There was the lash of a whip and the hoof sounds accelerated and there was the rumble of wheels.

Holmes, by the window, was peering out, but in a moment his face turned to me with a woebegone expression.

"I've been had, Watson. Outwitted, and by a pigmy, no less."

"But Holmes," I sputtered, "what happened?"

"I should have known when the little devil opened the window. We had him cornered, but he sailed out of the window and into a wagonload of hay, which is how he intended to leave our quarters even had he not been discovered. The hay wagon is four blocks away by now, and we shall never find it. Our little friend has made a clean getaway, but he didn't take what he was after. We can console ourselves with that."

"He was after the dagger, of course. Why?"

"Possibly that cartouche reveals something of its point of origin. Evidently, Chu San Fu doesn't want the ancient blade in our possession."

"Ah, then this pigmy was sent by the Chinaman?"

"You know Chu's methods, Watson. He employs dacoits, Lascars, and other unusual types with strange aptitudes. I'll give him credit for a most ingenious scheme of gaining entry here."

Holmes was closing the bay window as he spoke. "Fortunately, there was not enough sound to rouse the household. Best we not mention a barefooted pigmy to Mrs. Hudson, for she might not sleep soundly for a week."

His remark brought an alarming thought into focus in my mind.

"If the pigmy is one of Chu San Fu's bizarre entourage, then the Oriental must know of your involvement."

"It would seem so, Watson. I'll have the golden box taken to Mycroft tomorrow. Possibly it will be informative to him, though I doubt it. Just a device to get the little devil in here." Locking the front door, he made for the bedroom stairs again. "I'll also have the house watched during our absence."

"Then tomorrow it is off to Surrey?"

"Why not? We may pick up the trail of the insidious Chu San Fu quicker there than here in London."

"A moment, Holmes. This chap, Deets—or Spaulding—"

"For the time, let us refer to him by his assumed name, Deets."

"Very good. But I don't recall his giving you directions."

"Mayswood, the name of his residence, was enough, my good Watson."

And on this puzzling note, Holmes retired to his bedroom.

With my lights extinguished for the night, a myriad of thoughts tried to march down the corridors of my mind. Long experience with the affairs of Sherlock Holmes allowed me to erect roadblocks, and sleep was not long in coming. However, it was invaded by filmy figures spawned from the imagination. Wild horsemen thundered over an endless sea of sand with pyramid shapes in the background sharply defined by a blazing sun. Each nomad had sharply filed teeth and was swinging a huge, curved, scimitar-shaped weapon. Heads will roll, I thought before sinking into total oblivion.

Chapter Five

Surrey Interlude

Mid-morning on the following day found Holmes and myself at Waterloo Station where the sleuth purchased two tickets to Litchfield.

Our train journey to Surrey was uneventful. During most of it my friend leaned back in his seat with his hat pulled over his eyes, his chin sunk on his chest and his long legs stretched out before him. He might have been catnapping, or his brain could just as easily have been churning. I guessed that neither was the case and that he was, instead, disassociating himself from our discussion with his brother and the events of the previous evening so that he could approach the Deets mansion and its problems with a clear mind. It was Holmes's contention that a brain free of supposition and unclouded by half-truths was like an unused photographic plate, ready to take impressions.

A four-wheeler awaited our arrival at the station and whisked us into the countryside. The rain had passed through the area on its way to London and the greens were greener because of it. A spring sun projected lukewarm rays to brighten the scene, and everywhere was a soft, almost melodious sound as swollen rivulets attempted to drain off the surface water that had accumulated during the torrents of the past few days.

As we wound through curved lanes bordered by hedges and trees eagerly displaying the first new growth of the season, there was the musty but not unpleasant odor of wet leaves and moist earth. Into these tranquil surroundings a seeming contradiction sprang to my mind and traveled to my lips.

"Did Deets mention why he lived down country?"

"It would seem your interest in the racing world is confined to the equines that you wager on, ol' fellow."

I admitted as much.

"But they had to come from somewhere. Mayswood is well known as a stud farm."

"By Jove, I have heard of it."

"But did not associate it with our client. No matter. Possibly you can secure some hot tips on potential winners of the future."

Our road now left the trees and progressed up a slope towards an imposing marble building, much as Deets had described it. I noted a considerable cluster of buildings in the rear, obviously stables, and white rail fences that subdivided lush meadowland. In one area there were several jumps, and everywhere there was the neat and clipped white-on-green one would expect at a breeding farm.

As we reached the crest of the incline, our carriage swept round the imposing house and we found Clyde—I forced myself to think of him as Deets—speaking to two gillies in the stable area. He crossed towards us immediately, a smile creasing his firm face.

"I trust your journey was pleasant, gentlemen."

"Quite," replied Holmes.

His busy eyes were absorbing the scene as were mine. A number of horses were being released to follow familiar paths towards pastures. Some of the animals were mature, powerful beasts given to demonstrate their fit condition with leaps and lashing feet as they gained momentum and streaked into the fenced areas that surrounded the establishment.

Our host, in riding trousers and cavalry boots with an open shirt, was a far cry from the dandy of the previous day. As he led us toward the mansion house, I could not suppress a question.

"Any potential stakes winners among your animals?"

"We always hope. Several yearlings show unusual promise and their bloodlines are excellent. There's one, sired by Nurania, that we're excited about."

We were close by the dwelling now. A *porte cochere* was the main feature of this side of the mansion, and a large affair it was. Two carriages could have driven underneath it at the same time. Deets indicated puzzlement as to the next move.

"Would you care to wash up now before lunch, or does a visit to the scene of the incident appeal?"

"Being outside, let us view the balcony from the ground," suggested Holmes, and our host led us round the nearby corner.

The north side of Mayswood had an imposing flight of steps up to a formal entryway, this being the front entrance, though I imagined the major traffic passed through the door by the *porte cochere*. Further along, the smooth stone walls formed a right-angle recess allowing for a second-story balcony onto which five French windows opened. The break in the rectangular shape of the edifice was a pleasing architectural touch. The balcony was fronted by a stone balustrade on which were ornamental heads of savage beasts. In the center, a lion's head was slightly larger than its companions, a nice patriotic touch I thought.

"This being the balcony that you feel the intruder reached?" questioned Holmes in a manner that indicated his query was purely form.

Deets nodded. "For the life of me, I don't see how he made it."

I didn't, either. The windows on the ground floor were all effectively barred. Above them the walls were smooth, and any ledges or projections of some sort that would have given a cat burglar the handholds necessary to reach the balcony were just not there. Stout English ivy, which has served the lawless so well, was also absent.

Deets and I watched Holmes survey the side of the building and then move to a different position to view the balcony from another angle. When the horsebreeder looked at me questioningly, I indicated that I was as ignorant as he was to what was going through the sleuth's mind. This was not quite true, of course.

"Suppose I go inside and clean up," he suggested. "If you would care to view the sitting room, Dooley will show you up."

"Capital!" responded Holmes in a preoccupied manner.

As our client removed himself, I turned anxiously to my companion. Unless he had already come upon something, I fancied that he was viewing the scene and asking his agile mind what he would do were he a burglar intent on reaching the balcony. Before I could frame a question, Holmes's eyes found mine.

"A poser, would you say, Watson?"

"Indeed. I cannot imagine how even one of those human flies from the circus world could do it."

"Well, he did not climb the walls. He did not use a ladder. Such equipment could not have been removed in time. And," he added, chuckling, "he did not fly, lacking wings."

"Then how? There's certainly no clue."

"You are not at your best, ol' chap. By eliminating the more common methods, we must settle on a rope, an aid used by mountain climbers all the time."

My mouth sagged. Not at Holmes's simple explanation but at my idiocy for not thinking of it myself.

"Here I stand," continued the detective. "It is a dark and rainy night, important since the sound of falling water serves to cover any noise. In my hand is a coil of line attached to a light grappling hook. From right about here," he said, positioning himself, "I believe I could cast the hook upwards and over that stone balustrade. When the tines of the hook grip the railing, I keep the line taut and swarm up it to the second story. Now, if clever, I prepare for the worst by releasing the grappling hook, passing it under the rail of the balustrade, and lowering it to the ground. Now I have two strands of rope leading to the ground. I enter Mayswood via the French windows. But I hear approaching sounds. I flee back to the balcony and lower myself rapidly by sliding down the lines. Back at ground level, I pull the line free and disappear into the darkness. 'Tis done."

"Holmes, that's amazing. You have re-created the entire event."

"Not so, for I've revealed how I would do it. However,

should we discover some scratches on that balustrade that might have been made by the hook I envision, I rather fancy the matter is solved."

There was a certain self-satisfaction in his words that was grating. I banished my irritation as unworthy.

A venerable butler greeted us at the front entrance and led us upstairs. Mayswood was high-ceilinged, and most of the rooms were large enough to hold a meeting of the army general staff. But the feudal atmosphere of so many English country estates was completely lacking, no surprise since the mansion was certainly erected in this century and the furnishings were of no particular period but reflected the styles of many lands.

The upstairs sitting room was filled with sunlight from its four French windows, and the balcony revealed a breathless view of the surrounding countryside. Holmes was surveying the stone balustrade with his ever-present pocket glass when Deets rejoined us, now clad in tweeds. Holmes's movements had become more feverish as he moved from section to section of the stone railing, and finally he regarded us both with an expression akin to chagrin.

"I presented a plausable explanation to Watson regarding the coming and going of your uninvited guest, but the necessary corroboration eludes me."

I had begun to explain to Deets Holmes's idea when there was a sharp exclamation from the sleuth, who was now inspecting the outside of the railing.

"All is not lost," he exclaimed as we crossed to stand beside him, following the line indicated by his outstretched index finger. The ornamental lion's head on the outside of the balustrade rail was missing half an ear.

"What's this?" said Deets. "I wonder when that happened."

"Quite recently," replied Holmes in a triumphant tone. "Note how the newly revealed marble is not weathered as is the stone around it. My basic idea was sound, but I missed on the execution."

Deets was regarding him with a baffled expression that I recognized and well understood.

"Allow me to re-create the actions of your intruder."

Holmes shot me a quick glance. "This time, correctly. The man stood below, having no doubt seen you, Mr. Deets, depart. He held a light but strong line with a weight attached to its end, similar to the South American bolo. He spun the weighted line round his head, much in the manner of a cowboy of the American West with a lariat, and then cast it upwards. The weighted end wrapped itself round this ornament, knocking off part of an ear in the process. Holding the line taut, he climbed up. Once here on the balcony he removed the weighted end, ran it under the rail, and let it drop to the ground. I would estimate that on departure he could slide down the rope and pull the unweighted end free in a matter of fifteen seconds. Especially if he wore gloves or had heavily calloused hands."

Deets was shaking his head. "You have solved the mystery with a very clear explanation, Mr. Holmes. What do I do now?"

"I don't know. Nor do I know my next move unless I find out what the intruder was after."

This suggestive remark was allowed to dangle for a brief moment and I felt that we might be getting somewhere, but then Deets looked away. Was there an expression of guilt on his face?

"I can't tell you," he finally said.

This could have been read two ways, but Holmes did not choose to pursue the matter. Rather, he turned to admire the vista of rolling green fields.

"I note the horses all around us," he said casually.

Deets eagerly seized on the change of subject.

"We keep the brood mares separate, of course, but allow the yearlings and the stallions to roam at will. We're at the crest of the hill here and the fields stretch on every side. They are well fenced, and it gives the young fellows a chance to watch the sires. They seem to develop faster that way, chasing after pater as it were."

"I understand," said Holmes, "that horses, especially race horses, rather fancy companions. Roosters, dogs. . . ."

"Some do. Before my father bought Mayswood he raised dogs. But he developed a skin allergy that the doctors attributed to canine hair. That was the end of the dogs."

"Whippets? Greyhounds, perhaps?"

"Dobermans," was the reply. Holmes allowed this subject to drop as well.

By unspoken mutual consent, we all retired to the interior, descending the great stairs towards the dining room where we enjoyed a tasteful luncheon and some excellent burgundy that our host recommended highly. I was prompted to inquire as to where he had secured this vintage but suppressed the question as it seemed in poor taste.

Holmes informed our client that we would return to London via the afternoon train and that he would make inquiries as to the presence in England of a second-story man who had come from or had been in the Argentine. He used the word *gaucho* in connection with the suspect and said, in an encouraging manner, that a thief with a particular aptitude that was unusual was much easier to find. Deets seemed heartened by this fact, and we took our leave of Mayswood.

The click of wheels on rails along with the burgundy caused me to sleep much of the way back. When I did rouse myself on the outskirts of London, Holmes anticipated my question.

"Of course he knows, Watson."

"What?"

"What the intruder was after. I suspect we do, too. In response to my direct question you noted that Deets said 'I can't tell you.' By that, I assumed that he was bound by a promise, perhaps a fear. Then, too, the stationmaster at Litchfield who directed us to the carriage and the driver both knew our names, and I felt they were aware of the reason for our visit. It would seem that Deets enlisted our services as window dressing. 'Look you, beware, for Holmes and Watson are on the scene.'"

"Come now, that's stretching it a bit, is it not?"

"Possibly, but consider the matter of the horses and the dogs before them."

"You'll have to explain that."

"Captain Spaulding, retired from his explorations, settles down in England and raises dogs. Not the racing breed but Doberman pinschers, the fiercest watchdogs in the world. A reaction to canine hair causes him to drop this activity, and he turns to horsebreeding."

"What is unusual about that?"

"Nothing, until you consider the way Mayswood is laid out. Deets did say it was somewhat like a fortress. In addition, it is surrounded by fenced pastures containing, on all sides, high-spirited stallions and skittish yearlings. Were I intent on approaching the Deets ménage surreptitiously, I would think twice before crossing a field at the risk of being run down by a temperamental thoroughbred. When track champions are set out to stud, they evidence frisky ways. Captain Spaulding was intent on protecting something, and with his passing, his son has remained true to the task."

Holmes had given me plenty to think about. He was, as was his custom, diligently turning his theory this way and that in his mind to allow the light of reason to reflect on its various facets.

The remainder of our trip to Baker Street was made in silence.

Chapter Six

The Call to Colors

I well knew what twists and turns were in store at this point. The world's only consulting detective had involved himself in two matters, not unusually, for at times he had as many as a dozen cases that he handled simultaneously. His "calling out the reserves," as it were, merely signified that one or both ranked as a major challenge, and I had seen the sheaf of cables that Billy had dispatched two nights before. The harvest they produced had to be reaped.

Returning to our chambers was a signal for Holmes to depart after reading messages that had been delivered in our absence. In olden times I had chafed at being suddenly out of things, but I now realized that this was standard procedure in certain of Holmes's investigations. The cables had been dispatched to that ragtag army that his brother had referred to. Some Holmes met elsewhere, like Porlock, the informer, formerly connected with Moriarty of infamous memory. I had never seen the man, and Porlock was not his real name. But Holmes used him along with others whom I did know, some well.

They fell into two camps, this heterogenous crew with strange backgrounds and unusual, specialized talents. The outside group were seldom spoken of. On rare occasions, an unidentified person of either sex might make a surreptitious visit to Baker Street because of the exigencies of a situation. I took pains not to make note of their features and, as much as possible, to wipe them from my mind's slate lest an unwitting slip of the tongue would cause harm.

The inside group were known by name to Billy, Mrs. Hudson, and myself. They appeared at our chambers frequently and on most occasions I was privy to their conferences with the master sleuth.

I pictured my friend, possibly in one of the many disguises he used so well, now involved with the outside group. Certainly he would be loosening his hounds on the scent of Chu San Fu, and the memory of the Chinese criminal caused me to spend part of the dying day oiling my trusty Webley and checking its load. Holmes had a seeming disregard for his personal safety, which I tried to counterbalance by being as prepared as I could.

When nightfall came, I ate a solitary meal and tried to cushion Mrs. Hudson's concern about the eating habits of her famous tenant. The nutritive needs of the detective were one of the many worries of the dear lady and revealed her extreme patience. When Holmes disappeared, one never knew when he would return, and when he did, he would like as not decide to have a bite, which might range from a nibble of cheese to half a joint of beef. When frustrated by a case, and on the premises, he frequently sat brooding at the table, his meal untouched, and our landlady's wheedling was to no avail. But if Holmes has a problem, Mrs. Hudson had some cause to feel pride in her skill with stove and skillet. Even in those early days when I was still recovering from my wartime wound and subsequent illness, I had been blessed with a good appetite and consistently did justice to her provender.

The dishes had been cleared away and, possibly spurred by our trip to the Mayswood stud, I had made some check marks against entries in the Southgate Plate due to be run over the weekend. Our news dealer, who delivered copies of all editions, included a biweekly racing sheet that I fancied. I had narrowed my choice to Vortex out of Grand Dame by Nurania when there were footsetps on the stairs.

Before I could arise, Holmes opened the door and Slim Gilligan, a valise in one hand, followed him in. The former master-cracksman was our most frequent visitor from the inside group. His lock-and-key establishment, originally financed by Sherlock Holmes, was a successful business venture, small wonder since his workmen, mostly graduates of

Dartmoor or Princetown, were skillful indeed. Installing a lock on a front door or making a new key for a file case was child's play to one who has opened a Mills-Stroffner safe in the dead of night by the light of a bull's-eye lantern. It was bruited about in certain circles that Holmes was a silent partner in Gilligan's business, which must have acted as a deterrent should any of the employees consider resuming their wayward paths.

Holmes favored me with a quick nod as he crossed to the desk, unlocking the cash drawer. Gilligan, his cloth hat at a jaunty angle and an unlit cigarette stuck behind one ear, winked in my direction. His expression indicated, "We're at it again."

"There is an inn in the village, Slim," my friend was saying, "and I'm sure you can work out a good cover story."

"A breeze, Guv," was the abnormally thin man's response.

Holmes removed some currency from the desk, placed it in an envelope, and handed it to Gilligan.

"A cable here will reach me or Watson. If not, Billy will find us. I don't know of any other problems save those we've discussed. How about Styles?"

Oh ho! I thought. Slippery Styles, the human shadow, is involved.

" 'E's at Waterloo, waitin' fer me. You'll 'ave yer cable, Guv—in jig time."

With a cheerful wave in my direction, the cracksman was gone. I did not hear the downstairs door open or close, but when Slim came or went I never did. He just seemed to materialize like a genie at Holmes's call and then vanish. For a time, I had thought that by night he came and went via the roof. Gilligan was a great fancier of rooftops. Of late, it had crossed my mind that he might know about the house next door and the secret entrance to our establishment. I refrained from bringing this matter up. If Holmes wanted me to know, he would tell me. One of my friend's catch phrases was: "I tell as much or as little as I choose." Usually, he modified this somewhat cavalier statement with the additive: "That is the advantage of being unofficial." The years had taught me that this was an elastic phrase meaning that he alone possessed carte blanche. In truth, he had on occasion chosen to appoint himself as the prosecution, judge, and jury as well, but no harm had come of it.

During my musings, Holmes had gotten his pipe going and now saw fit to break his silence.

"Any visitors, Watson?"

"None. Nor messages, either."

"No matter."

Followed by a trail of smoke, he began to pace our sitting room with that purposeful manner. Holmes was tall and amazingly strong, the best amateur boxer I had ever seen. As a result, his movements were graceful and his footfall light. Had it not been so, I imagine there would have been paths worn in our carpets, for he did like to think on his feet. I imagined that his mind, so capable of absolute concentration, was completely immersed in the Deets matter and whatever errand he had sent Gilligan on. Slim's mention of Waterloo had led me to associate the cracksman with the Mayswood affair. As usual, Holmes surprised me.

"I agree with your selection, Watson. Vortex should win the Plate with ease."

"There must have been exasperation on my face as I followed his moving figure. My racing sheet was on the end table, though how he spotted it and my pencil work I could not fathom.

"Look here, Holmes, I checked at least four of the horses."

"But you underlined Nurania, Vortex's sire, said former champion being the leading stud at Mayswood Farm. Your final choice is obvious, is it not?"

I suppressed a sigh. Everything was obvious, once Holmes explained it.

Having produced his surprise, which gave him joy, the sleuth switched to the matter at hand. His words, presumably directed at me, might well have been delivered to the walls in my absence. But I was a fixture like the commonplace books and his voluminous files, a sounding board that he had become accustomed to.

"Chu San Fu has been positioned for me and there is no

undue activity in his lair, which means he hasn't heard, as yet, of our trip to Mayswood."

"You think he has an information source in Surrey?"

"If I read the signs right. One, there was an intruder at Mayswood. That ornamental lion's head gave us a corroborating clue there. Two, the nighttime visitor was not a robber but a one-man survey team. Getting the lay of the land, as 'twere. Three, the Chinaman is after the Sacred Sword."

"Hold on!" Occasionally I rebelled in my role of Greek chorus, a fact that did not nettle Holmes. In fact, he welcomed it since it gave him the opportunity to test the steel of his reasoning. "Your first two statements had a foundation of fact, but now are you not moving a bit out on a limb? Do we know that this sword that intrigues you so is not just a myth?"

"Touché, Watson. We must visit Sir Randolph Rapp to secure an opinion."

An expert one, I admitted to myself. Sir Randolph had figured in a previous adventure of Holmes's and was the *dernier cri*, to my way of thinking.

"One thing Rapp will mention is that most myths and folklore are not just flights of fancy. The Midas legend for one—"

Whatever other tales, lost in time, Holmes intended to cite I did not learn, since there were sounds from without and he crossed to the door and flung it open. Filling the aperture was the robust form of Burlington Bertie.

" 'Ere we be, Guv. Mite late but I did me best."

"Ah, Bertie. Do come in."

As Holmes stood to one side, I fear my eyes must have of a sudden resembled saucers, for behind Bertie there was another figure.

I'm sure it was an illusion, but when this apparition followed in Bertie's footsteps, it seemed that he had to step sidewise to make his way through our substantial doorway. He was no taller than Holmes, but his width dwarfed the burly Bertie. His hair, so blond as to be almost white, topped a round face devoid of wrinkles with no traces of a beard. It was the face of a child set on a sturdy neck that terminated in a huge upper frame. He was, almost literally, as broad as tall. His legs were short but had to be like the trunks of oak trees to support him. There was a smile seemingly painted on his face, and his wide blue eyes had a dreamy quality as though he had just awakened.

I rose to my feet hurriedly and noted that Holmes was regarding our unusual visitor with a surprised look as if wondering if the body was real and not carved by a wood-worker using Gog and Magog as models.

"This 'ere's Tiny," said Burlington Bertie.

"I see," replied Holmes. I admired his sangfroid.

"Do be seated, gentlemen."

The humor of Lambeth and Limehouse, Chelsea and Croydon, is of a simple nature. How could this gargantuan be named anything but "Tiny"? I watched his progress into the room with alarm, trusting that our furniture would survive. Holmes directed traffic in such a manner that Tiny was aimed at our largest chair by the fire.

"Tiny don't say much but 'e's a good lad."

"Quite," replied Holmes. "I can see that he would not need many words."

The movements of the good lad fascinated me. They were delicate, as though he trod on eggs and maneuvered in a doll's house. Of course, I thought, the poor chap has to be careful. An inadvertent gesture and he's liable to push down a wall!

Tiny lowered himself into his designated chair in so fluid a manner that there was not even a creak. He sat with his hands placidly folded in his lap, his face slowly moving between Holmes, Bertie, and myself with interest, and his smile never wavered.

"You said there might be some business, Mr. 'Olmes, so I brung the boy along to see if 'e'll pass muster."

"He'll do just fine," replied my friend.

Tiny was obviously listening and capable of understanding, for he started to rise but was forestalled by a gesture from his companion.

"There's more yet."

As the giant resumed his seat, Bertie turned again to Holmes. "Loik I says to yer earlier, Mr. 'Olmes, there's not a sign of that third bloke wot I caved in on the docks when I hies meself back there t'other night."

"You mentioned pursuing some leads," replied the sleuth, who had managed to drag his eyes away from Tiny.

"I 'ad in mind Blind Louie, the beggar. 'E lives not far from the docks and wot 'e don't see ain't worth viewin'." As though this required additional verification, Bertie turned towards me. "Sharpest eyes between 'ere and Land's End, Doctor."

"Blind Louie?"

"At's roight. Oi 'ad me a good idea for Blind Louie was comin' 'ome 'bout the time of the fracas wot 'e seen. 'E's got the end of that white cane of 'is weighted and was goin' ter lend a 'and but 'e sees me and the late Negro 'ad got things under control. Anyways, after I leaves, Blind Louie is thinkin' 'bout gettin' on the dock to see if the cove I coshed ain't got a few pence wot 'e don't need, but Louie is cautious, 'e is, and a good fing, fer some Chinks comes by and picks up the body, and carts 'im away. Now Louie don't know 'oo the Chinks is but 'e figgers maybe the boyo I coshed is Sidney Putz."

Holmes shook his head, disclaiming knowledge of this sinister citizen.

"Me, neither, Mr. 'Olmes, but Louie says Putz used to work fer Weisman, the usurer. And 'at's all I could dig up."

"A good job, Bertie." My friend was crossing to the desk again as he spoke. "We'll see if we can learn more of Sidney Putz. Meanwhile, I am expecting some action and I want you and Tiny to be on call." Holmes secured more notes from the cash drawer and passed them to Bertie. "I don't know what is involved, but I'll get a message to you at the usual place."

"Right-o, Mr. 'Olmes. Wotever the caper, you just do the thinkin' and Tiny and me, we'll make out."

"Of that I'm sure," stated Holmes with deepseated conviction.

Fascinated, we both watched Bertie and Tiny depart.

I sank back in my chair and mopped my forehead with Irish linen. "Really, Holmes, life is never dull at 221B Baker Street."

"How fortunate for us. Keeps us young, you know."

He did have the good grace not to let the matter drop at that.

"As you gathered, I spoke to Bertie earlier. Almost as an afterthought, I recalled those two giant Manchurians we came in contact with once before. Followers of Chu San Fu. Now Bertie is no midget, so I asked him if he could locate another good man in a brawl."

"I would say," I answered, "that Bertie filled the bill."

Chapter Seven

Special Commission

The following morning when my senses sluggishly saw fit to rise from the sea of the subconscious, I guessed that the hour was not an early one. The warmth of my blankets held appeal, but I resisted the impulse to lower my lids again and deny the world of reality.

I rose with a half groan, my feet searched the cold floor for my worn bedroom slippers, and shortly thereafter, clutching my dressing gown round me, I descended to the sitting room of our bachelor abode. The possibility that Sherlock Holmes, habitually a late riser, might still be abed was disproved by the acrid smell of the strong shag of his morning pipe which assaulted my nostrils on the stairs. I found my friend seated at the desk regarding messages.

"My good Watson," he said without looking up, "the heel of one of your slippers is loose. Do have it looked after before you come acropper."

"How did you—!" I began, and then bit back the words. "A revealing sound during my descent, no doubt," I concluded.

"Exactly. We readily detect the sounds of others but tend to ignore those we make ourselves." Holmes rose to knock out his pipe in the fireplace. "But we cannot ignore some news just in. Action is called for, and I have a special commission for you."

My spirits brightened. It had been some time since the disappearance of Lady Frances Carfax, but the adventure remained etched in my mind.* Holmes had deputized me to conduct an investigation relative to the lady, and his critique had been to the point.

"A very pretty hash you have made of it" were his words, and, he had twisted the knife further by later adding: "I cannot at the moment recall any possible blunder that you have omitted." Since that moment, I had yearned for the chance to redeem myself.

"It is vital that I have someone on the scene at Mayswood," continued Holmes.

"But Gilligan and Styles—" I began.

"I have a cable from Slim on the desk. But I need an inside man, Watson. Matters are coming to a head with greater rapidity than I anticipated. You can catch the late morning train for Surrey at Waterloo."

"And my mission?"

"You will inform Clyde Deets that I have uncovered a warm trail as regards his nocturnal intruder. Let me impress upon you, ol' fellow, that this is true. We are not telling the gentleman the whole story, but that's neither here nor there." Holmes was regarding me closely. "Deceit is not one of your strong points, and I want you at ease with your conscience."

"Oh, come now—"

A hand gesture stifled my retort, a good thing since this subject was shaky ground for me.

"Tell Deets that you wish to make inquiries in Litchfield and the surrounding area. You can be a bit mysterious about it. Clients rather like that. He will offer you the use of a carriage, but you suggest that you could perform your investigations better from horseback."

"Holmes, would you have me on a racehorse?"

"Tut, tut! Have no fear of that. I'm sure he can provide a hunter suitable to your needs."

"Well, it's been a while since I've been in a saddle, but I suppose I can carry it off."

"Assuming our duplicity holds water, as I fancy it will, ride off in the direction of Litchfield. Out of sight of

* Surely Watson is in error here. "The Disappearance of Lady Frances Carfax" is generally agreed to have been in the Summer of 1902, long after this adventure.

the establishment, circle the area carefully, making note of the roads and where they lead. You'll have to ride into the hamlet itself to preserve the facade of conducting an investigation. Pay particular attention to the railroad, Watson."

"I'm to survey the terrain, then. Sounds a bit like a military campaign."

"Agreed," said Holmes with an approving smile that banished some of my doubts. "Also, I want you to acquaint yourself with the stables at Mayswood, especially those devoted to the riding animals. Locate the tack room. Mention that you are addicted to strolls after dinner. I want you familiar with the stable area in the dark. Deets may volunteer to accompany you, so much the better. Horses are his business so he'll readily give you a guided tour. Now, one other thing: when you arrive at the breeding farm, manage to be at the window of the room made available to you between nine and nine-thirty at night. Extinguish the lights and use a candle. Pass it three times back and forth before the window. Then await an answering signal, three flashes from a lantern. Repeat the process, if necessary, until your signal has been acknowledged."

I regarded Holmes with an expression akin to astonishment.

"But why this hocus-pokus? Reminds me of that Baskerville affair."

Holmes's concerned and serious manner was swallowed up by a chuckle. "So it does. Hadn't occurred to me. But consider that for my peace of mind I must know your exact location. You play such an important part in the weapon that we are forging."

His words produced a glow of pride, and my spirits rallied at the thought that he placed such faith in me. Later it occurred to me that his words actually revealed nothing, and when I was on the Surrey-bound train, I experienced a moment of panic at the realization that I knew so little of Holmes's plans. His instructions did not appear to involve anything vital at all. But I banished my misgivings, determined to let the drama unfold. I really had very little choice.

Holmes had cabled ahead, alerting Deets of my arrival,

and the same carriage and driver, Alfred, awaited me at the Litchfield station. My host had held luncheon for me, and as indicated previously, he set a fine board. He was seemingly delighted to learn that Holmes was "on to something," as I put it. My revelations were flimsy fabrics indeed, but I managed to introduce some suggestive silences and wise looks, all of which he readily accepted.

Suddenly I realized that the threadbare information with which Holmes had dispatched me had been no oversight by the master manhunter. Detailed explanations were not needed, and I felt that I had earned some scattered applause interspersed by a few faint "bravos!" Not for my performance as the supposed investigator, but for the fact that my words were honored without question. The career of my friend was at this period certainly approaching its zenith, and his name was a household word, due in part to the recountings of certain of his adventures that I had made available to the reading public. When Holmes was on a case, his methods were immune to criticism, and in truth the solution was considered a fait accompli. Such was the aura of infallibility that surrounded his name that even a sophisticated man of the world like Deets was caught up in the cloak of invincibility worn by the man from Baker Street.

When Dooley, the butler, showed me to my room, I found that my valise had been opened and my things hung up. The aged family retainer, during the serving of lunch, must have heard my request for the use of a horse, for there were riding pants available along with boots that suited me nicely. The butler was a bit long in the tooth for the trade of espionage, but I felt he would be pleasing to Mycroft Holmes, who put such store in "anticipation."

Deets took me personally to the stables and had a groom saddle up a chestnut mare, all the while assuring me that she was a gentle animal. As Holmes had instructed, I made note of the area where the saddles, bridles, and blankets were kept, resolving to revisit it come nightfall. Deets gave me simple directions to Litchfield and mentioned that should I get lost, my steed would, if given a free rein, return me to Mayswood without fail. I sensed that, with the eye of an expert, he placed little faith in my horsemanship.

I had managed to make a fair mount and set off with high resolve to emulate cavalry officers I'd known when with the Fifth Northumberland, my old regiment. I must have been holding the curb rein too tight, for the chestnut, "Fandango" by name, worried at her bit and was lathering at the mouth, showing a disposition to introduce short, nervous side steps. I loosened the reins and contented myself with indicating my desired direction by the pressure of my knees, an arrangement that seemed to suit the horse, who relaxed so that we both were able to enjoy the warm afternoon sun and bracing air.

Some distance from Mayswood, I diverted from the main road to the neighboring village and started a wide circle round the breeding farm. Now Fandango introduced another little trick in her repertoire. Since we were not moving away from Mayswood, at every crossroads she chose to veer in the direction that would return us to its pastures. After some urging on my part, we reached a meeting of the minds and my mount abandoned visions of her stall, oats, and a rubdown.

The winding country roads were in good condition considering the spring rains, and the whole area, in contrast to Mayswood itself, was heavily timbered. Hemlock, chestnut, and elm were in profusion, and it occurred to me that the coloration of Fandango blended well with the surrounding trees. My riding apparel was beige, and were I to pull off the road and remain motionless in the timber, I fancied my mount and I would be difficult to spot. The lane I had chosen inclined upwards after a while, and soon I was on a bluff looking down on a pleasant valley. The gleam of rails was discernable to the left, and as I followed them visually I noted a freight terminus of some size with a variety of tracks on which boxcars and freight carriers stood, many empty and with their doors open. This puzzled me somewhat, being removed from Litchfield, until I realized that the rails I had first noted were probably a branch line and that sizable freight trains were assembled at this terminus and then dispatched for the run into the metropolis of London.

It was a country freight yard that I had chanced upon. Well, Holmes had drawn my attention to the railroad so I abandoned my proposed circuit of Mayswood and rode a little way along the path until I found a trail leading down from the bluff and into the valley. I made note of the area in case my side journey turned into a dead end and I was forced to return this way. Once on level ground, I followed the rails towards Litchfield. When we turned away from Mayswood, Fandango again showed a disposition to sulk, but she finally became reconciled to the situation and mustered a presentable single-foot that did not bounce me too much in the saddle, though certain portions of my posterior gave promise of tenderness.

The single-foot segued into a canter, and I realized that Fandango was a gaited horse when she accelerated into a rack that ate up ground with a gentle rapidity. The horse, like Deets, sensed my ineptitude and seemed to be making things easy for me, or perhaps she was in a hurry to get the matter over and get back to a nosebag.

On the outskirts of Litchfield Fandango decelerated into her single-foot, probably her most showy gait, and I fancy we made a sporty pair as we entered the hamlet, which was little more than one street of about two city blocks in length terminating at the railroad station.

As I suspected, there was a cable office adjacent to the station, and I drew up before it and, carefully and slowly, quitted my saddle with no more than a few grunts. I led Fandango to the horse trough in approved style and then secured her reins on an adjacent rail right next to a mounting box. I'd gotten off without falling on my face, and perhaps I could resume my seat with dignity as well.

At the cable office I entered and made a show as though inquiring about a message. Actually I just exchanged some words with the telegrapher about the weather, and he must have thought I was a lonesome soul indeed. Vacating these premises, I noted that the local inn, a small establishment, was named "The Red Lion." Were I to possess a pound note for every inn by that name in Britain, I might well have a box at the races next to Lord Balmoral! "The Red Lion" had to be the center of Litchfield's limited social life, so I set my feet towards it resolutely. Then I saw them! Two Chinamen on the opposite side of the street and coming towards me. Well, I had not been friend and biographer of Sherlock Holmes for so long without recognizing the makings of a shrewd move. Orientals don't just happen in the depths of Surrey. Contrary to the experience of our American cousins, English hands iron English shirts, and most of our railroads were built with the assistance of the Welsh and the Cornish. The Chinese had to be visitors and, hence, had to be residing at the inn.

I hastened my steps and preceded them into the edifice by way of the pub door conveniently available. Being already on the premises, they could not suspect me of following them should they make an appearance. Chinese spelled Chu San Fu, and while the grip of the former crime czar on Limehouse had been broken, it made sense that many of the retainers he still had left would be of his race.

I assumed a stance at the empty bar and wished I had a riding crop to tap against my boots as I ordered a stout.

The barkeep was a man of few words, but when he filled my order he summoned seven of them, revealing in the process his Scots ancestry.

"I ken you're nae from these parts."

"A visitor, my good man, as you have discerned."

I felt that a sop to the Scot's powers of observation might lead to more discernment on other subjects, but he indicated little interest in my length of stay, point of origin, or anything else.

After giving the polished wood surface a perfunctory swipe with a bar rag, he retired to the end of the room to throw darts at the inevitable board. Keeping his eye sharp for some bets with the evening trade, I thought. However, said practice was interrupted, to my delight, by the entrance of the Chinese. In very broken English, they requested tea and retired to a side table and low conversation in their native tongue. The barkeep relayed the order through a service window in the back of the bar and resumed his dart activity.

I was considering ordering another draft and wondering how I might get closer to the Chinese, a fruitless task since I could not understand one word of their conversation. Then there was another entry, a disconcerting incident to the barkeep, who had just scored two center hits and was intent on making it three. As it happened, his services were not required. A thin little man in nondescript clothes found his way inside with some difficulty, holding his throat with one hand and gesturing at his mouth with the other. When he spoke, it was in a croak and with some effort.

"Is there . . . is there a doctor round?"

Lifelong training took over. "I am a doctor," I said, promptly crossing to him.

"Got somethin' stuck in my windpipe," he wheezed.

I removed his hand from his throat and, using two fingers, pried his jaws apart, peering down his gullet, but the light in the pub was dim. I ran a finger in an exploratory move past his tongue, for this could be serious, but he started to choke and I removed my digit while I still had it.

He gestured towards the door and I seized him by the arm with a gesture of agreement, leading him outside and into the afternoon sun. With his back to the door, I started to open his mouth again when things took a singular turn.

"Just give it a fake look-see, Doctor Watson, for it's a dodge. Me throat's tip-top."

I started to draw back from the man with a shocked expression, and alarm bells rang in my ears.

"Keep lookin', Doc," he urged in a low voice, raising his chin as though to aid my efforts.

As I made a dumb show of peering into his orifice, he spoke quietly and distinctly, no mean feat with his mouth wide open.

"Pay no attention to the Chinks, Doc. Mr. 'Olmes don't want those boyos to get a wind up. Just make yer way back to Mayswood, and we'll watch for your signal tonight."

"Then you are—?"

"—Slippery Styles, Doc."

Good heavens, I thought, the human shadow! I'd never seen him close to before, but when Holmes wanted someone followed, Styles was the man he called for. My friend contended that Slippery could follow a sinner into hell without getting his coat singed!

Momentarily inspired, I whipped out a pocket handkerchief, holding it to Styles's mouth and slapping him on the back. The little man made a nice show of apparently coughing up a chicken bone or some such object. There lurks in all of us the desire to perform, even in an empty theatre, and I was so imbued by this adventure that I had a happy inspiration.

"My room is on the front of Mayswood," I mentioned as though I were telling the chap that he was all right now.

"Got yuh, Doc. Till tonight."

With the feeling that all was not amiss, I returned to the pub to pay for my drink and departed full of self-approval since I had not cast a single glance at the mysterious Chinese.

As I managed, with the help of the mounting block, to straddle Fandango and get my feet into the irons, I reasoned that Holmes must already be alerted to the presence of Orientals in the vicinity of Mayswood. No doubt from Gilligan's cable.

Going down the street, Fandango gave indications of following a different route and seemed to harbor definite ideas about it. It occurred to me that the horse would take me back to the breeding farm in the most direct manner if allowed to, so I was content to let her take charge. After all, there is a limit to the patience of a five-gaited show horse. Such she had to be to successfully transport a middle-aged doctor of sedentary habits safely up hill and down dale through the Surrey countryside.

Back at Mayswood Stud, I had ample time to wash up and change for dinner before joining Deets in the drawing room. His Irish whiskey was on a par with his burgundy, and seated next to a pleasing fire, my blood running faster from the day's ride, I resolved to treat said spirits with respect. My host had a pleasing personality, as I had noted before, though he was not as loquacious or rapid in his speech as he had been during our first meeting at Baker Street. I informed him that my afternoon had produced no results and considered mentioning the two Chinese but abandoned the thought. It could do no good and might do the reverse.

I tried to lead the conversation to horsebreeding. Deets spoke easily and fluently on that subject, and I resolved to give more attention to the bloodlines of my racing choices in the future. Whenever the conversation dragged, I resorted to previous cases of Holmes's, a conversational crutch that I could use with facility and that always found ready ears. I did mention that I thought Holmes would conclude his London investigation shortly and would join us in the country. It seemed the sporting thing to do and apparently this proved welcome news.

Butler Dooley, like all of his rare breed, appeared with seeming omniscience whenever needed and gave indication of having a sharp pair of ears to boot. His master had absented himself for a moment for some undisclosed reason, and the butler inquired with concern if it were possible for Mr. Holmes to share my room should he be arriving shortly. He explained that Mrs. Deets had been in the process of redecorating all the other bedrooms, save the master suite, prior to her sudden departure for her sister's home on Tuesday. The reference to "sudden departure" rather pricked up my ears, and then the day of the week mentioned caught my attention. It now being Thursday, this would mean that Deets's wife had been bustled off to her sister's on the day that he visited us at Baker Street.

I forestalled the servant's departure with the indication that a refill would be acceptable, and thought furiously.

"Was it Tuesday that your mistress left, Dooley?" I asked, with what I hoped was a casual air. "I was of a mind that it was Monday."

"Oh no, sir, the mistress left on Tuesday all right, for it was the same day that Mr. Deets went to London."

Well, our client had specified that his wife had taken her trip before the incident of the intruder. I also thought it singular that the lady was removed from the estate immediately following the happening. Obviously, Deets was more concerned about the matter than he had indicated, or possibly his wife was of a nervous nature, though this did not coincide with my picture of an English lady satisfied with the rural life of a country estate, as high-toned as it might be. I decided to abandon this subject when I realized that, for all I knew, Mrs. Deets was not English at all and her life at Mayswood might not be a happy one either.

"Dooley," I said, accepting a refill that I noted was liberal. "Mr. Deets tells me you have been with the family for some time."

"I had the honor of serving his father."

"After his travels?"

"His travels, sir?"

The question to my question was delivered so immediately and honestly that I almost spoke of the famous Captain Spaulding and his explorations, but drew back in time. I was getting in too deep and was rather glad that the present master of the house returned at this moment.

Shortly thereafter we dined, following which my host graciously took me for a stroll round the grounds, providing excellent cigars for us both to enjoy during it, though I have always felt that the taste and aroma of a cigar loses something in the open air. They, like good brandy, are meant to be enjoyed in a comfortable easy chair, to be savored, as 'twere. I told the equine expert about the monograph Holmes had once published dealing with the ash of every known brand of cigar and tobacco and rather lengthily titled: "Upon the Distinction between the Ashes of the Various Tobaccos."

This so intrigued Deets, who obviously enjoyed the good things of life, that I was able to guide our footsteps without seeming to into the area of the stables containing the riding horses, and I used my eyes as well as I could and managed a few leading questions as well.

Life on a breeding farm evidently began at an early hour. It was with no difficulty that I was able to reach my bedroom before nine. My riding habit of the day had been carefully brushed, and the boots polished to a fine sheen. But the container in which my toilet articles were kept had not been opened. A tiny piece of wax was still under the cover when I opened it. This was a trick that I had learned from Holmes years ago. Within was the small candle that I had taken the precaution to include with my razor and the rest of my kit.

Extinguishing the lights on the hour, I lit the candle and passed it three times across the center window of my room. I then snuffed out the flame and blinked my eyes to allow clearer vision in the darkness, another trick of the sleuth.

In short order there were three answering flashes from the woods. Quick work, I thought, but then Gilligan and

Styles already knew which side of the house to watch. My trip into Litchfield had been of some benefit.

Clear country air, free from the oily smoke of channel coal, has a soporific effect, and I felt myself drifting off to sleep almost immediately.

My final thoughts were that it had not been a wasted day and I could think of no grievous errors I had made. Possibly I had some aptitude in the sleuthing line after all.

The following day gave promise of being a repetition of the previous one. Fandango seemed more familiar with my ways and allowed me, with a resigned air I thought, to make a complete circuit of the estate. I noted the various roads and paths as best I could along with the general terrain. Then we traveled to Litchfield where I avoided "The Red Lion" but, from habit, visited the cable office. I was somewhat surprised to find a message there, not yet dispatched to Mayswood. It was brief, as Holmes's cables were wont to be: "Inform those concerned of my arrival tomorrow. S.H."

I allowed Fandango her head returning to the stud farm, and she made a rapid job of it. A good thing, too, since I had noted a number of aches and pains when we had set out, and our brisk return trip seemed to relieve them rather than compound the problem.

I informed Deets of the contents of the cable and he finally expressed curiosity, reasonable under the circumstances.

"I wonder what he has learned?" It was a general question, but I sensed he expected an answer and might be a little suspicious if he didn't get one.

Well, ol' boy, I thought, you'd better make this good. Holmes has remarked often that subtlety is not one of your talents. Let's prove him wrong. Holmes was not a fabricator; he did not have to be. But I had noted that when he found it expedient to lay a false scent, he employed as much of the truth as possible. I determined to follow this principle in my first attempt at flim-flammery.

"I seldom know all of Holmes's moves until after the checkmate." Well, that was certainly true. "As he mentioned," I continued, "the fact that the intruder used a bolo-type device alerted him to a South American as a possibility. I can give you a guess."

Deets indicated this would be appreciated. .

"Holmes's knowledge of the criminal classes is extensive, and in addition he has access to the files of Scotland Yard and the Sureté as well, if need be." I didn't dwell on the Criminal Arkiv of the Berlin police. No sense in overdoing it.

"I think he has selected possibilities from known second-story men who are agile, strong, but small."

"Why small?" The wary look in Deets's eyes was fading away.

"He pulled himself up to the balcony in short order and descended in a trice; otherwise you would have seen him. That's not easy for a weighty man. Holmes pictures a type like a tumbler or acrobat, who is also adept with a weighted line. He has been narrowing down the list, and his cable indicates that he now has a prime suspect."

"But how does this tie in with your presence here? Not that your company hasn't been welcome," Deets hastened to add, with the true instincts of a proper host. "Your stories of Mr. Holmes's cases have been of great interest."

I hope I exhibited a magnanimous air. For safety's sake, I resorted to the oft-used device of a Socratical response.

"Would you think it possible that a man of that description might have been seen in this area?"

He nodded, of course. What else could he do?

"In fact, the culprit might still be in the vicinity planning a second attempt. If so," I stated with a touch of bravado, "my presence on the scene might deter such an idea."

Deets's boyish smile had returned.

"You detectives really have to touch all the wickets, don't you?"

"Detail. Painstaking detail. The sifting of all the facts and, finally, the forming of the relevent elements into a mosaic, a design that throws the harsh light of truth on what happened or, possibly of more importance, what might happen."

As well to be hung for a sheep as a goat, I thought. Deets didn't really know what I was talking about, for I didn't know myself. But it had a good sound to it and ob-

75

viously played a pleasant tune in his ears. I resolved to attend future discussions between Holmes and our client lest some of my words come back at me.

I was present, but not at all in the manner that I had anticipated.

Chapter Eight

A Harrowing Night

I had no sooner retired to my bedroom, the footsteps of the attentive Dooley fading down the hall, when I was so startled that I must have jumped a foot. Out of nowhere came a voice, and it took a moment to realize that it was a familiar one.

"Is the coast clear, Guv?"

As I stood petrified, Slim Gilligan assumed that my silence indicated an affirmative and rolled out from under my bed.

"Good Heavens, Gilligan, what brings you here?"

"Mr. 'Olmes wants you ready to move, Guv. 'E's got a nose fer such things, 'e 'as, and tonight's the night."

I did not bother asking the cracksman how he had gained my room. With his record, a country estate presented no problems. To my credit, I acted in a businesslike manner. "What's the plan?"

"If yuh waits a bit, till the master of the 'ouse 'as folded up shop, you're to go downstairs. Tell the butler that you want to take another turn 'round and then nip out to the stables and saddle a couple of ridin' 'orses. Then you come back, see, and the butler—"

"Dooley."

"—'ll lock the place up fer the night. You get inter your ridin' togs and stand by. Mr. 'Olmes figures there's goin' to be a real hullabaloo durin' the night with a lot o' runnin' 'round, and you slips out in the confusion and gets the 'orses. Ride round back and make fer the main road, stayin' away from the tree line."

"Then what?"

"Just keep goin' away from the 'ouse. Mr. 'Olmes'll hail yuh."

"Is he here?"

" 'As been fer a while. Good luck!"

Gilligan listened for a moment at the door and then slipped through it and was gone.

I sat on the bed for a moment, my thoughts awhirl. Holmes had said that I would play an important part in the drama to unfold, and suddenly it seemed that I would. It struck me that this was the greatest miscasting of all times. Night alarms with a somewhat overweight medical man riding over the countryside like a supporter of the ill-fated Stuarts fleeing from a company of roundheads? Holmes's drama might be played out like a farce comedy!

But the Watson spirit rose within me, and I banished such thoughts as self-defeating. Holmes had dressed me in the clothes of an adventurer, ready to take center stage, and I resolved to play the part with conviction, though I felt more like assuming Gilligan's hiding place under the bed, with a blanket over my head.

After a suitable period, I walked jauntily down the great stairs of the mansion and made for the rear. In the butler's pantry adjacent to the huge kitchen I found Dooley, who slipped a copy of *La vie Parisienne* out of sight and took me to the rear door, which he unlocked for me. Outside in the bracing night air, I walked casually and apparently aimlessly until well removed from the house and then made a beeline for the stables. None of the grooms were about, and I was able to secure the riding equipment from the tack room.

Locating Fandango's stall, I spoke to the horse in a low tone and allowed her to get used to the idea of my presence before slipping a bridle on her. I then led her from the stall and arranged the saddle. There were sounds from the other horses but I ignored them. Either I was going to pull this off undetected, or I was not. With the girth cinched tight around the mare, I secured her bridle in front of the next stall, figuring that the horse within, conscious

78

of Fandango ready for action, would get the idea and accept the bit from my unfamiliar hands. Such proved the case, and with the two horses saddled, I returned them to their stalls to await their moment. I don't think my foray took more than fifteen minutes, and when I tapped on the back door, Dooley opened it for me, indicating no suspicion. Feeling considerably the better for having accomplished the first part of my task, I returned to my bedroom and wondered what the signal for the second act would be.

Seated in an armchair, I steeled myself for the waiting, always the most difficult period in a situation like this. It had been such a short time ago that I had thought of the peaceful atmosphere in our snug quarters on Baker Street, and here I was in a Surrey mansion waiting for who-knew-what in connection with the Deets affair. It had begun like such a pedestrian matter. The introduction of our client's deceased father into the list of dramatis personae had added the fillip of dark and sinister motives.

And what about the agent of Mycroft who had died in our presence? This bizarre occurrence combined with the invasion of our quarters had been momentarily jettisoned it would seem, though I knew Holmes's manner too well not to accept the fact that the two cases had connective tissue. The association of all this with one John H. Watson in Surrey was remote indeed. But if Sherlock Holmes's nostrils had quivered, there was a scent in the air.

My musings were suddenly interrupted with an energizing thought. My activities on this night had just begun, and I hastened to my feet to don my riding habit, on loan, to be ready for the action when it came.

It did come, finally, with a rush and a roar of sound that snapped me awake and out of the chair that I had been slumbering in. There were indistinguishable shouts transformed to alarms by their tone of anguish and terror. There was a smell in the air and, for a ridiculous moment, I thought it might be Holmes's pipe. But no, it was not the scent of his shag, but there was smoke. As I made for the stairs, it became more apparent. My God! It came from a conflagration!

Darting out the side entrance by the porte cochere, it being the most readily at hand, I saw flames lighting up the night sky. They were at or adjacent to the horses' barns wherein the racers were stabled. Despite a tumult of sound and running footsteps, I was completely alone. Every man jack on the place was at the fire, desperately trying to save the priceless thoroughbreds.

I made an instinctive move to rush to join the rescuers, but Holmes's instructions came to mind in the nick of time, and I bolted to the stalls of the riding horses, somewhat removed from the center of activity. There were whinnies and neighs as I made my way to Fandango, for the horses, sensitive to the aura of excitement, nay panic, were moving nervously in their places. Fortunately the wind was such that the smell of the fire had not reached them, or they might have been unmanageable. My presence seemed to have a calming effect on the chestnut mare, and I led her from her stall and then secured the reins of her neighbor.

When I mounted Fandango, the tenseness of the moment lent springs to my legs. With the other animal in tow, I urged the mare into motion. The moment we cleared the barn door, Fandango spied the not-so-distant flames. I was urging her in a direction that would take us around the country mansion, and she cooperated in a manner that jarred my back teeth. We swept by the house at a full gallop and thundered down the main road leading from Mayswood. I had all I could do to hang onto the reins of our companion animal, who was in just as much of a hurry as my mount.

I dropped my curb and was riding to the snaffle, and that was not true in a moment, for in desperation I dropped my bridle entirely and gripped the pommel of the saddle with one hand. For no reason, the name of the other horse flashed through my mind. "Mystique" she had been referred to. A suitable mount for Holmes, but Mother of Heaven, would I ever reach him!

Out of the night loomed a complication. The white picket horse-gate was closed across the driveway to Mayswood as it would be in the night hours. The gallant Fandango, flanked by "Mystique," was bearing down on the obstacle at a speed that defied stopping in time, nor were there reins in my hand to try it or the strength in my arms to do it if they had been there.

The gate, a low affair, assumed the proportions of a Grand National hurdle as we thundered towards it. Its white planking, touched by a spring moon that suddenly sailed free of high clouds, assumed a ghostly glow. To think that I, dedicated to the saving of life, was to end my days with a snapped neck or speared by a broken plank! Little did my dear, departed mother picture my emulating one of the ill-fated riders of that desperate charge in the Crimea!

The gate was upon us. Still gripping the saddle with one hand and Mystique's reins with the other, I instinctively leaned forward as I had seen huntsmen do when clearing a stone wall in pursuit of the elusive fox. Then the thunder of hoofs ceased, and for a glorious moment I had the feeling of flying, soaring through the air as if in fulfillment of man's age-old dream. I was suspended in a nothingness as those two splendid horses with their muscles uncoiled, their legs outstretched, cleared the barrier in unison. Oh, it must have made a wondrous sight—which I never saw, for my eyes were screwed tightly shut and I was just hanging on for dear life without even time for a fervent prayer.

The moment of weightlessness passed with a crash as we made contact with the road beyond the gate. I was jarred to my heels and lost a stirrup, coming within an ace of losing my seat as well. Then, by some miracle, the loose iron snapped back over the toe of my riding boot and I had the support of two legs, which allowed me to regain a portion of my balance.

As though in relief at clearing the obstacle, Fandango slackened her headlong rush and I was able to loosen my death-hold on the saddle and snatch at her flying reins. Leaning back in the saddle with the reins as support, I succeeded in slowing my mount and Mystique as well even further, and it was then that I heard the call.

"Watson! Over here!"

I saw Holmes in the semidarkness waving a white handkerchief by the side of the road. I was so startled at hearing his voice, so amazed at even being alive, that a surge of unknown strength welled up within me. My left arm, which a moment ago had threatened to fall off, swung the reins to the right and I leaned in that direction as well, throwing the head, neck, and withers of Fandango against Mystique and somehow bringing both animals to a skidding, sliding halt right where Sherlock Holmes stood.

The great sleuth grabbed Mystique's reins as I let them drop. Securing the animal by the bit, he anchored Fandango in the same manner, all the time looking upward at me in complete amazement. The horses were sucking in air in great breaths and their forequarters were lathered a foamy white. Somehow my riding bowler was still on my head, though askew. I was as drenched and as breathless as the steeds but managed to keep my backbone straight. Had I sagged a smidgen, I would have fallen headlong from the saddle like a sack of grain. The moment was tense and the situation critical, but Holmes stole time to gaze at me as though unsuspected vistas had suddenly been revealed to him. I have always contended that my intimate friend had the rare ability to seize a situation at a glance, to read the book of a happening in a fleeting second, but this time his instant appraisal deserted him.

"Watson, good fellow, were it possible for me to be rendered speechless, I'd be as mute as an oyster! That gate is fully five pegs high and I could but think, as you came upon it, of a Cossack in full flight. And to clear it with not one horse but with two, in perfect form! If Deets were to give you a mount, I'd place my wager on your colors, dear friend."

I was goggle-eyed, but the sincere conviction of Holmes's words and the light in his eyes kept me from swaying. I could not and would not destroy an image nurtured, however incorrectly, in the mind of the kindest man I have ever known. I made a weak half-gesture towards the breeding farm in the distance. "Holmes, Mayswood is afire."

"Naught but haystacks, ol' chap," replied Holmes, swinging into Mystique's saddle. "Sufficiently close to the stabled thoroughbreds to create a menace, but something that Deets and his crew can handle. Come, let us observe the follow-up of this diversionary tactic."

The sleuth reined Mystique from the road into the line of trees, and I had little choice but to follow in his wake. Brushing through branches and bending low in the saddle to clear outstretched boughs, we made our way through the trees to a point at the end of the timberline that I assumed Holmes had scouted and chosen in advance. From there, we commanded a fine view of the front of the mansion. The flames were dimly visible around the side of the residence, and the firefighters were still intent on their task. We were at our station but a moment when I spied at least four men who seemed to materialize from the ground before the house. There was a flash of metal in the air, and objects flew into the night sky to descend on the stone balustrade of the balcony.

"My thought of using grappling hooks was not amiss, Watson," whispered Holmes as the shadowy figures tested their lines and then swarmed up them hand over hand.

"What are they after, Holmes?"

"Regard the balcony. What do you see?"

"Five French windows . . . then there—"

"Enough. It is so true that one looks but does not see. That American, Poe's, concept of the purloined letter was accurate."

"Holmes, what are you—?"

"Think back to when we were within the gallery before walking out on the balcony. What is the picture that comes to your mind's eye, Watson?"

"Well, we walked towards the four French windows and made our way—" I stopped abruptly, shafted by a thought. "Four windows! But five are staring me in the face."

"The fifth is a dummy. Look, they are making for it even now. In but a moment they will have the aperture open."

The figures that had gained the balcony were doing as my friend said. Huddled round the fifth opening, there was a pause in their feverish activity, which allowed me to protest, to give vent to my mental rebellion.

"I assume it is a door to a secret chamber, Holmes, but why not have it concealed?"

"Because someone's eye wandering over the face of the building would note an unusual distance from the real window on the end to the windows of adjacent rooms. They would wonder where all that space was, how it was used. As it is, you see a charming exterior in proportion and note the openings but do not count them. From the inside, things have a different perspective. You cannot consider a room you occupy in conjunction with adjacent ones."

"But when we went out on the balcony?"

"Did you notice anything unusual? Your eye was captured by the view. There were windows behind you, how many you did not count. You walked right past the false one, never conscious of the fact that you were passing an entry to a vault, a hiding place for whatever treasures Captain Spaulding brought back from his expeditions."

"You noticed it, of course."

"Ah, Watson, I have trained myself to look and to see as well. Ah ha! They've forced the door."

Two of the figures on the balcony suddenly disappeared within the house. The third posted himself by the real windows. The remaining one went to the edge of the area at the side of the building nearest the fire as a lookout should anyone note something amiss. Apparently confident that their arrival was undiscovered, as it certainly was, both men on the balcony then moved to the balustrade. Loosening the grappling hooks, they passed each one over the railing and dropped it to the ground. It was a re-creation of Holmes's suppositions several days before.

Suddenly I tightened my hold on the reins, lifting Fandango's head as though in preparation for a charge.

"This, then, is what Deets feared. That his uninvited visitor would suspect the location of the family vault. We must stop them, Holmes."

My friend's lean and sinewy arm reached out to grasp me by the shoulder and pull me back in my saddle.

"Hold tight, Watson. We have not planned this so carefully to stop them. We want to see what they do."

"Do? They're after that sword. You were right about that, of course. If left to their devices, they will spirit it away."

"Not so easily, good chap."

I noted flashes of light from the interior of what we assumed was the Deets' family vault.

"Gilligan and Styles are waiting on the Follonsbee Road, which is the only direct thoroughfare back to London."

Holmes gestured to our left. "Now there's a path in that direction, is there not? For I think the Chinese came from there."

"Oh, they are Chinese, are they? Let me see."

My mind raced back over my journeys round Mayswood, and fortunately the mental pictures meshed in my mind.

"Yes, there is a good-sized lane running in a half-moon direction that way," I stated, pointing towards our left and rear. "It splits at a fork; one branch continues round by a bluff and curves back to the road to Litchfield, the other terminates at a railway assembly point down in a valley. Actually, there's a path down the bluff that reaches the same point much quicker. I chanced upon it."

"Good show, Watson! In former times that Confederate cavalry genius, Jeb Stuart, might have grown fond of you. The junction you mention must be for making up freight trains for the run into the city. I suspect that is the key to the Chinaman's plan."

His musings were interrupted by the reappearance of the men on the balcony of the Deets mansion. They were carrying something with them, though I could not make out its form. Had I to hazard a guess, I would have said it was a crated object. Holmes suddenly lost interest in the nocturnal attack squad. I noted they were securing the door they had forced, no doubt seeking to delay the discovery of their thievery.

Holmes swung Mystique to his left.

"Take my horse's tail in your hand, Watson, and let us be as silent as possible."

With some reservations, I secured the end of Mystique's tail in my right hand and, leaning low in the saddle, let Holmes choose our route through the trees. The arrangement was efficient since Holmes had uncanny night vision, which served him well on this occasion as it had many times in the past. My position was an uncomfortable one, but it saved me from being brushed from my saddle by tree branches on at least two occasions.

After a period of swerving round trunks, Holmes drew to a stop. I heard a cautionary "shush" from him, and then he was out of his saddle. Passing Mystique's reins to me, he was gone into Stygian darkness, for the trees blocked out the high-flying moon. My heart was pounding, half in reaction to what had been and half in anticipation of what was to come, and I cannot say how long he was gone. Suddenly I was conscious of another presence and felt Holmes retrieve his horse's bridle. I could make out his form dimly now, and he patted Mystique encouragingly on the muzzle, then took Fandango by the bit and led both animals in what I assumed was the general direction of Litchfield, though my directional sense was nonexistent at this point.

After another short period, we came out of the woods. Standing by Fandango's forequarters, my friend posed a question.

"Is this the lane you referred to?"

In the added light of the clearing, I looked up and down the country road and nodded. "That path would be . . ."

I suddenly regained my confidence. A little light and visibility does have that effect on one.

"Here, I'll show you."

I urged Fandango forward as Holmes remounted and followed. Hopeful of recognizing landmarks I had noted previously, I kept a sharp eye and even then passed my objective. But the gleam of railroad tracks from the bluff reoriented me and I backtracked to the opening by the roadside and the narrow trail that my mount and I had traversed before. Holmes's hawklike eyes had been sizing up the situation.

"I may call you 'pathfinder' in the future, Watson."

Forced by the trail to ride single file, I was unable to dazzle him with a retort, but then I could not think of one either. We had our hands full negotiating our passage, much more treacherous by night, I soon realized.

At last we reached level ground, and the shadows of freight cars dotted the scene. But there was sound as well. A stationary locomotive puffed in readiness, and there was movement and sporadic conversation. I realized that a train was being built up, probably carrying agricultural produce for early morning delivery to the hungry metropolis. Holmes kept us in the shadows, and since we had come from a heavily wooded hillside by a thin and tortuous trail,

I had no doubt that our presence was unsuspected. The locomotive suddenly sprang to life, moving backwards, and there was a clang of metal as other freight cars were hooked on to a growing line.

"What is our next move, Holmes?"

"We've gained considerable time, which is fortunate. The Chinese had a delivery wagon on the roadway. With their cargo they are making for here by the branch road you mentioned, and the Sacred Sword will ride into London on the early morning freight whilst they return via the Follonsbee Road. It will mean that Gilligan and Styles are following a dead trail, but no matter."

Holmes's voice dwindled away and I shot him a quick glance, noting that his brow was furrowed. Then the lines disappeared and he was looking at me with that boyish half-smile.

"Merely anticipating, Watson. Do keep an eye cocked for the delivery wagon, like a good chap."

Again he dropped from the saddle and glided swiftly across the open ground towards the small building that seemed the nerve center of the junction. His movements reminded me of descriptive passages I had read regarding the American Indians' amazing ability to flit from one object to another when engaged in a stealthy approach.

Fandango gave indications of a whinny and I reached quickly forward, placing the palm of my hand over her nose. Really, that horse was most intelligent, and she curbed her desire to communicate. Then I saw, vaguely, a wagon coming round a bend in the distance. I hastily dismounted, holding both our steeds by their bits in an attempt to keep them silent. Suddenly, Holmes was at my side.

"If you ever wish to incriminate me, Watson, you have me dead to rights, for I have just stolen an object from the Great Eastern Railroad. I note our Chinese are on the scene, so let's get in the saddle once more."

He was displaying a piece of marking chalk as he spoke, standard equipment with freight handlers. I forestalled Holmes's move towards Mystique.

"Look here, I've been leaping on and off for half the

night, Holmes, or so it seems. Would you be kind enough to give me a leg up?"

"Certainly," he replied, intertwining his long fingers. With one toe in his hand-cradle and his shoulder as a fulcrum, I managed to get astride of Fandango once more. As my friend swung upwards with a grace that was revolting, I saw the moon glisten on his white teeth and realized that he was laughing at me, but his words brought me up short.

"I've said before, Watson, that you occasionally display a pawky humor. I'm not fooled, you know, being convinced you are descended from Attila the Hun himself." So it is that reputations are born.

With Holmes leading the way, we progressed a distance away from the junction but parallel to the rails that were the feeder to the main line.

"The Chinese have arranged to have their crate placed in one of the freight cars, of that I am sure. This train is carrying naught but foodstuffs, so when the object is removed, it should be readily spotted. However, we shall facilitate the process."

Holmes had reined to a stop now and was looking back at the junction, and my eyes followed his. The wagon had drawn adjacent to one of the freight cars. Here in the valley the moonlight was quite bright, and I noted that an object about four feet in length was passed from the wagon to one of the railway roustabouts, who took it towards the line of freight cars. I looked at Holmes and realized that he was counting from the engine back.

"The twelfth freight car, Watson," he said happily.

Of course he was enjoying the whole thing, as he always did. Especially when he managed to keep one step ahead of the opposition.

Now he reined round again and we traveled further towards the main line. Drawing to a halt in the shadow of a clump of small trees, we waited, and then came the methodical and lugubrious chug of the locomotive as it slowly gained momentum with the cars behind it jerking into motion like reluctant children making for school in single file. Every thrust of the steam-driven pistons increased the speed of the metal serpentine, and it was proceeding at a good rate when it passed our place of concealment.

88

"Hold fast, good Watson," said Holmes as he broke from the trees, gigging Mystique to a fast gallop. I saw now that he had chosen the location carefully, for it was a stretch where the roadbed was level with the adjacent ground. Without realizing it I was counting cars, and then Holmes swerved his mount in close to the swiftly moving train and, leaning forward and out, he reached with one long arm to chalk an "X" on the twelfth freight car. Then he guided his mount away from the train and raced for the shelter of the trees.

As the train disappeared round a bend, I rejoined Holmes to find him patting Mystique with all the affection of a highland horseman for his bonny steed.

"Now that the pace of our nocturnal adventures has diminished, you might explain to me what is going on," I suggested.

"Things are going swimmingly, and now we shall make our way to Litchfield. This freight makes frequent stops along the line. We can catch the one o'clock flyer from Litchfield and reach London before it. I assume we can follow the rails to the rural hamlet."

"I've done so."

"Capital! Upon arrival, you make for the station and secure tickets. I will roust the cable-office attendant, for a message must precede us to London. A message to Deets will not be amiss if only to locate his horses for him."

Not long thereafter, I lowered myself gingerly into the seat of our compartment on the morning flyer with a deep sigh of relief. Stretching my aching legs, I mentally forced strained and knotted muscles to relax. There was the familiar click of wheel on rail and trestle. At last we were headed back to London, far more suitable surroundings for two staid, middle-aged bachelors, one of whom was intent on a steaming tub positively alive with Epsom Salts. Holmes had been right, of course, about the schedule of the flyer now hurtling through a countryside covered by the blackness of night. The man's knowledge of trains, both in Britain and on the continent, was positively encyclopedic, and I drowsily made mention of this.

"Ah, Watson, those ribbons of steel that are the warp

and woof of the tapestry of transportation so indispensable to the empire. . . ."

At this point, I fell asleep.

It was Holmes's long, violinist fingers on my shoulders shaking me gently that summoned me from the land of Nod.

"Come, ol' chap, we are pulling into Waterloo, and the curtain has not yet fallen on this playlet."

It is with chagrin that I confess to a small, nay mean, streak within my nature, for it was pleasing to me that my companion seemed to arise from his seat with a hesitant manner as though testing the steadiness and capabilities of his extremities. I sprang upright, and it was with the greatest difficulty that I suppressed an exclamation of anguish. But my tottering legs stiffened at the quick glance of surprise tinged with envy that the sleuth flashed my way while unlatching the compartment door to the high-pitched background music of grating brakes as the train came to a halt.

My friend's firm hand on my arm guided me through the station and into a carriage without. Holmes's directions to the sleepy-eyed driver were inaudible to me, but at this point, I had lost interest in our next destination.

It proved to be a vehicular bridge over the vast checkerboard of Great Eastern rails converging towards the hub that was the transportation empire's London station. Holmes's suggestion that I remain with the carriage was accepted with alacrity. He removed himself to stand on the walk-across of the bridge, his eyes in the direction of Surrey. The appearance of his cigarette case and the lighting of one of the Virginia blends that he fancied suggested a lengthy vigil, and I fell asleep again.

Possibly it was the sound of an approaching freight or the peculiar tocsin that alerts us in some mysterious manner when action is imminent, but my eyes blinked open to catch Holmes watching the cars of a freight train passing beneath the bridge. At a particular moment, his white handkerchief waved in the half-light of the early morning. Since this was obviously a signal to someone positioned further down the line, I now understood the cable that he had taken pains to dispatch from Litchfield.

Not waiting to check the results of his improvised semaphoring, Holmes returned to our carriage, his knuckles rapping on the box. When the trap opened and a bewhiskered and heavy-eyed face peered down, Holmes finally delivered the curtain speech to our nighttime saga:

"221B Baker Street, my good man, with all possible speed."

Chapter Nine

Holmes Assumes the Trust

It was well into the afternoon when I finally stumbled from my bed, giving vent to a series of jaw-straining yawns as I rubbed the vestiges of sleep from my eyes. Like an incoming tide, a flood of questions inundated my poor, lethargic brain, but I shoved a mental finger into the dike, effectively plugging the sea of conjecture. At the moment I cared not a whit as to the dramatic happenings of late or the potential fate of the Sacred Sword either.

After steaming in a hot tub, performing my toilet, and dressing with care, I descended to our sitting room feeling more the man and less like an archaic bag of protesting bones.

Holmes was not alone, for Clyde Deets at the moment was depositing his hat and gloves on the end table.

"I have remarked before about your intuitive timing, Watson. Mr Deets is just upon the scene."

Our client's face was a blend of perplexity and fatigue with a soupçon of haunting fear.

"Gentlemen," he said in a harrassed tone, "recent events are just too much for me. A fire at Mayswood, Doctor Watson's disappearance, your message, Mr. Holmes, which arrived with the two riding horses—"

"I trust," interjected Holmes, "that there was no damage to buildings or livestock last night."

"None. I can be thankful of that."

Deets's words terminated abruptly as though he were at a loss, and Holmes came to his aid.

"Best we shred the fabric of secrecy. A confidential inquiry agent cannot operate at a level of efficiency without all the facts. In this case, personal knowledge along with deduction filled some gaps for me."

"You know then. I might have guessed that you did. But do you both—" his eyes flashed to me "—understand the potential peril involved?"

"More than you do," replied Holmes confidently. "For simplicity's sake, let me sum this up. The subject of your father, Captain Spaulding, and his explorations in Egypt and the Sudan is very much off limits in your household, and not once have you made mention of his fame. It was your father's hope that his name and activities would fade into the mists of time, for he wished to become a missing link with the Islamics of the desert."

Holmes was speaking with such fluency that I suspicioned a communique from Sir Randolph Rapp. The ex-Regius Cambridge professor, turned motivational expert, was a veritable reservoir of vague incidents and half-known truths round the world, as indicated by his monumental work, *The Motivated Minds of Mankind*.

"Now I resort to surmise, though I'll stake my reputation on it," continued the sleuth. "Your father had a peculiar affinity with the Arabians. During his expedition to the Sudan he came upon a kindred spirit, a chieftain or sheik, no doubt, who had found wisdom with the passage of the years. This unknown hero realized that the Sacred Sword, a relic and supposedly the weapon of the prophet Mohammed, represented a potential catalyst, a symbol that, in the hands of a wild-eyed zealot, could launch a flood of fierce horsemen on neighboring territories. Faced, as they would have to be eventually, with modern artillery and disciplined troops, they would become the ingredients of a bloodbath, but oh! what carnage they could cause before their onrush could be stemmed."

Deets made as though to summon words but then leaned back with a shrug of acceptance, indicating that Holmes had already said them.

"The sword does exist, authentic, no doubt, and the chieftain saw a means of forestalling the possible annihilation of his people. He entrusted the relic in the hands of

94

your father to be secreted in England. Captain Spaulding fell in with the idea and may have later regretted it, for he accepted an awesome responsibility. The thought of some rebellious nomad faction tracing the symbol to our shores is a bit far-fetched, but agents of an advanced nation might well do that. Great powers have been known to foment insurrection where it will do harm to their adversaries."

"That was my father's fear," said Deets simply.

"But now another piece has been placed on the board," said the sleuth, his large eyes traveling to the hearth fire as though conjuring pictures from its dancing flames.

"Last night, the fire was, as is obvious, a diversionary tactic to draw the attention of you and your household while the employees of a master criminal stole the Sacred Sword. I could have forestalled the happening but chose not to for the simple reason that Chu San Fu, a name unknown to you, would just try again."

Deets was sitting rigidly upright in his chair.

"Do you mean you know where the sword was taken?"

"Of course. Would I let it disappear? I, sir, am Sherlock Holmes."

Our client leaned back as though abashed.

"Of course. Forgive me. But what is your purpose in allowing this—this Oriental—to gain possession of the relic?"

"To learn of the plot that he has conceived. Chu San Fu is the former crime czar of Limehouse and the entire Chinese community. I entertain suspicions as to his sanity, but he is a wily opponent with vast financial means at his disposal. I would not for a moment allow him to possess this potentially dangerous symbol if I thought he was working on behalf of another agency, but that is not his way. He has some personal plan involving the sword, the outlines of which are but vaguely discernible to me at this moment."

"Then you intend to give this criminal rope . . . ?"

"Hoping to hang him with it, of course."

"Mr. Holmes, what would you have me do?"

"Nothing. Was anything else removed from the vault?"

A negative shake of the head was Deets's response.

"Then I have assumed the trust placed in your father's

hands in far-off Arabia. It is I who must see that the sword does not fulfill a fateful destiny. I suggest that the fire at Mayswood was the only incident that night. The robbery just never happened."

Deets's lips were pursed as though tasting the sour fruit of decision. He was regarding his hands, nervously clenched in his lap, and then his eyes rose to meet those of Holmes, and the haggard expression seemed to fade from his face.

"I really have little choice, you know. Were I to report to the authorities the taking of an object not even known to exist, they might well send me back to my brood mares with patient words and comforting pats on the back. So be it, Mr. Holmes. The Spaulding trust now rests on your capable shoulders."

When our visitor had taken his leave, I regarded Holmes with a touch of exasperation.

"The fact that you insist on assuming the burdens of troubled people on three continents is not unknown to me, but Holmes, by all that is holy, what have you got us enmeshed in now?"

"A tasty problem, ol' fellow."

"And one that, in future times, will prompt the remark: 'Only Sherlock Holmes could have solved it.' "

"I trust that is so," replied the sleuth, rubbing his hands together with satisfaction. He could never be faulted for underestimating his potential.

"All right. I must concede that the historic sword exists and you have allowed Chu to secure it, though it seems to me you are somewhat casual about that fact. Where is the object now?"

"Safely in the hold of the Hishouri Kamu, a tramp steamer that raises anchor at Southampton with the flood tide."

Holmes's answer to direct questions were sometimes vague, but this one was not and I could only stare at him.

"Burlington Bertie and his friend Tiny were positioned in the railway yard when the slow freight from Litchfield arrived. My signal from the bridge allowed them to keep the proper boxcar under observation, and they followed the crated sword to the Hishouri Kamu. The object is not listed on the manifest, but another singular one is under refrigerated cargo. The coffin containing the body of one Sidney Putz."

"Who?"

"The man on the dock. One of the attackers of Mycroft's agent that Bertie coshed."

"You mean he killed him?"

"Doubtful. More likely he was disposed of by Chu's order, having failed in his mission. His coffin is marked for delivery in Alexandria."

I was shaking my head in a confused manner and Holmes continued, a sharpness denoting impatience in his voice.

"Come, come, Watson! The sword is taken to the freighter, which just happens to list in its cargo the final remains of Sidney Putz, in life employed by Chu San Fu as an assailant. Surely, too much coincidence there. The sword is by now concealed in the coffin, and since we know that it is ticketed for Alexandria, that is the sword's destination. Can you conceive of any reason why the body of a yegg of the London underworld is being transported to Egypt save to provide a place of concealment for the fabled weapon?"

"But why, Holmes, is the sword going to Egypt?"

"As is your wont, Watson, you have stumbled over the main problem facing us. Why indeed? That is the answer we seek, and fortunately we have time. The Hishouri Kamu, being of the tramp variety, is slow, with many ports of call on her schedule. Until she reaches Alexandria, the sword is completely safe and we are allowed a breathing spell."

"Which we certainly need," I began, but before I could expound further on this subject, Holmes interrupted as though in haste to clear the air and move to other matters.

"Spare me, good chap, a lament regarding questions breeding more questions. The sword exists, that we know. Chu San Fu has it, for we saw his minions steal it. We know where it is and where it is headed. Now we must find a connective link, for surely Egypt brings to your mind Mycroft's dead agent, his mention of Chu San Fu, and the unusual and ancient relic that he had secreted on his person."

"But was not Mycroft imbued with the idea of an ancient tomb? The prophet Mohammed antedates ancient Egypt not by centuries but by thousands of years."

"Three, at least," agreed Holmes. "You put it well, ol' fellow. We must think more on this."

When Holmes thought, he required facts to form a framework for his speculations. This meant research, and there is no searcher more detailed than the one who does not look for knowledge but augments knowledge already acquired. The latter is armed with the indispensable, for he knows where to look for what he seeks.

Our rooms at Baker Street, with the numerous case histories in which I took great pride, and Holmes's commonplace books along with the newspaper files, produced a semilibrary atmosphere. This was augmented by an inflow of work on Egypt and the Valley of the Nile that captured all available table space, spilling over to piles on the floor that I tried to keep orderly. I recalled those early days when fate, in the form of my chance meeting with young Stamford at the Criterion Bar, had first thrown Holmes and me together. I had estimated his fund of knowledge in a rather cavalier manner. While conceding that he had a profound grip on chemistry and an immense familiarity with sensational literature, I had listed his understanding of philosophy and astronomy as nil and his grasp of politics as feeble.

Things had changed during the years. First my friend had become well versed in astronomy, spurred, no doubt, by the fact that the infamous Moriarty had penned *The Dynamics of an Asteroid*, which enjoyed a European vogue. Then his facile mind reached out into other fields, not all connected with the solution of crime. His ability to sustain feverish periods of intense mental activity allowed him, once his teeth were implanted in a subject, to stay with it until it was wrestled into a workable form with familiar features.

I had lived through Holmes's flirtation with medieval architecture as well as his romance with sixteenth century music, which climaxed in his mongraph upon the polyphonic motets of Orlandus Lassus, considered by experts as the final word upon the subject. Now it was Egyptology that the sleuth was gripping by the throat, albeit it was not a choice dictated by whim but motivated by our activities of late. Possibly it was also a rebirth of a previous infatuation dating from his Montague Street days. Whatever, most hours found my friend immersed in some volume or another, more often three or more simultaneously.

Such was the retentiveness of his splendid mind that several days later he devoted our entire dinner hour to delivering a detailed recounting of Giovanni Balzoni's Egyptian and Nubian operations, a man unknown to Holmes a week before. Egyptian architecture, jewelry, religions of ancient Egypt, a number of suggestions as to how the pyramids were constructed—the list was endless. Finally I chose to ignore the whole matter before I began to imagine desert sand in my food! Holmes was on an Egypt spin, and he was looking for something. Painfully obvious was the fact that he wasn't finding it.

However, all the ensuing days and nights were not sedentary. My friend had his pack sniffing up wind. One day, having concluded several patient calls, I wasted some time pleasantly with a medical friend at the Bagatelle Club bar. Then I chose to walk back to Baker Street. In the vicinity of the Strand, I spied Holmes standing under the awning of a book dealer, an open volume in hand. Next to him, also in a studious pose, was Slippery Styles. That they were conversing in monosyllables without moving their lips I was sure. A bookstore as a meeting place was a favorite device of Holmes's, and I now knew first hand that he was keeping Chu San Fu under close observation.

Chapter Ten

Sir Randolph's News

Our Surrey adventure began to seem like a dream, for the activity associated with it came to such an abrupt end. I grew accustomed to Holmes's presence in our quarters, a rarity when a major case dominated his working calendar. Then one morning I rose somewhat early and found that he was gone. But he rejoined me as breakfast was being served, even disposing of a rasher of bacon with eggs and some of Mrs. Hudson's toothsome scones. His manner seemed grave, but I did not note the nervous restlessness that indicated he was at loose ends as regards an idea. Actually, he seemed resigned. I waited him out, and finally he chose to tidy up and package the recent days of seeming inaction.

"We have reached an impasse, Watson, one that a crash course in Egyptology has not bridged, nor have events as reported from our sources provided a clue. At the end of a tether as regards my own resources, I am forced to go elsewhere, and as a first move I visited the Diogenes Club this morning. Recall that Mycroft came to us at our request, so I returned the courtesy."

"And found your brother similarly bemused?" This was but a shot in the dark.

"Let us say that his concern has grown, not lessened. There have been a series of meetings. First in Afghanistan, then Babylonia, Syria, Palestine, Persia, and Arabia. These being religious gatherings, Mycroft's information is very sketchy. One meeting in the Grand Mosque in Damascus was extremely well attended and a lengthy affair. The main point is that a spirit of unrest is spreading in the east and heading, like the Sacred Sword, towards Egypt. Islam blended a hundred scattered races into one, but the religion is split into many sects, more than seventy-two to be exact. If some revelation, some apparent miracle, were to unite the followers of the Crescent, you can anticipate the possible results."

In a sudden flash of understanding, I spoke automatically.

"The second coming of the Prophet."

Holmes's nod of agreement was grim.

"As another move towards assistance, I have secured an appointment with Sir Randolph Rapp. Are you free to accompany me this morning?"

I accepted this invitation with alacrity. The unusual household of said gentleman was extremely interesting to me, as was the man himself. His theories rather paralleled Holmes's thinking on certain matters, and his influence, though indirect and unsuspected, was enormous.

But as I prepared for our journey to Mayfair, another matter was brought to our attention. Wiggins, titular head of the Baker Street Irregulars, that motley group of juvenile street urchins that Holmes had recruited as his eyes and ears in the streets, came calling. The young rapscallion brought no news of his own but was the bearer of a message.

"The thin man sent this fer yuh, Mr. 'Olmes."

Holmes took a handwritten note from Wiggins's grimy paw and, after reading it, dismissed his ally with thanks and a shilling.

"Slim's on the job, Watson," he murmured thoughtfully. "It would seem that Chu San Fu and his entourage will depart by private yacht for Venice within twenty-four hours."

"What sense does that make?"

"None, unless my memory has played me false." Holmes was beside the bookcase extracting a copy of Lloyd's Shipping Guide, which he riffled open. "I was right. The Hishouri Kamu does not touch at Venice or any other Italian port."

"The sword is en route to Egypt and the Chinaman to Italy. Has a new element been introduced into this overly complex matter?"

"Would that I could answer you, ol' fellow. Come, let us make for Mayfair. Having kept Chu San Fu in my sights till now, I don't intend to lose that advantage, so we may have a trip in store.

The Rapp estate in Mayfair seemed unchanged. Portions of the rambling house were visible through the trees, and the surrounding iron-spike fence provided an impressive barrier broken only by the driveway gate presided over by an occupied gate house. Being familiar with this unusual domicile, Holmes and I dismissed our hansom at the entrance and made ourselves known to the large, truculent-looking man who did not unlock the outer portal until we were identified. It clanged shut as soon as we walked through and began making our way towards the house.

Clumps of trees were effectively positioned to shield the residence from the street, but nothing grew near to the establishment save close-cut lawns. The area was as devoid of cover as the top of a billiard table. There was a chorus of low growls in the distance, and I knew the Doberman pinschers were nervously pacing their kennels. When the establishment was darkened for the night, the dogs would be let loose to roam between fence and house, and to walk then as we were now, without the presence of a known member of the household, would be akin to suicide. Randolph Rapp was important to the Empire, and considerable pains were taken to assure his safety and privacy.

When the butler, whose contours were those of a regimental blacksmith, ushered us within, Holmes and I were again observers of a picture of tasteful English home life. Costly Oriental rugs chose at intervals to modestly reveal highly polished floorboards before resuming their figured designs. The pristine white glove of an admiral of the fleet could have been run over any piece of furniture in the brightly lit drawing room without surfacing a dust mote or dirt particle. The logs in the fireplace and those in the attendant wood basket were of uniform size and cut, and I felt they would not dare allow a secretion of sap to flare or pop. Paintings were hung in precisely the right places as though positioned to the centimeter. Two large oils bore the imprint of John Everett Millais, and surely that was a Bellini over the great couch.

If the drawing room and entrance reflected the meticulous taste of the most proper Amanda Rapp, Sir Randolph's study, to which we were led, had to be his sanctum sanctorum and an untidy one at that.

As the butler retreated, the former professor, now motivational specialist, rose from behind his large desk, which was festooned with notes, letters, and reports in a helterskelter manner. His ruddy face, rounded and smiling, emerged from an oversized head crowned by a shock of unruly hair. He was short, and his balloonlike body bounced as he came towards us, from his work area, on bandy legs.

"Ah, Holmes," he said, extending his hand. "Always delighted! Do sit down." Indicating a leather couch, worn in spots, a short distance from his overflowing desk, he seized my hand in both of his. His short, spatulate fingers, like those of a pianist, were strong. "And, my good Watson. You both look fit."

Leading me to a somewhat lumpy easy chair, he indicated humidors containing cigars and tobacco that were in evidence round the room. There was a jade case on his desk from which he extracted a long Egyptian cigarette. The index finger of his right hand was marred by a nicotine stain, which he suddenly seemed to notice, picking at it in an absent-minded fashion as he reseated himself.

I lit up one of Rapp's rum-soaked cigars with appreciation as the professor shoved papers aside, merely increasing the confusion. He gestured towards it with a sigh.

"Order is the virtue of the mediocre. Can't recall who said that, but the idea gives me comfort." He retrieved his cigarette, puffing on it. "But what has been happening in your active lives? You fellows get round a mite whilst I am chained here."

Holmes and I knew this wasn't true, and Rapp knew that we knew it. When it suited him, he wandered at will through government offices, and few indeed were the files not open to him. As like as not after one of his forays into what he called "the outside world," a series of reports would emanate from the very room we were sitting in and find their way by official courier to departmental heads, frequently with a shake-up as the result.

"Have you," questioned Holmes, "been privy to reports from the Middle East of late?"

"Sent to me by your brother," was the reply that accompanied an affirmative nod. "Bad show, that. Especially the gathering in the Grand Mosque of Damascus. Present were at least seven of the leading Islamics. When factions begin to agree, watch out! Especially the followers of Mohammed, for the Bedouin has always loved violence."

Preambles were wasted on one such as Randolph Rapp, and Holmes was delighted to dispense with them.

"If the diverse Islamic sects are untied by some miracle, the jehad, the holy war that they cry for, could result."

"Islam . . . La illah il'allah," entoned Rapp.

"It's the miracle I'm searching for."

"There is the Sacred Sword."

I must have given a start of surprise, and Rapp favored me with a gentle smile.

"It was not long ago that I inquired of Holmes as to the disappearance of Captain Spaulding. Now, with a Mid East outbreak threatening, I must assume that you have considered the sword as a tool to stir the masses."

"My brother runs to the theory of an undiscovered tomb, and there is tangible evidence to back him."

"Also good thinking," replied Rapp crisply. "I see where his mind is going."

There was a pause, and I could not let this statement dangle.

"Well, I certainly don't."

"Consider, Watson, the matter of the Mahdi." Rapp's tone did me the courtesy of not sounding tolerant. "The outbreak he instigated is of recent vintage. The Mahdi got away with the prophet deception because of a resemblance, especially the construction of his teeth and the lisp. Even primitive minds bent on pillage and plunder will not respond to the same stimulus twice. Mycroft Holmes pictures a movement based on something more conclusive than a zealot waving a sword."

"An ancient prophecy, perhaps?" said Sherlock Holmes. "The very word 'ancient' leads us to Egypt."

Rapp seemed intrigued. "That cradle of civilization had a plethora of gods, but even among them, there was a one-god reformer. Ikhnaton, in the fourteenth century before Christ, banned all other deities in favor of Aton, the sun god. However, he was no Mohammed, and his monotheistic attempt failed. Upon his death, worship of the old gods returned, and the Egyptians attempted to eradicate that particular pharoah from their history. I don't really know if his one-god faith lived on a bit or not."

"You don't?" I asked.

Despite my many years with Holmes, there was always the element of surprise when he confessed to being baffled. In a similar vein, to hear Randolph Rapp in doubt about anything made my eyebrows jump.

The professor was shaking his head. "There are still so many things we do not know. Especially about Egypt."

"But I thought the Rosetta Stone—" I began.

"Oh yes. One of Napoleon's soldiers discovers a black basalt tablet that provides the key to the deciphering of the hieroglyphics and the rediscovery of the culture of ancient Egypt. Quite amazing, but not completely satisfying. We have never been able to decipher the hieroglyphics of Crete, Watson, which may predate those of Egypt. Aztec and Mayan inscriptions remain a puzzle. In a similar manner there are the so-called secret writings."

Holmes was leaning forward on the couch.

"This is something new," he admitted.

"It is reasonably certain that they originally were in the pyramids, though possibly later tombs from which they were stolen, for they were inscribed on tablets of gold. But some have shown up through the centuries. As to their message, who knows?" Rapp shrugged and then another thought intruded.

"There is one chap, Howard Andrade, who I'm told has cracked the riddle. He based his study on the Cretan hieroglyphics, using them as a basis or key to the cuneiform symbols of the secret writings. Evidently he has succeeded."

"But," I said, "if this Andrade fellow has deciphered an

106

ancient form of writing, wouldn't there be a bit of a stir? I'd think the journals would pounce on it."

"Dear me, no!" protested Rapp. "Things move a bit slower in the field of antiquity. Andrade is a brilliant chap. I'm inclined to believe he has pulled it off. But he will make no claims until he has absolute proof. Remember, every other Egyptologist will desperately try to prove him wrong simply because they haven't deciphered the secret writings themselves."

"A competitive field."

"Ruled by pride," agreed Rapp. "Andrade removed himself from the country to complete his research. Doesn't want his near-triumph to leak out. Last I heard he was living in Venice."

I almost jumped out of my chair, and even Holmes had the good grace to register surprise.

"Venice, you say?"

"I do, never expecting this reaction. Here we are discussing ancient religions and a potential holy war, then of a sudden you give every indication of going somewhere."

"We are," said Holmes. "To Venice."

Chapter Eleven

Adventure in Venice

Of course, it was not as simple as that. Holmes had other questions regarding Andrade to pose to Randolph Rapp, and on our return to Baker Street messages flowed from his pen. But on the following day, we resumed our travels, nothing new to one associated with the greatest manhunter of all time.

Holmes, for no reason that I could fathom, chose to take the train to Dover, and from there the steamer to Belgium. In the great harbor station at Ostend, he conferred at some length with the stationmaster, a meeting to which I was not privy. Being a bad sailor, I was attempting to sip some passable tea and consume dry biscuits with no great success. My stomach was not in the best condition, and the table at the station restaurant where my friend left me seemed disposed to tilt on occasion, purely an illusion.

When the sleuth fetched me, the stationmaster was by his side with a veritable sheaf of rail tickets and an enthusiastic expression on his face. I knew what that meant. Holmes's knowledge of rail traffic had suggested a varied route festooned with connections, which had positively enthralled the stationmaster who would certainly wire ahead to assure us of superior service during our journey. It was a procedure that Holmes had followed on previous cases. Whatever strange stations we dropped off at to await an inbound train, whatever intricate route we followed, we were certain to arrive in Venice in the shortest possible time. Holmes's travel plans invariably depended on perfect timing, which was always forthcoming. In the minds of Anglo-Saxons, possibly other races as well, there lurks the tendency to attribute a personality and sex to inanimate objects, even such awesome things as thundering locomotives. The beautiful Blue Train to the south of France has always seemed feminine to me, whereas the luxurious Orient Express is associated with the masculine gender. If, amidst the pistons and wheels of a great train, there lurks a smidgen of soul, I know of a certainty that it is aware of the presence of Sherlock Holmes and would never dare be behind schedule when carrying the master sleuth. Call me mad, but the results bear out my fancy, and after four changes en route, we arrived at the pearl of the Adriatic in an amazingly short time indeed. The St. Lucia railway station was as irrational as ever, but Holmes had us out of it and into a suite in the Venezia Hotel on the Grand Canal in short order.

During our rush through western Europe and down the boot of Italy, one thing was glaringly obvious. Our route had been relayed to others, for cables had arrived for Holmes at various stations during the trip. He did not choose to make me privy to all of their contents, but I gathered that Howard Andrade resided in a private home on the Rio di San Canciano. I assumed Holmes had made arrangements to approach the gentleman, since this seemed his intent, but my native curiosity as to his methods and plans was diverted by my queasy stomach and travel fatigue. Once installed in the Venezia with assurances from my friend that nothing would happen of an immediate nature, I devoted myself to the healing arms of Morpheus and, in early evening, awoke considerably refreshed and feeling quite the new man.

Holmes was pacing the sitting room, clad in his purple robe and puffing on his pipe, giving no indication of fatigue from our journey. I sensed that he had not rested since our arrival and confirmed this thought when I spied the butt of a thin Mexican cigar in an ashtray.

"Orloff has been here!" I cried instinctively.

My friend's eyes twinkled. "Watson, what a delight! You spy the only clue to the presence of our somewhat sinister friend in a trice. Truly, our years together have not been wasted."

"But what is he doing here?" I snapped my fingers suddenly. "Ah ha! You contacted your brother, and Wakefield Orloff followed us to Italy."

"I certainly contacted Mycroft after our interesting meeting with Randolph Rapp. However, this led to a trading of information. He was most interested to learn that Chu San Fu is en route here via yacht. After a bit of prodding he revealed that Orloff has been in Venice for some time keeping an eye on Howard Andrade, the expert on ancient writings."

I was regarding the sleuth with knitted brows. "You mean, your brother anticipated Chu San Fu's trip to Venice?"

"Not at all, but Mycroft has been captivated with the idea of something in Egypt being at the bottom of the Mid East unrest. He knew of Howard Andrade's work on the secret writings of the pharaohs, and very reasonably put two and two together."

"Holmes, you'll have to be more specific than that."

"Then I must blend fact with conjecture," he replied, his hands clasped behind him as he strode the length of the room and back again. "The ominous meetings of Moslem leaders being fact. As to what has stirred the Mid East cauldron, we must look for some new element, some occurrence out of the ordinary that has brought these various factions together at this specific time. If the catalyst is in Egypt, conjecture leads us to Andrade. If he has decoded the secret writings, that is certainly new and could lead to additional breakthroughs in the unraveling of the history of the ancient civilization. Remember, Watson, it was but in 1822 that the Frenchman, Champollion, using the Rosetta stone as his key, cracked the hieroglyphics. Since Egypt's history was recorded in stone and preserved by the unique dry climate, Champollion's discovery allowed modern scholars to learn more about life in ancient Egypt than we know of our own original Saxons. The Rosetta Stone was discovered in 1799, but it took almost a quarter of a century before that black lump of basalt fulfilled its destiny."

111

I realized that I was shaking my head. "I'm a little vague on that, Holmes. As I recall from school days, there were some fourteen lines of hieroglyphics and fifty or so lines of Greek based on them. Since the Greek message was a translation of the ancient carvings, what took so long?"

"Actually, the message was in three forms, Watson. It included thirty-two lines of common demotic script, but that's not important. The difficulty in decoding the hieroglyphics lay in the fact that some of the signs are alphabetic, some phonetic, while others simply represent ideas. Trying to translate ideas is a bit of a problem, is it not? Lot of guesswork involved.

"Now about those secret writings, can we not assume that they were composed in part or whole by the rulers themselves, privy because of their position and authority to the as-yet-unrevealed secrets of the land of the Nile. The Rosetta Stone recorded a decree by priests of Memphis praising the pharaoh Ptolemy Fifth some two hundred years before Christ. Little of importance there. But what if one of the golden tablets, as yet undeciphered, dates back three thousand years before Christ and contains the secret of the Khufu pyramid?"

"What secret?" I said instinctively.

"King Khufu, or Cheops in Greek, built the great pyramid, ol' chap. It's size alone is staggering, but its orientation is truly amazing. The mass of stone covers thirteen acres, and its sides run almost exactly to the cardinal compass points. Its deviation from true north is but five arc minutes. Such an alignment could not happen simply by chance. Do you know the shadow it casts can be used as a calendar, and an accurate one at that?"

Holmes's eyes were burning as he spoke, and it took no genius to realize that he was, for the moment, caught up in the myriad of unanswered questions of ancient Egypt. I mentally chided myself for a clod. What more reasonable that the solver of mysteries would be captivated by the greatest puzzle in the history of mankind! My own poor brain was dazzled by the thought of a civilization, predating ours by five thousand years, that could construct edifices so colossal as to defy the skills of our mechanical age!

The light faded from Holmes's eyes to be replaced by

112

the cold, analytic look that grounded his flight into the mysterious fantasies conjured up by the pharaohs of so long ago.

"But come, Watson, our duties are of a more practical nature. Either Andrade has cracked the carvings of the ruling class or he has not, and we'd best find out. Wakefield Orloff has arranged an appointment with the hieroglyphics expert, who lives but a short distance away."

Outside the hotel Holmes secured a gondola for us, which I regarded with some trepidation. The waters of the Grand Canal were as smooth as glass, and my erratic stomach was of no concern. However, the thirty-two-foot craft leaned to the left, by design of course, and being only five foot in width it did not appear seaworthy to me. However, similar vessels studded the waters of the canal, and I overcame my reservations and gingerly gained a seat as Holmes directed the gondolier, who promptly put us in motion with his single oar.

The small craft had a unique rhythm, not unpleasant, and I actually began to enjoy our journey, though convinced that this type of conveyance would never replace the dependable hansom. There was considerable traffic, but our oarsman was skillful. Holmes pointed out some truly striking mansions on the Riva del Vin, and then I spied the Rialto Bridge. It was an imposing stone span over the Canal that inspired a sinking feeling within me as we made for it.

"I say, Holmes, that bridge has shops on it."

"Two rows, old fellow, and well trafficked."

"But the thing's overloaded! It will collapse on us."

"Rest easy, Watson. It does seem a bit inelegant, but gondolas like ours have been sailing under it safely since 1591."

This silenced me and reassured me as well.

Shortly after passing under the Rialto Bridge, we abandoned the Grand Canal for the San Canciano, on which the Egyptologist lived. This being a much smaller canal, there were frequent stone footbridges that curved overhead as we moved down its still waters. The houses on both sides were private dwellings of varied heights and designs though universally constructed of stone.

Our destination proved to be of two stories with its main entrance on the Rio di San Canciano and one side facing a tributary canal. There was no porch or float and, of course, no sidewalks. One simply rowed to the front door and stepped into a small vestibule. At the corner of the house was a bow window overhanging the quiet waters of the canal and sufficiently different from the general architecture to catch my eye. Some thoughtful builder had conceived of a view of both the canals the house faced on, and a pleasant sight of an evening it must provide.

Holmes instructed our gondolier to await our return and knocked on the impressive door. I noted that the adjacent house had ivy growing on its outer surface, which was dotted with small stone balconies from which tendrils of vines dangled, providing a pleasing, slightly bohemian look. Everywhere there were curved arches, stone overhangs, and the general appearance of well tended, though ancient, construction. Many of the buildings must have been at least three hundred years old, I thought, perhaps older. They had to take good care of the stonework, for Holmes had mentioned that seasonal high tides sometimes raised the level of the water to the first story. Doors must be jolly well tight set, I thought as the one in front of us opened.

I did not know what I expected to find on the other side, possibly a servant or the Egyptologist we wished to contact, but here was a familiar and welcome face: the straight nose, the small, military moustache, and the moon-shaped visage of the portly and deadly Wakefield Orloff. Those fathomless green eyes defrosted with an alien warmth as they flitted over us and, by habit, checked our backtrail. Then the security agent stepped to one side, indicating for us to enter. We were constantly meeting, usually in unusual places, and greetings were superfluous. Ever since the matter of the Louvre robbery so brilliantly handled by Holmes, Orloff had been ranked as an associate, and I was always grateful for his presence, which carried with it an insurance value as sound as the pound sterling.

"Gentlemen," said Orloff, in his low, mild voice, "this is Howard Andrade."

A figure leaning over a huge table turned towards us and, with a departing glance at the subject of his scrutiny, crossed in our direction. The Egyptologist was beardless, with flaxen hair streaked here and there with gray and a broad, pink, good-humored face. His waistcoat had apparently given up its efforts to compass his girth, but he moved quickly enough and his handshake was firm.

"Mr. Holmes, of course, and this must be Doctor Watson, whose words have provided many a fascinating hour. I'm honored, gentlemen."

It was immediately obvious to me that Andrade was a splendid fellow. As he indicated available chairs in the very large room in which we stood, I surveyed the interior of this quaint Italian house. That the hieroglyphics expert or a predecessor had instituted extensive remodeling was apparent. The walls to what had to be a combined living room and study rose two stories to an ornamental plaster ceiling that was quite magnificent.

There were numerous bookcases well filled as befitted the home of a scholar. The south wall was interesting indeed, containing a first-story gallery running the depth of the house and reached by a curved staircase. Off the upper landing, guarded by a wooden balustrade, was but one door, and I assumed that the master bedchamber was there. Windows, which formerly served the original first story, now provided two rows of apertures for the large central chamber. During the day, I imagined, the area was brightly lit by sunlight even though there were no windows in the walls other than the one that constituted the front of the house. Behind us and to the right of the entrance door must be the kitchen facilities, possibly servants' quarters as well, I thought. The remainder, save for that portion of the first floor facing onto the gallery, was one large open room lit by chandeliers and with Hepplewhite furniture tastefully positioned. The walls were festooned with pictures, all of Egyptian scenes. There was a delightful feeling of space. The room was dominated by the oaken table Andrade had been at when we arrived. It was strewn with pictures, calipers, dividers, parallel rules, and other equipment that I could not recognize. I sensed that Andrade worked mainly on his feet, circling the table that was the focus of his area of activity.

Having seated his visitors, Andrade leaned against the table and surveyed us with a half-smile.

"I came, Mr. Holmes, to Venice to insure privacy and must admit that I was a bit put out when Mr. Orloff appeared on the scene." He shot a quick look at our friend, who was in the process of lighting one of the thin Mexican cigars that he fancied.

"However, his credentials were so impressive that I could not refuse him an audience, and a good thing, too, since he has done me a great service." Andrade's eyes shifted to a pile of photographs on the table and then he moved to sink, somewhat slowly, into a large armchair. "Then he requested that I meet with you, Mr. Holmes and Doctor Watson. Now, I would be a dullard indeed if I did not think that a visit from the world's foremost detective is connected with the Egyptian research I'm involved in."

"It is," replied Holmes. "My—our—investigations are not of an archaeological nature, but they do seem to point to Egypt, and you are the first new element in hieroglyphics since Champollion."

Andrade's full lips twisted in a slight grimace. "The Frenchman gets all the credit. Not that he doesn't deserve it, you know. Positive genius. Spoke Latin, Greek, and Hebrew by the age of eleven. Mastered Arabic, Syrian, Chaldean, and Coptic in two years. However, our own Thomas Young is rather overlooked. It was he who deduced that in hieroglyphics the royal names were inscribed in oval frames."

"Cartouches," said the sleuth.

The Egyptologist's eyes brightened and he regarded Holmes with even more respect.

"Exactly, sir. You have a familiarity with the subject. But I take us from the matter at hand. You want to know if I have been successful in decoding the secret writings."

"That's it," replied Holmes.

Andrade stirred uncomfortably in his chair. "Of course, you understand that our discussion is highly confidential. Later this year I will deliver an address to a group of skeptical and, in many cases, antagonistic colleagues. It will serve my purposes best if they are not aware of my full revelations. Then I intend to publish a paper that might

116

have the same reception as Champollion's 'Letter to M. Dacier in regard to the alphabet of the phonetic hieroglyphics.'" His mouth pursed for a moment and then he gave vent to a sigh of resignation. "Well, not quite as earth-shaking, since Champollion was first. No matter, I can give you an answer for the first time."

As though the thought of his quest produced a sudden surge of energy, Andrade rose from his chair and crossed nervously to the table. Turning, he slid his posterior onto its surface. Had he crossed his legs beneath him, there would have been a resemblance to a seated Buddha. His arms behind him, he leaned back and there was a creak of protest from the oak, but the table was stoutly constructed. Andrade's eyes had an almost dreamy look as though he was reliving the work of years, which in fact he was.

"It was the temple of Abu Simbel that first aroused the curiosity of scholars, myself included. It lies a hundred miles south of Karnak and is the largest monolithic sculpture in the world. The temple is cut into a solid sandstone cliff, and its facade is covered with huge effigies of Rameses Second. Inside the temple, in the inner sanctuary, is another statue of Rameses Second, and underneath it a number of inscriptions that have defied translation. Thomas Young became intrigued with the idea of another form of hieroglyphics, and this theory, to which I subscribed, was buttressed by certain golden tablets that had shown up. They are very rare. Graverobbers must have melted them down in times gone by. Then, with the coming of our modern era, they realized that the genuine article was worth much more to a great museum or wealthy collector than the basic worth of the precious metal.

"Three of the tablets are in the possession of the Egyptian Museum, and I have seen copies of the inscriptions but never the tablets. In the beginning, all I had to work with were the inscriptions at Abu Simbel. I did decode the secret writing, developing certain ideas of Young, but that's another story. What I needed desperately was confirmation of my findings. Now it is common knowledge in the field that Giovanni Balzoni, the Italian archaeologist and adventurer, came upon two more golden tablets not long before his death early in the century. He got them out of Egypt,

117

for things were very easygoing in those days, but they disappeared. Then they turned up fifty years later and were purchased by Mannheim, the great German collector. Since they were the only golden tablets outside of Egypt, Mannheim made quite a fuss about his acquisition, and they were stolen from him and have not reappeared to this day."

I could not contain myself any longer.

"But what have these ancient tablets to do with your discovery?" I asked. Happily, Andrade seemed to welcome my question.

"Proof positive, Doctor Watson. I have translated the Rameses inscriptions along with all the copies of the known tablets that I could secure, but I needed more material to work on."

He waved a large hand in the direction of Wakefield Orloff. "It was here that this gentleman came to my aid."

Holmes was regarding the security agent with surprise.

"Don't tell me that in such a short time you located the Mannheim tablets?"

As Orloff laid aside his cigar, it was Andrade who fielded the conversational ball.

"Almost as good, Mr. Holmes. He secured photographs of them."

Andrade slid off the table and spread a pile of large photographs on its surface.

"Here, gentlemen, are pictures of the Mannheim tablets, which I have translated as conclusive proof that the riddle of the secret writings is no more."

We all clustered round the table. The pictures were of rows of inscriptions taken from various angles. To me they were but a series of carvings bearing no relation to a written language, but Holmes seemed intrigued and Andrade was positively bubbling with joy as he pointed to various lines of ancient text.

Holmes's eyes had gone to Wakefield Orloff.

"Rather nice piece of work, this," he said, indicating the photographs. "How did you get them?"

There was a fleeting shadow of self-satisfaction on Orloff's impassive face.

"Memory helped. I recalled that Mannheim is a great

118

believer in pictures, most often of himself, and in the newspapers whenever possible. He is no shrinking violet. His photographer, Werdelin of Berlin, was evidently influenced by his greatest patron because he is a collector as well. Of photographs. I had some dealings with the gentleman once and knew that invariably when on a big job he made copies of his work, which he carefully filed."

"So you went to Berlin and secured the copies in Werdelin's files," said Holmes.

"He owed me a favor," was the security agent's reply, accompanied by his quiet smile.

"In any case, with the pictures I saw the end of the road," continued Andrade. "I have been at work for thirty-six hours, gentlemen. My poor assistant gave up the ghost three hours ago and is in my room upstairs in an exhausted sleep. To be frank, I don't feel the slightest fatigue."

"The adrenalin of victory," I stated automatically.

Since the Egyptologist seemed intent in going over various inscriptions and had a courteous audience in Holmes and Orloff, I withdrew from the scene slightly. The ancient writings had little appeal to me, and I moved to the bow window that had captured my attention upon our arrival.

On the San Canciano canal there was an endless procession of boats and gondolas, and I noted skyrockets from the direction of Campo San Marco. There was a drumbeat of sound, almost like muted gunfire, which I identified as fireworks, concluding that it was but another festival night in the city noted for such celebrations. As my gaze swiveled towards the small tributary canal running at right angles to the San Canciano, I shook my head for a moment and blinked my eyes.

"I say," I exclaimed, turning to the others, "there seems to be some sort of rope made of knotted sheets dangling from a window of this house."

My words had an immediate effect. A quick glance passed between Holmes and Orloff, and the sleuth darted for the curved staircase leading to the upper story. I was right on his heels and as I stumbled after Holmes, I saw, out of the corner of my eye, a remarkable sight. Orloff had not made a move towards the stairs. Instead, as though levitated, he was now on the top of the stout table, but for no more than an instant. Two steps forward on the table surface and his steel legs dipped and then straightened with a surge of power and he was in the air, arms outstretched and above his head. His leap would have been admired by a ballet dancer! Then widespread fingers gripped the top of the balcony railing and the amazing power of his arms and shoulders took over, propelling his body upwards. His legs tucked in and then swung between those knotted arms with exquisite grace, the hands were released and, catlike, he was on the gallery as Holmes and I came round the curve in the stairs.

Orloff's movements were without pause. Already he was flowing across the floor and his shoulder crashed against the door of the bedroom, knocking it asunder like a battering ram. There was a flash of light from within the room and the thunder of a gun, but the security agent had dropped to the floor in a rolling movement. Scrambling to the head of the stairs, Holmes and I could see the bedroom interior. By an open window, an indistinct figure had one leg through the opening. Three more flowers of light blossomed from the vicinity of the man's right hand, and the roar of sound was continuous. The ever-moving mass that was Orloff had rolled behind a substantial chair and was coming to a semierect position, his hand reaching to the back of his neck and the chamois sheath attached between his shoulder blades. His arm was no more than a blur, and then there was the flash of metal, but the Toledo steel of his Spanish throwing knife buried itself in the window frame, for the figure had dropped through the opening.

I thought I heard a splash from without as I reached the bedroom door. Orloff had moved behind his knife, brushing the chair in front of him away as though it were a toy. Then the first interruption in his continous flow of movement from the floor below to the bedroom occurred. Crossing like a quicksilver shadow towards the window, his foot stumbled over a small stool, unseen in the dim light, and his legs came out from under him. But it did not stop him. The man's reflexes were truly of another world, for in midair he dipped into a forward roll, his thick neck and shoulders caressing the floor and, of a sudden, he snapped erect on both feet beside the window.

His actions really defied description, for though they were made with a speed that one could not accept in retrospect, such was his grace that he seemed to float in slow motion, an illusion fostered by the total absence of any wasted movement. When danger crooked its ominous digit and invited mischance, Orloff seemed to embark on a programmed path, always one step in advance of fate's finger.

An outstretched palm halted Holmes's progress towards the window, and I bumped into him from behind.

"They've fished him into a gondola," said the security agent in a calm voice suitable for an invitation to tea. "They're turning into the main canal." As he spoke, his right hand dipped to his wasteband and a small-calibre revolver seemed to materialize. "I could—"

"No." stated Holmes flatly. "The fireworks have covered the gunfire, but let's not have target practice in the San Canciano. By the time we reach our waiting gondola they will have lost themselves in the canal traffic, so we'd best write this matter off."

Holmes raised the flame in a gas lamp, throwing additional illumination into the room.

"No aspersions on your marksmanship, good fellow. I know you could have picked the intruders off like clay pigeons, but I'm not sure that's the way we wish to play it."

Orloff's green eyes were locked with the sleuth's for a moment, and a shadow of understanding touched his face. Then the handgun disappeared, and he calmly retrieved his throwing knife from the window frame, tucking it back between his shoulder blades with an automatic movement.

He then indicated a makeshift rope anchored to the bed and running through the window. "How about this?"

Holmes shrugged, having already noted the bedsheets hurriedly knotted together. "Improvised, which tells us this incident was not preplanned."

As Orloff drew the line of bed linen back through the window there was an exclamation from the landing, and Howard Andrade, puffing from his ascent, was regarding us with wide, startled eyes. I had quite forgotten the good man, but his appearance served as a further reminder of all that had happened in such a brief period of time. Our host had been spectator to the abrupt departure of his three visitors, then the sound of a shattered door, a burst of gunfire, and finally silence. Having recovered his wits and made his way upstairs, he found nothing but two men calmly analyzing the scene and another, myself, looking befuddled.

"I say," Andrade stammered, "what have we here? A mameluke revolt?"

His voice was a full octave higher than normal. Suddenly his eyes darted round the room. "Where is Aaron?"

"Your assistant?" questioned Holmes.

"Aaron Lewis. I secured his services in Venice."

Suddenly I shook off the dazed feeling that had enveloped me.

"Look here, you said this Lewis chap was exhausted and had retired before collapsing. This is your bedroom?"

"Yes," replied Andrade. "Lewis normally resides in a small room on the ground floor. I sent him up here so that my potting around would not disturb the poor fellow."

"Why, it's as plain as a pikestaff," I said triumphantly. "The intruders were after you, and spirited away your assistant by mistake."

"Good Lord, why?"

Since neither Holmes nor Orloff seemed disposed to offer a comment, I elaborated for the benefit of the startled cryptographer.

"Someone wishes to learn the code of the secret writings. That's rather obvious."

"I think," said Holmes gently, "that a discussion is called for."

Falling in with his thought, I rather led Andrade towards the stairs and the living room below.

Questions bubbled to the surface of my mind but were submerged by my medical training. Andrade seemed to be suffering a reaction from all the excitement, and I thought it well to get him seated below, securing some alcoholic stimulation for him from a well-stocked cabinet.

In a moment the Egyptologist's color improved, and he was able to regard the three of us with a whimsical expression.

"This rather bizarre occurrence is much more in your line, Mr. Holmes, than mine. Am I to assume that there might be more of the same?"

It was Wakefield Orloff who spoke up. "I think not, sir. At least, I shall take suitable precautions to make sure your domicile is not invaded again."

I well knew what that meant. More of Mycroft Holmes's faceless men would appear. For all I knew, Orloff might already have associates at his beck and call in Italy.

Andrade took another sizable sip of his libation. "What is the meaning of all this melodrama, gentlemen, and what about Aaron Lewis, my poor associate?"

Warned by the haunted look in his eyes and fearing palpitations, I spoke instantly and in my most soothing doctor manner.

"Once the hoodlums learn they have the wrong man, surely they will release Lewis from their clutches."

"Let us hope so," said Holmes. It struck me that his manner was surprisingly casual. "About your assistant, Mr. Andrade. How did he happen to come into your employment?"

"I am a bachelor, so it was easy for me to pull up stakes and come to Venice in search of solitude to complete my project. The house is mine by virtue of a generous, now departed, uncle. I knew that I was on the verge of a break-through, and my work was intensified. At this point, much filing was required. I was at my wits' end when Lewis appeared at my door, much as Mr. Orloff did but recently."

"Possibly for the same reason," commented Holmes quietly.

The Egyptologist did not notice this remark, but I filed it away.

"Lewis said he had heard of my project and had excellent references, including a rather glowing letter from Flinders Petrie. I know Petrie and recognized his distinctive script. Lewis seemed well up on the Egyptian picture and took charge of my files, putting them in workmanlike order. It was such a relief to have the paperwork attended to that I was able to progress much faster towards what is now the final solution."

"What did he look like?" asked Orloff.

"Lewis? Tall, thin-boned. I suppose 'cadaverous' is not amiss as a description. Very quiet chap, used to the simple life, but then those who have been on expeditions to the

Nile most often are. Had a nasal problem and tobacco smoke bothered him. Fact is, that is why I suggested that he use my bedroom today. With the successful translation of the Mannheim tablets a fait accompli, I was terribly keyed up and smoking like a blessed steel mill. Lewis is along a bit, agewise, and I was concerned for his physical well-being."

"As I am for yours right now," I interjected. "You've been on your feet for a day and a half, and the recent events have been wearing. I'm prescribing bed rest immediately."

There were other questions that Holmes wished to ask, possibly Orloff as well, but both stifled their instincts in consideration of Howard Andrade's condition. One of the dividends of my profession is the delight in having the last word. When a doctor says "that's it!" there are seldom arguments, from a prime minister on down.

We took Orloff in our gondola to the Grand Hotel, where I assumed he was staying. I had the idea that he would join us at the Venezia after resolving matters that claimed his attention, one being to throw a net round Howard Andrade. On our journey, Holmes pointed out the beautiful Palazzo Dario to me, planned by Pietro Lombardo, as well as the huge and luxurious Piazza Corner della Ca' Grande, planned by Jacopo Sansovino. Lombardo and Sansovino were unknown to me, but my friend seemed to place great store in their names. I recalled that he indulged in a passion for Renaissance architecture at one time. It was in relation to an old case, not without points of interest, which I may make available to readers some day.

The hour was late but Venice is cosmopolitan, and Holmes and I were able to secure a satisfying meal in the hotel dining room at an hour when most Englishmen would be dawdling over their last brandy and seriously considering their beds.

The same thought was crossing my mind as we occupied ourselves with a bowl of fruit augmented by some fine cheeses. It was then that we were joined by Orloff. Our waiter hastened to secure a chair for the security agent. Whether he knew Orloff, who was well traveled, or just

reacted to the commanding presence of the deceptively rotund man I do not know. During dinner Holmes had been
preoccupied and I had not disturbed his thoughts, but now
revelations would be forthcoming, which delighted me.

Orloff was no Randolph Rapp, but then who was? However, his experience, honed to a fine edge in the shadow-
land of international espionage, was extensive. Being a man
of acute perception and few words, his conversations with
Holmes frequently had a staccato quality, and I was invariably hard pressed to keep abreast of the two.

"Andrade is well covered?" This was more a statement
than a question from Holmes as he sliced the peeling from
an orange.

"Cooks himself. Simplifies things. Cleaning woman
comes in three times a week. We'll check her out." Orloff
accepted a wedge of cheese that I offered him. "May put a
man on the premises. Butler, courtesy of Her Majesty's
government. The cryptographer won't object. Rather keen,
you know. Must realize that his discovery has touched off
a bit of a chain reaction.

If not, I thought, you will convince him. Orloff was to
the manor born, and I could picture said gentleman plying
a thriving trade selling sand in the Sahara.

"What news of the Chinaman?" queried Holmes.

"His yacht should be here shortly."

"Hmm! You'd think Chu San Fu's arrival would have
signalled the move on Andrade's residence."

"Whole thing was rushed. Sloppy job."

I had poured Orloff a tot of after-dinner liqueur, and he
was regarding Holmes over the rim of a sparkling glass.

"I've a mind as to what hurried them. You."

It was at this point that I threw patience to the winds.

"Could you translate this interchange for my dull ears?"
I fear my manner was somewhat huffy.

"Chu San Fu's agents are in Venice," explained Orloff.
"They hastily removed Aaron Lewis from Andrade's home,
ahead of schedule, I'd say. The answer has to be Sherlock
Holmes."

"How do you figure that?"

Orloff's lips twitched, a sign of satisfaction rarely seen on
his features.

"Noticed your friend here react when Howard Andrade described his assistant."

My gaze shifted to Holmes, whose eyes were twinkling.

"Dear me, I have become transparent, but Orloff is right. The description of the assistant, Lewis, bore a remarkable resemblance to Memory Max."

My inquisitive stare was undiminished, for I did not share Holmes's encyclopedic knowledge of members of the criminal classes.

"In his early years, Max did a turn in the music halls as a memory expert. Answered any question. Photographic memory, you see. However, he turned his not inconsiderable talents to less legitimate pursuits and became one of the leading forgers of our time."

"How strange," I exclaimed. "A man with a freak memory turning to forgery."

"Not so, Watson. Those with an unusual mental aptitude frequently find great relaxation in working with their hands. Max's dexterity with tools and dies proved most embarrassing to the government."

Well, I thought, you rather disprove that, old fellow. But then my mind rejected this thought. Holmes did, in moments of relaxation, derive great solace from his violin.

Orloff was sipping his liqueur thoughtfully. "Max specialized in guineas and sovereigns. I know of him."

"But I *know* him," said Holmes, and there was an instant gleam in Orloff's eyes.

"I was instrumental in laying Max by the heels, back in '81 as I recall. An early case. He's been safely in Dartmoor for years, but obviously is out now."

"Wait," I blurted. "You mean that Memory Max was a . . . a plant next to Howard Andrade?" I was pleased at coming up with a suitable colloquialism.

"Of course." Holmes's tone, not by intent, indicated that a five-year-old child would be *au courant* with this.

"But the mysterious 'they' were after Andrade himself. They got into his bedroom, you know."

"I allowed your re-creation to stand, Watson, since it served as an alarm to Howard Andrade. However, you had it all wrong. Bed sheets torn and knotted together to form a rope to allow one to descend from the first-story room to the canal level are not a means of entry but of exit. What happened is clear enough. Memory Max was used as a means of getting close to Andrade, to memorize his files and learn the secret of his decoding of the secret writings. At an appropriate time, the arrival of Chu San Fu's yacht, I presume, he was to be spirited away to join the master criminal. Destination? Egypt. But an unforeseen element was introduced when we arrived in Venice.

"Were I to come face to face with Memory Max, I would recognize him, so the 'they' you refer to had to prevent our meeting. They signalled Max to get out, setting a time for a gondola to be under the window of the master bedroom. Using the plea of exhaustion, the forger arranged to be in the bedroom, and fashioned the rope of bed sheets to facilitate his escape. Your spotting it almost upset their plans."

I leaned back in my chair, more than a little pleased with the last statement. Holmes's eyes adopted that opaque look that I knew so well. Silence fell on the table, and I exchanged a look with Orloff that drew a shrug as a reply. Finally the security agent said softly, "What now?"

"There is," responded Holmes in an almost dreamy manner, "a bit more surmise than I approve of. Chu San Fu has the Sacred Sword and it is headed for Alexandria. The Chinaman's yacht is en route here. Beyond these facts, we are guessing. My thought is that Chu San Fu will pick up Memory Max here in Venice and then continue to Egypt. But what of the Mannheim tablets? I have a feeling those writings in gold are a part of the puzzle. I recall that they were stolen from the Mannheim collection and believe that the thief was captured. Without my files and commonplace books, details elude me. Can you prompt me on this matter, Orloff?"

"In part. One Heinrich Hublein was convicted of the theft and is in prison now. The tablets were never found, but the why of that I do not know."

"Wolfgang Von Shalloway might," said Holmes. "I will cable the esteemed Chief of the Berlin Police tonight, and if his answer proves interesting, we shall resume our travels tomorrow, Watson, in an attempt to add more pieces to this international jigsaw."

Chapter Twelve

The Madman's Tale

The Berlin police chief's response to my friend's cable must have been encouraging, and Holmes must have waited at the cable office for it. At dawn I was rousted from my comfortable bed, and we were soon on the Hamburg Express, which passed through Berlin en route to its eventual destination. Our journey is vague in my mind. I dozed fitfully a great part of the time, which was just as well since Holmes was indisposed to talk and there were lines of worry and concern around his eyes and noble forehead.

As was our custom whenever in the German capital, we checked into the Bristol Kempinski, where I was grateful to wash away the dust of our journey. The following morning we made our way to the Alexanderplatz and the nerve center of the machinelike Criminal Investigation Department of the Berlin Police Force.

Holmes had for years enjoyed an *entente cordiale* with Von Shalloway, famous Berlin police chief, and Arsene Pupin, the pride of the Sureté. It was a fortuitous "you scratch my back" arrangement for all three, augmented by actual admiration and friendship. In the matter of "The Four Detectives" they had actually worked together on a case, but that is another story indeed.

Wolfgang Von Shalloway was his small and dapper self, and after greetings got to business more rapidly than is customary on the continent. To have his fellow investigator contact him was to summon his best efforts, for it was a matter of pride that the German Eagle display a sharp beak in the presence of the British Lion.

"He is dragging you all over Europe, *nicht war*, Doctor?"

I summoned a weary smile of agreement.

"I did not think you were in Venice for your health, and now, Germany. It must be something big to entice Holmes from his beloved London."

"It could be," replied Holmes.

"Well, if you can throw some light on the matter of the Mannheim tablets, I will be in your debt."

"You have the thief, do you not?" I asked.

"We have Heinrich Hublein in a facility for the criminally insane. That is all we have. The tablets? Poof!"

Von Shalloway's hands gestured expressively. There was a look of distaste around his firm mouth.

"Not satisfied?"

"Far from it, Holmes. This happened four years ago. Hublein was not my only problem." The chief indicated a file on his desk, then tapped it with his index finger.

"Four cases, gentlemen, all unresolved. You Britishers would call it a blot on my escutcheon, and it is. They are. Never mind. One thing I will say for Hublein. He was good luck. After he confessed, no more unresolved cases."

"The thief confessed?" I asked.

"Is crazy *nicht war*? And the doctors say he is crazy. 'Catatonic' they call him. Withdrawn into a secret world within himself. Possibly this is so."

Von Shalloway rose from behind his desk as though to remove himself from the file he had referred to. There was a soft knock on his office door and an assistant entered, registered on a gesture from the chief, and disappeared without saying a word. I recalled Holmes once saying that when Von Shalloway said "Jump!" his aides asked, "How high?"

Holmes surprised me. "Tell us about the unresolved cases."

He surprised Von Shalloway also. "I thought you were interested—" His jaw abruptly clamped shut. "Never mind. Perhaps you can came up with something. I should not look a gift . . . a gift . . ."

130

"Horse in the mouth?" I suggested.

"Ya. Watson is up on the, how you say, 'lingo.'"

"He reads sensational American literature," commented Holmes dryly. "About those other cases."

Von Shalloway was back at his desk with the file open, but that was purely a gesture of habit. Obviously, he knew the contents backwards.

"Better than six years ago, we have a robbery in Morenstrasse. The thief jimmied the door to a built-in stairs that served as the fire escape. It was a well-to-do apartment house and out of all the residents, he picks a suite occupied by a supposed financier who we know is a big-time fence. His door is jimmied, too, and a lot of money is stolen."

"Ah ha!" I exclaimed. "A receiver of stolen goods would keep a lot of ready cash on hand."

Von Shalloway pointed towards Holmes. "That he learned from you and not from sensational literature. Anyway, we went over the locks. Hammer was on the case."

"Good man!" said Holmes.

"I trained him," replied Von Shalloway. "Something about the scratches on the locks rang a bell, and he went to the Meldwesen."

Fortunately, this was not gibberish to me. A mind like Sherlock Holmes's had to be fascinated by the machinelike logic of the Germans and their genius for organization. I had heard from him all about the Meldwesen, the huge catalogue of cards that constituted the most exhaustive body of information on criminal matters assembled. Holmes referred to it as a crime machine, and since it took one hundred and sixty rooms to house, I judged it to be a big one.

"It was the jimmy that was the clue. It was a special design used by only one man according to our records. We picked him up soon enough. It had to be him, only the night of the robbery he was in jail on suspicion of involvement in a casino robbery in Bad Homburg."

"The case fell apart?"

"Completely." Von Shalloway was on his feet again. "All four cases the same. In Bremen, a jewel robbery. The victim, we think maybe he is a smuggler. His wife's jewels are taken. Possibly, also some diamonds that he spirited through customs. But, no mind. The thief gets in with a glass cutter. Everything about the job spells one man whose modus operandi we have catalogued. So what happens? The suspect, the night of the robbery, is acting as a snitch in a *weinstube* we are raiding in Berlin. My own men give him an alibi."

Von Shalloway accepted a Capstan cigarette I offered him and lit it nervously. "Danke, Doctor. Hmmm! Tightly packed, no? The American cigarettes, they are better."

"I prefer them," said Holmes.

"Anyway, we have constructed a machine. Our Meldwesen and Kriminal Archiv cannot fail. But still I have those four cases."

"What about Hublein?"

"Make that five cases, Holmes. The two gold tablets were stolen from Mannheim's home in Spandau. As you know, Herr Mannheim has one of the largest collections of art objects in the world. The thief gained access through a fourth-story window. There is only one man who could have done it. Schadie, also called 'The Shadow.' "

"He had an alibi?" I asked enthralled.

"We have never found him. We know all about him, of course. He uses suction cups on his hands and attached to his knees. He can go up a wall as smooth as glass. The Mannheim case, uhh, we heard a lot about that from high places. Herr Mannheim's steel mills are important to Germany. There were traces. Our technicians found indications of rubber on the outer wall of the building. It had to be Schadie. But, into headquarters comes this Hublein. No record. He is pretty wild-eyed, but he insists that he stole the tablets."

Von Shalloway thumped his desk with exasperation.

"It had to be Shadow Schadie, but try to convince a jury when they are facing a man who has confessed. Hublein was convicted. He made no defense. The few words the lawyers could get out of him were incriminating. Then the doctors got hold of him. I agree with them. Hublein has bats in his, how you say . . . ?"

"Belfry?"

"Ya! Und now he is in the booby . . . booby . . ."

"Hatch."

"That is so, Doctor."

"You say he had no record?" asked Holmes.

Von Shalloway regarded us both with an embarrassed expression. "Tanks Gott the journals did not make much of the case. A confessed criminal is not news. Gentlemen, Heinrich Hublein was a female impersonator."

I half rose from my chair. "Come now, Von Shalloway, you're pulling our legs."

"I wish it was so. But, *nein*, Hublein was entertainer. He had what they call 'a good act.' He is small, dark of hair with thin bones and classical features. Always, he makes himself up as a blond and he sings in high voice and pretty good, too. Then at the conclusion of his turn, when the applause comes, he sweeps off his wig and audience realizes that he is not woman at all."

"A female impersonator and a crime of the century," mused Holmes thoughtfully. "I rather feel your newspapers missed a bet. Can I see this most unusual prisoner?"

"Of course. But you will look over the four cases I mentioned, no?" Von Shalloway was leafing through his records and extracted some typewritten sheets, which he handed to Holmes.

"Study them, please. Every day I come in here and I see that file, and then I think of Hublein and it is not such a good day suddenly."

The sleuth nodded. "Might I first have a go at the Meldwesen? You know how it delights me."

Von Shalloway turned to me with twinkling eyes.

"Ach, he is looking for something." His bright eyes shifted back to Holmes. "I shall have Hammer escort you, and while you are going through files, Doctor Vatson and I will have luncheon. I know a beerstube which has the best bratwurst you have ever tasted, Doctor."

I winced. The German chief of police was as trim as a dancer despite an astonishing capacity for dark beer and rich food, whereas I. . . . But Holmes urged me to accept, and so it was that I spent the better part of two hours with Von Shalloway and returned to his office feeling much the better for it. Holmes was waiting in the anteroom.

"I had a delightful time in your files, Von Shalloway.

The good Hammer offered to take me to see Hublein, but I felt that Watson's presence would be beneficial. Medical opinion, you know."

"Of course," I said, belching slightly. "By all means, let us be off to the crazy house."

The facility for the criminally insane was adjacent to the city jail. Holmes suggested that I have a discussion with the doctor in charge while he inquired amongst the personnel as to Hublein and his attitude during his incarceration. Sergeant Hammer was taking us to the man's cell when I reported my findings.

"A model prisoner, Holmes. Makes no fuss and actually says nothing at all, symptomatic of his mental disorder. He has become a mute."

"Save on certain rare occasions, usually at night, when peals of laughter come from his cell," said Holmes. "One attendant I spoke to described the sound as devoid of mirth and of a mechanical nature, interrupted only by pauses for air."

I shuddered instinctively. "The man is not dangerous, in any case."

"But silent. The worst kind for our purposes."

We were at the cell door now, which Hammer unlocked for us.

Heinrich Hublein was as Von Shalloway had described him. He was sitting erect on the cot in his room, staring at the wall in front of him with small, button-black eyes. I noted that his mouth twitched, but he made no notice of our entrance. Hammer closed the cell door and stood by it, alert. Hublein was classified as nondangerous, but we were in a mental institution, and a complete reversal of temperament was possible.

Holmes remained motionless, studying the figure on the cot and possibly waiting for him to register on our presence. In appearance Hublein seemed fragile, with a flat chest and delicate, pipestem bones. I felt that his nervous system and sensory tissue had relatively poor protection, a contributing cause to what I diagnosed as a breakdown followed by a deliberately enforced withdrawal from a world that was unbearable. He seemed the type that would react dramatically to a shock or a situation from which he demanded escape at all costs. Like many who have fled from reason, he was youthful-looking.

"Hublein?" It was Holmes using a soft tone in an inquisitive manner.

The man nodded slightly, as though we barely existed on the periphery of his existence.

"The famous entertainer?" continued the sleuth. There might have been a sudden flash in those dull eyes. I could not be sure.

"This really will not do," said Holmes. His voice had a faint, chiding sound to it. "They will never know what you did."

Hublein's eyes slowly, reluctantly abandoned the wall, and an inch at a time his face turned in our direction, the rest of his slight body remaining motionless. It was like a diver allowing the buoyancy of his body to bring him to the surface. When his head had made a forty-five-degree turn, he seemed to be looking through us and beyond.

"They don't think you stole the tablets, you know. They certainly don't know about your great performance."

The dark eyes came slowly into focus, regarding Holmes's expressive face and, I felt, actually seeing him for the first time. The sleuth's words seemed to have drawn him from another dimension.

"It's never been done before, you know. Nobody ever thought of it but you."

There was a flicker of understanding now, of interest.

"How do you know?" His voice was husky, as though rusted from lack of use. I was conscious of Hammer stiffening. Words from Hublein had startled him.

"I am Sherlock Holmes."

The thin-boned, delicate face was fastened on the sleuth, and he pushed a lock of dark hair off his narrow forehead.

"To use the machine against itself. A revolutionary concept."

The lips twitched again, and a half-smile forced itself shyly onto the pale face with almost translucent skin.

"It was a good idea," he admitted. His words came easier this time.

"But you must have had to practice. How did you learn to use the jimmy?"

Now there seemed an actual desire to speak, to explain, to indulge a starved vanity.

"They had diagrams of the tool in the files. Besides, you meet all kinds of people when you work in cabarets."

"So you got some tips from a swag man. Also some instruction on how to use a glass cutter." Holmes might have been a professor congratulating a student on good marks.

"I can do things with my hands. I started out working with puppets."

"Before you took up female impersonating."

Irritation flitted over Hublein's face. "There was more money in the impersonating. I could sing in a high key and dance enough to get by. Men in the audience used to try to grab me. They felt like fools when I took off my wig."

"But you never liked it."

"No. People thought I was a freak."

"So you wanted to do something truly dangerous. Be a Robin Hood." Holmes corrected himself: "William Tell."

The veil was completely brushed aside from the eyes now. They glowed.

"It wasn't wooden puppets or cosmetics and wigs. It was exciting, no make-believe. The darkness, the silence, and the thrill when you got away and knew that you had done it. You'd fooled them."

"Fooled everybody," commented Holmes factually.

"But I was fooled in the end." The thought was a bitter one, and the shutters of Hublein's eyes started to close again. I sensed he was beginning to drift back into the catatonic escape, but Holmes was alert to this danger as well.

"What about Frau Mueller? That was the finest touch."

This bait proved irresistible, and the performer was with us again.

"That was easy. No one suspected me."

"Because you always impersonated beautiful women."

The small face nodded jerkily.

"Frau Mueller was a crone. I blackened several teeth. Her wig looked like frayed hemp. I penciled in lines and used a wart right here." A slender finger indicated an area between chin and lips. "One look at Frau Mueller was enough. She was an unpleasant sight. I had to give up the cabaret work, of course."

"So that you could pose as a night cleaning woman at headquarters. Not being an old or arthritic woman at all but young and agile, you could fulfill the duties of the job and have some extra time to search through the Meldwesen files until you found the cards you wanted."

"The first four robberies were trial runs. I wanted to do something big. Something that would be in the papers and that people would talk about for years."

"So you decided to 'steal the act' of Shadow Schadie."

Holmes's show-business colloquialism pleased Hublein. "I had to practice for months. But finally I mastered the suction cups. I am very light, you see. That helped."

"And you turned yourself into a veritable human fly."

Hublein nodded. "The papers were full of the purchase, by Mannheim, of the golden tablets. I thought that would be the great robbery, the one that would cause the most talk. The tablets were so valuable that I could sell them and retire. No more cabarets and no more Frau Mueller either. But they were white gold. No fence would touch them."

There was anguish in Hublein's face now and the suggestion of moisture in his eyes.

"I'd done it. I'd worked so hard and planned so carefully and I had ended up with nothing. When the Chinaman approached me and offered me so little for the tablets, I felt my whole life was for nothing. I was a puppet with no one on the strings. I sold him the tablets, and then . . . and then. . . ."

The voice dwindled away. The seated man's head slowly turned back so that his unseeing eyes were fastened on the blank wall again. Heinrich Hublein had retraced his steps back to the kingdom of forgetfulness, of silence, of nothingness.

Holmes's eyes encountered mine. There was a resigned expression in them, as though he realized that he had no more bait to tempt the vanishing personality back into the world of reality.

He signalled to Hammer, who opened the cell door. Hublein was not conscious of our departure.

137

An aura of sadness enveloped me when we left the poor, misguided, unbalanced man, but it vaporized in the heat of excitement liberally spiced by wonderment.

"Holmes, how did you ever deduce that Hublein was the perpetrator of five crimes? And that he created the character of a spurious cleaning woman?"

There was a thin smile on Holmes's aquiline features that I recognized as an indication that he was pleased with himself.

"When Von Shalloway described the robberies in his office, did not something strike you?"

I cast my mind back in a determined effort to locate the tell-tale that had allowed Holmes to cut the Gordian knot, but in my heart of hearts sensed that it would elude me.

"Each crime bore the trademark of one criminal who had a cast-iron alibi."

"The alibis were happenstance. Think, Watson! The Morenstrasse robbery involved the flat of a fence. In Bremen, the jewels were stolen from a suspected smuggler. It immediately occurred to me that someone was using the Meldwesen files not only to copy the methods of certain criminals but to select the victims as well. Who, besides the officials, would have access to the files? Someone invisible."

"Oh, come now, Holmes!"

"Patience, old chap. Mailmen have a certain invisibility. We see them on their appointed rounds with such regularity that after a while we cease to see them. A cleaning woman falls in the same category. And we had Hublein, a female impersonator. The Germans file and list everything, so I was able to learn that one of the nighttime cleaning force, a certain Frau Mueller, failed to show up for work the day that Hublein surrendered himself to the police. She has not been located to this day."

"Until the elusive Frau Mueller was unmasked by Sherlock Holmes," I stated proudly. "Your discoveries will certainly delight Von Shalloway, but how do they affect us?"

"Hublein mentioned a Chinaman who purchased the tablets from him at bargain rates."

"Chu San Fu?"

Holmes shook his head. "An agent of his, no doubt. This

was four years ago, and Chu was still in the role of the collector. I suspect he secured the tablets because they were too good a bargain to miss. Since then something has happened that has made them precious to him."

We were almost back at Von Shalloway's office when another thought struck me.

"Hublein mentioned white gold. What is that, Holmes?"

"Pure gold is twenty-four carats. In modern times, most gold is mixed with an alloy to provide rigidity. The most common, fourteen-carat, has a large percentage of brass. Pink gold uses copper. White gold can be produced in two ways: with nickel, which is inexpensive; or with platinum, which is rarer and more valuable than gold itself. The sacred tablets used platinum as an alloy, not for the sake of rigidity, it being as malleable as gold, but for ostentation."

"No receiver would touch the tablets because of the platinum content?"

"I think they misled Hublein there. The man was not a trained criminal but merely a mimic. A fence could have had the tablets melted down and then separated the gold and platinum. I think the robbery was just a little too hot, and it scared them off."

Not long thereafter we returned to the Bristol Kempinski, leaving a delighted Von Shalloway in Alexanderplatz. The police chief with his unresolved cases solved and the matter of Hublein cleared up as well was much inclined towards hosting a victory dinner, but Holmes begged off, I regret to say. He stated that duties beckoned, and Von Shalloway was too acute to inquire as to their nature.

Back at the hotel, Holmes indulged in one of his disappearing acts. I suspect that he beat a hasty path to the British Embassy and made use of the diplomatic wire to contact his brother in London. What other messages he may have sent or received I do not know. On his return we packed, which was not time-consuming since we were traveling light.

Now Holmes was intent on reaching Egypt. I mentioned, somewhat snidely perhaps, that I hoped the freighter carrying the relic stolen from the Spaulding mansion had not altered its plan of sailing and beaten us to

Alexandria. Holmes, as usual, had an answer.

"The Hishouri Kamu was missing two stokers just before they weighed anchor, Watson. They were forced to sign on two new crew members: Burlington Bertie and Tiny. The freighter is on schedule and will not reach Egypt for some days."

So, Holmes, had planted his men on the cargo ship to keep an eye open. I had thought him somewhat casual about the Sacred Sword to which he attached so much importance.

I suggested that we augment our limited wardrobe at one of the fashionable Berlin shops, but there was no time for that. Holmes booked us by rail to Constanza, Romania. The train trip was dull, but there was a surprise when we arrived at the port on the Black Sea. A carriage took us to the waterfront, where we boarded a destroyer of Her Majesty's Navy, a means of transportation provided without a doubt by Mycroft Holmes. Wasting no time, the needle-thin craft traversed the Black Sea to the Dardanelles, and soon we were pitching and tossing in the Mediterranean.

I shall draw the curtain of charity over this trip. Suffice to say that I was pale, wan, and frightfully sick throughout. Holmes did his best, I must say, staying with me in the little cabin in the officers' quarters that we shared. In an effort to distract me from my misery, he did speak in unusual detail about the matter that we were involved in, opening up a new line of thought completely.

"You know, good fellow, ancient Egypt was a literate society completely capable of leaving a clear history, and after Champollion deciphered the Rosetta stone, it was reasonable to expect answers to age-old mysteries. But such was not the case."

"You feel the golden tablets might unlock hidden doors?" I asked, and then made myself available of the tin basin that Holmes had in readiness.

"Or I may be in fear of it. We are very vague on how they built the pyramids, you know, and have no idea of why they are aligned with the four compass points. Or why the Sphinx and the Colossi of Memmon both face east, parallel, by the way, with the axis of the great Amon-Ra temple at Karnak."

"Simple, Holmes," I sputtered, wiping my face and mouth with a wet towel. "The rising sun. They did worship the sun along with other deities."

"I'll accept that," he said. "But consider that other ancient structures, seemingly impossible to build in a nonmechanical age, are also lined up to risings and settings of the sun and moon. I refer to Stonehenge and the Mayan temples in Yucatan, to name but two."

"Good heavens, do you suspect some cosmic significance, some secret power?" I never got an answer to that, for I became deathly sick again and lost all interest in the subject.

Chapter Thirteen

Back Alleys of Cairo

"Of course," said Colonel Gray, "all of the seven wonders of the ancient world were constructed B.C., for the Greeks listed them in the second century before Christ. All gone now save the oldest and the largest." His right hand, which had been fanning him with his hat, gestured westward towards the Nile. "The pyramids of Giza remain as the sole survivors. Built two thousand years before Nebuchadnezzar conceived of hanging gardens. Infinitely old when the bronze fragments of the toppled Colossus of Rhodes were carted away by a junk dealer."

The skin on the colonel's hands and arms was ebony dark, but his face was the color of new brick. He took a sip of gin and lime and continued in his drawling, somewhat bored, voice.

"And, Doctor, when we are gone and when England is gone, they'll still be there. I'll take you to see them tomorrow if you wish. No trip at all. Over the Nile bridge and you're practically there."

I shrugged, disinclined to be definite about anything at the moment. When we had arrived in Alexandria, it was immediately apparent that Holmes had been burning up the cables and that there were definite plans afoot. He had placed me in the hands of Colonel Gray for safekeeping to Cairo whilst he involved himself in who-knows-what in the port of Alexandria and, possibly, that of Rosetta as well. The Colonel was obviously an old Egyptian hand, though what his exact duties were in the protectorate was not made clear to me. He got me to Shepheard's Hotel, which was all I cared about. That sedate establishment, center of British society in Cairo, was welcome indeed, and I'm sure some color came back to my face at the mere sight of it.

We were seated on the veranda acceding to a hallowed custom of the area known as the "sunset drink." Gray, a fountain of general knowledge, regaled me with stories of Richard Lepsius's German expedition in '43, his excavations at the Sphinx, which had led to mention of the adjacent pyramids.

Frankly, I was rather surfeited with discussions of the wonders of this ancient land and sought to divert the conversation to more modern and informative channels.

"Colonel, aren't there an unusual number of military in the area?"

For a moment his eyes registered surprise over the rim of his glass. Then he grunted. Colonel Gray commanded a large variety of grunts, all uninformative.

"Has there been local trouble?" I persisted.

"Nothing on the surface," he finally said cautiously.

"A feeling, then? Understand you chaps can sense that sort of thing."

He agreed with this and set about to prove that I was right.

"Egypt has closer ties with the Orient than with Europe, you know. Orientals are, underneath, a frightfully superstitious lot. Then, one of those religious revival periods is overdue among the Moslems. The native town seems to have the wind up over some prophecy or rumor. Probably the latter."

Since he seemed disposed to drop the matter, I prodded him.

"Not something like that Mahdi business?"

"Heavens, no! A wild tale, no doubt. Something about a prophet from the grave. A squib appeared in the *Al-Ahram*—"

He registered on my puzzled expression.

"—Our leading paper. Unusual for them to comment on the gossip of the mosques and bazaars, but. . . ."

Colonel Gray's glass made contact with the table between us. "Care for another?" he asked tentatively.

"Thank you, no. Look here, awfully grateful for your acting as guide and what-not, but I rather imagine I am an inconvenience. I'll have dinner here at the hotel and fancy a good long sleep."

"Mr. Holmes did express concern about your condition," said Gray. I sensed he was glad for the opportunity to unload me.

"I'll drop by, come morning, and see if Mr. Holmes has showed up," he said, shaking my hand perfunctorily. This idea produced another of his grunts, and he delayed his departure.

"You know, in London it is a bit hard to understand how things are out here."

"On the borders of the Empire, as 'twere."

"Humph! But your friend seems rather up on things."

How Colonel Gray had become aware of this fact puzzled me. I wondered if he was really the choleric-faced, sterotyped colonial official that he seemed to be.

I luxuriated in a cool tub in the suite secured for us by Gray, donned a suit of lightweight that the Colonel had helped me select in an arcade shop opposite the hotel, and dawdled over a dinner. Still somewhat weak, I ate lightly.

Afterwards I walked through the lobby and out onto the terrace of Shepheard's. It was comforting to have solid ground beneath my feet. With the setting of the sun the Egyptian heat had moderated, though the evening was muggy. However, in my tropicals I was comfortable enough. With no news from Holmes I was a bit at loose ends and debating whether to cross the street and view the arcade shops or return to my room when I saw him.

He was walking on the Sharia Kamel, squat, short-legged, and progressing at a fair rate of speed. It is said that to an Occidental all Chinamen look alike, but I disproved this by recognizing the man immediately. It was Loo Chan, the Chinese lawyer employed by Chu San Fu. As he passed under a street lamp I noted the perpetual sheen of his olive features and the drawn lips, revealing alarmingly white teeth so large and perfect as to seem false.

I did not even consider my next move but threw aside my cigarette and took after him. The lawyer was headed in the direction of the Ezbekiyeh Gardens and, with a flash of inspiration, I hastened to the other side of the street to continue my pursuit. My brain was working feverishly, trying to recall what I had heard of the exploits of Slippery Styles, whose uncanny skill at trailing men was a legend. There was sufficient traffic so that my presence was not noticeable and plenty of shop windows available to turn towards if the Chinaman happened to take a look over his shoulder.

Having acted instinctively, I now mentally paused to take stock of the situation. The fact that the London lawyer was in Cairo was at first surprising, but with Chu San Fu headed for the Nile, what more reasonable than that members of his criminal group were already in Egypt. Could I but locate Loo Chan's place of residence, I might be able to relay important information to Holmes on his arrival in Cairo. It occurred to me that it would be most comforting if the great detective were with me now as I walked the streets of a city virtually unknown to me on the heels of a member of a criminal conspiracy. But this was no moment for the faint-hearted, especially since my task was becoming more demanding.

We were on the outskirts of the European city, and ahead were the bazaars and narrow streets of the native quarter. Pedestrian traffic thinned out, and soon the thoroughfare we followed was deserted. Loo Chan continued forward, never once looking back, which might have seemed strange to a wiser dog on the scent. Then the Chinaman did pause and glance over his shoulder before turning into an alley. His move could not have happened at a worse time for I was, though on the opposite side of the street, badly positioned near one of the infrequent street lamps. However, Loo Chan made no note of me, turning purposefully into the dark alley, and it was then that some sense forced itself upon me.

"He's leading me into a trap," I thought. "Somehow he or a cohort spotted me at the hotel, and he has baited me into the open. Well, two can play that game," I thought with a surge of confidence.

I continued down the street, steeling myself not to even glance at the alley mouth into which the lawyer had ducked. At the next intersection, I turned to the right and

146

passed the corner. The native quarter was deserted, all inhabitants having withdrawn to their lodgings. No surprise that, since Cairo was known to wake early. With no observers about, I accelerated into a trot that brought me, somewhat short-winded, to the next corner. I did not round it but rather peered towards where I felt the alley opening might be. If Loo Chan emerged, I would have him under observation whilst hidden myself. But there was no sign of the Chinaman. Now I faced an impasse. My best bet seemed to be to try to return to Shepheard's, but if the minions of Chu San Fu were after me, they could well overtake me in the darkened streets of this quarter of Cairo and no one would be the wiser. I had no weapon to forestall them and chided myself for leaving my revolver in my suitcase at the hotel. But then I had not anticipated a foray into nighttime Cairo after dinner.

Well, peering round a corner was getting me nowhere, so I took a deep breath and rounded it, cautiously making my way down the block. The alley did open on the street I had chosen and I slipped into it, feeling somewhat the better for the total darkness that enveloped me. I could see nothing but could not be seen either. Such was my thought. Loo Chan must have entered a building facing the alley. Perhaps after all he was not conscious that he was being followed. I could traverse the narrow footway, regain the street on the other side, and beat a hasty retreat, making note of the locale for a report to Holmes.

Keeping the fingers of one hand on the wall on my right, I moved in the planned direction at a snail's pace indeed, for I was in horror of stumbling over some obstruction like a baggy-pants clown in a circus. Somewhat surprisingly, I moved silently in the Stygian darkness and was conscious of the dim light at the alley end, which spelled escape. Then I heard the soft, sibilant sound of a voice, and a curtain was raised almost by my head, allowing a shaft of light to split the night. I froze, and then instinctively moved to the wall beside me, pressing my back to it.

The voice was a mumble of sound, and then I heard a chair being moved within the ground-floor room on the other side of the wall. A shadow crossed the light emanating from the window. I eased closer to the aperture, removed my hat, and, summoning all the nerve at my command, stole a peek into the room. Loo Chan had seated himself at a plain round table, and standing opposite him was the impressive form of the Manchurian wrestler who had been my jailer when Chu San Fu had kidnapped me in London. The Chinese lawyer was looking upwards at the muscular figure, something he would have had to do even if he were not seated.

"The yacht should arrive sometime tomorrow," he said. Evidently this statement had significance, for the Manchurian nodded.

Good heavens, I thought with a flood of elation! I am privy to a conference here! Possibly the key to the strange series of events will be revealed to me. What a coup!

"We must be prepared for his coming," continued Loo Chan.

Whatever else he intended to say I did not learn, for a horny palm was slapped across my mouth, stifling all but my faintest sounds of protest. Nor could I put up an effective struggle, for an arm, more like a nautical hawser, encircled my arms and body. I did get in a couple of backward kicks with my heels, but to no avail. Suddenly the arm encircling me slid away, as did the one over my mouth, and to my amazement I was free. There was the soft sound of a falling body, and I turned and found a large form motionless on the pavement of the alley. It was the other Manchurian, for there were two of them, brothers, employed by Chu San Fu. I hadn't the slightest idea of what had happened. Possibly a falling object, like a flower pot, had fortuitously felled my captor. One thing was clear. They were on to my presence. In a flash I recalled that to the Chinese, surprise is akin to fear and is the breeder of it. This fact, well tested by experience, had to be used, or my goose was cooked to a turn!

Steeling myself, I marched through the door on the far side of the window into an odoriferous hallway and then through another door into the room I had observed.

Loo Chan wore a bland expression of satisfaction, and there was a gleam of cunning in his small, obsidian eyes, which faded when he realized that I was present without escort.

"Good evening," I said in a matter-of-fact manner! "If you will send your bully boy here into the alley, he can drag his unconscious brother within."

As I sat down opposite the lawyer, I was delighted to note his startled reaction.

"Your attempt at strong-arm tactics was ridiculous, of course, since I'm here to have a word with you."

"You are—what?" Chan was completely unnerved, and rattled to the Manchurian in Chinese. The wrestler left the room.

"Surely you don't think your clumsily baited trap would fool anyone but a child," I stated contemptuously. "Even the sometimes obtuse Inspector Lestrade would have laughed at it."

Alarm had flooded Loo Chan's eyes, and I pressed on.

"Dear me, I can see clearly that you have overdramatized again. The open window, the sound of a voice, and the curiosity of the Anglo-Saxon will entrap him. Do you think me a dunderhead? Had you not been aware of my presence, would you have spoken in English? Surely not, but in your native tongue."

I leaned back in the straight-back, regarding Loo Chan with disdain. In the alleyway this thought had not occurred to me, but the Chinese didn't know that, a knowledge gap that I hoped to preserve.

"Why . . . why then would you come here, on my footsteps, if you suspected a trap?" As he spoke, Loo Chan was mentally stumbling round, trying to regain firm footing.

"Because—in the patois of the American dime novel— the jig is up! Lawyers are reputed to be a cautious lot, and you had better get out now."

Consternation and confusion fought a battle on his face. Since the best defense against a counterattack is to never let it get started, I continued to knife him verbally, all the while trying to preserve an icy facade.

"I can afford to be generous with advice. Surely, here, I am completely safe." I indicated my dingy surroundings airily, as though I were seated in the commissioner's office at New Scotland Yard.

Loo Chan almost sputtered. In fact, he did. "You, the

intimate and associate of that devil Holmes, think you are safe with us?"

"Completely." I leaned over the table, spearing him with an outstretched finger. A very effective gesture that, and one that I had seen Sherlock Holmes use to enforce a point.

"If Chu San Fu arrives tomorrow in Cairo, you cannot have him meet me. What might I tell him about the destruction of his London organization?"

Loo Chan's round face froze. He did not grasp what I was touching on, but the sound was ominous. His worried eyes were fastened on me with an unspoken question. I summoned an answer.

"You recall that the Limehouse Squad just happened to have a veritable blueprint of every part of Chu San Fu's operations in London. Where do you think it came from? Your files. Rather careless to have such information in your safe, don't you think? I'll wager Chu San Fu will."

"My safe was not opened."

"Wasn't it?"

"Furthermore," he continued desperately, as though trying to forestall the fatal moment, "none of my records were missing."

I actually laughed. It wasn't easy, but I believe I pulled it off rather well.

"They were photographed."

"But that's illegal."

"So it is. You should have a good case. Let's see, who will you sue? The master cracksman who got into your office? The photographer?" I did not choose to reveal that Slim Gilligan had performed both jobs. "Possibly, the man who planned the whole thing?"

"Holmes!" he exclaimed, and the taste of the word was gall and wormwood. Emotion twisted the Chinaman's face as he imagined disaster. Then the spark of cunning reentered his eyes.

"If you could not tell Chu San Fu—"

I used an upright palm to stem his words before he gained confidence by uttering them.

"You can't present him with a dead body. Do you think

150

he would believe that you and those two gargantuans could not take me with ease? Impossible!"

The flicker of hope was erased from Loo Chan's face, and then the passivity of resignation settled over it.

"What is your thought?"

I had of late listened to so much of the history of Egypt from Holmes, Sir Randolph Rapp, and most recently Colonel Gray that I decided to make use of it.

"The ancients of this land made a habit of obliterating from history certain distasteful matters, which is why the reign of some of their pharaohs is hardly known at all. I suggest that tonight never happened. I was never here. If you can control the Manchurians, I see no problem."

I could sense the lawyer trying this thought for size and searching it for a flaw. Evidently he did not find one, for he rose to his feet, indicating the window.

"So be it. Best you leave this way. I will take care of the Manchurians."

While clambering out of a half-opened window in a dark alley in Cairo is not my idea of a dignified exit, all in all I felt that the matter had been well handled. True, I had consorted with the lawless, but surely this was better than filling a shallow grave in the shifting sands of Egypt. Or being the prisoner of Chu San Fu, whose feelings towards me were hardly benevolent.

As I scurried out of the alleyway and hastened back to Shepheard's, it jostled my conscience to accept the fact that I had played the role of the blackmailer. However, I was alive and free, so surely this transgression had been in a good cause.

If I could muster an alibi for my solo flight into dark doings in far-off places, I cannot, in conscience, deny a certain pride that provided me with great joy when I regained the lobby of the hotel only to run into an irate and anxious Colonel Gray.

"Good God, Doctor, where have you been? My men are searching the city for you!"

The high color of his face was more pronounced and the banality of his personality was a thing of the past, a mere cover, as I had already begun to suspect.

I regarded him with a cool manner, tinged with surprise.

"I was conducting an investigation of my own, Colonel. Please explain your concern." It was but a little thing, and yet I shall always cherish it in my memory.

"You were what!" Gray verged on apoplexy. "You realize that they would have handed me my head in London had something happened to you unless Holmes beat them to it right here!" He seemed ready to embark on more of the same when a new thought segued into his mind. *Possibly there is more here than meets the eye*, he was thinking. *This Doctor may be an unknown quantity, and I'd best walk softly*. Discipline forced his severe mouth into a semblance of a mirthless smile.

"Forgive my concern, sir, but you are a visitor to these shores." These were but words to cover an awkward situation. Gray knew it and suspected that I did as well. He was grateful to have an escape hatch.

"A Mr. Orloff from the Foreign Office has arrived, Doctor, and has been asking for you. I took the liberty of allowing him entry to your suite."

"Excellent, Colonel. I am in your debt." Gray almost clicked his heels as I made my way towards the lift with, I hope, a preoccupied expression.

Now there was no doubt in my mind regarding the Colonel's activities in Egypt. A squad of men were searching the city for me, and he could maneuver the hotel staff at will. Gray was Military Intelligence. The dark shadow of Orloff had shown up in Cairo. We had been transported by a naval vessel. Obviously, Holmes was not the only one concerned by the doings of Chu San Fu in the land of the Nile.

Outside our suite, I took the precaution of knocking on the door before fitting my key in the lock. Bursting unannounced into a room containing Orloff was no way to insure a safe existence. The rotund security agent was comfortably seated in a chair, the steel-rimmed hat that he so often employed, such an awesome weapon in his hands, close by. I may have detected a smidgen of concern vanishing from his green eyes. There was about him a quality always helpful to my ego. Orloff habitually treated me as

152

an equal, an abrupt departure from his usual good sense, but I always felt the better for his faulty judgment.

"I trust," he said with his lazy smile, "that Colonel Gray knows of your return. The gentleman tends to be excitable."

"Chu San Fu's people are here in Cairo," I blurted out. "You spotted them?"

"The lawyer, Loo Chan, and those two Manchurian bodyguards, one of whom you laid out like a mackerel as I recall."

"Ah yes, the altercation on Baker Street. It would seem that you have been busy."

"Happy chance. I just happened to spot Loo Chan."

"Or he let you do so," replied Orloff.

"That thought did occur to me," I said, and was thankful that the security agent didn't pursue the matter.

"That Chu would have some of his apparatus here awaiting his arrival is reasonable. I wonder if they know what he has in mind?"

"I doubt it," I said, expressing a thought that had crossed my mind when closeted with Loo Chan in the native quarter. "In fact, I'm not certain his people are too enthusiastic."

"Dissension in the ranks?"

"They may feel they are following a falling star."

Orloff's eyes could not suppress a slight glow.

"There are times, Watson, when you do surprise me."

And myself as well, I thought. Then I wondered how I was going to explain all this to Holmes. The sleuth would insist on the details that Orloff chose to ignore.

The moment of truth was close by, for there was the sound of a key in the lock and Holmes's thin form entered the room.

"Ah ha!" he exclaimed, tossing his deerstalker on a chair. "The eagles gather."

"To do battle with the forces of darkness," was Orloff's contribution, and a surprising one since humor was not prominent in his makeup.

"What news?" inquired Holmes. "You do look much better, Watson," he added as his eyes swiveled to Orloff.

"What you expected," said the security agent. "Voices have been bought and tongues have been wagging. Like the snowball downhill, a rumor has gathered strength. I judge it to be an expensive but effective bit of propaganda."

"You mean the Moslem unrest?" I asked, and noted that both Holmes and Orloff looked at me in surprise.

"There was mention of it in the local paper," I added.

"Do tell," said Orloff.

"An indication of how far this groundswell has progressed." Happily, Holmes elaborated. "In a land, nay continent, where the printed word is in the hands of a few, a tale told on a caravan trail or a whisper in the bazaar carries more weight than the front page of the *Times*. In Egypt, we are not far removed from the town crier. And when a story goes from mouth to ear, it never loses in the telling."

Holmes and Orloff were looking at each other, and a silence fell. I began to get that feeling again. The same that I experienced when my friend consorted with his brother, Mycroft, and one sensed that there was unspoken communication as two minds evaluated facts, each knowing the line of thought that the other was following. However, this was not as unusual as it seemed at first glance, for Wakefield Orloff was an extension of Mycroft Holmes. "The Walking Arsenal," as Holmes described him, was the steel forged to strike terror in the hearts of the enemies of the nation. That this unusual man chose to display an antagonism towards the enemies of Sherlock Holmes was another matter. Finally the detective broke the vacuum of silence.

"You have been in touch with London?"

Orloff nodded. "Finally, Whitehall and Downing Street seem aware that there is a pending crisis out here. A cabinet meeting was called and a lengthy, sometimes heated, debate followed. In the end, it was agreed that since a British subject who had been of service to the Empire was on the spot, he should approach the matter. It is hoped that it can be resolved without embarrassment to the Crown."

There was another pause as the security agent's words sank in. Orloff continued in a casual tone.

"If you pull this off, you may have to refuse knighthood a second time."

Holmes dismissed this idea with a gesture. "Poor Mycroft will be accused of nepotism."

"It was Bellinger and Lord Cantlemere who swung the day. I understand Cantlemere was quite grandiose in his references to you, mentioning, among other things, 'wooden ships and iron men.' "

"The aged peer may not be original, but I have no doubts as to his eloquence," was Holmes's dry comment. His eyes captured my startled ones.

"Well, Watson, we'd best come up with something or we dare not show our faces on Baker Street again."

"We, indeed! As near as I can figure out, you are practically Viceroy of Egypt."

"Let us not dramatize, ol' chap. Surely the word 'unofficial' will be used in all dispatches and echoed by that august personage in Balmoral Castle."

Orloff distrusted politicians and disliked anything but the direct approach, but he tried to be fair. "Really the only solution, you know. 'Investigation' is a very elastic word and does present the government with a disclaimer if 'private' is used in conjunction with it. The news has been relayed to the right quarters. You can count on the cooperation of the authorities, as reluctant as they may be."

"All right," said Holmes, springing to his feet. "The matter is coming to a head, that we know. Our first move is to keep that yacht of Chu San Fu's under observation. The Hishouri Kamu should also arrive shortly. Now, if there is to be some revelation to the Moslem world, it must take place in the Mosque of al-Ashar right here in Cairo. It has been Islam's center for religious study for a thousand years."

"That concurs with the feeling of the local men," said Orloff.

"Then we'd best to bed," said the sleuth. "Why don't you stay with us?" he asked Orloff. "There is ample room."

"I was hoping you would ask. The sofa out here will be fine. Let me tend to a few things, secure my bag, and rejoin you."

The only entry to our suite was the main door, and I saw what the security agent was up to. Holmes's presence in Cairo had become vital, and any unwarranted visitor would have to pass Orloff before reaching our bedroom door. Since Orloff had the nighttime instincts of a Bengal tiger, I ranked such an attempt as impossible.

Before extinguishing the lights, I recounted my adventure in the back alleys of Cairo to Holmes, and his face reflected sternness, then gravity, and finally relief.

"Good heavens, Watson, had your quick wit not come to your aid and you'd come to harm in the hands of Loo Chan, what would I have done?"

These few words were Holmes's most emotional reaction since that day when I had been superficially wounded by a bullet from the gun of Killer Evans. Once again I had a brief glimpse of the great heart that lurked behind his usual cold and austere manner. As though ashamed of himself, he shook off the mood.

"But Shakespeare was right. 'All's well that ends well.'"

The next morning, following breakfast, there was a parade of local authorities to our suite, and I recognized that the situation was an uncomfortable one. It was they who had put in the time here on the edge of the Arabian desert, yet in a moment of crisis, an unofficial investigator from London was to call the shots. To have his associate, a doctor no less, in attendance would have added to the strain. To vacate the premises, I contacted Gray and asked if he would take me to the pyramids as he had volunteered the previous evening. I could tell that the Colonel felt he was being shunted off again, but he stood by his invitation.

So it was that we passed through the city to the Nile bridge. In the morning hours, Gray informed me, one encountered a true cross-section of natives and animals, and I agreed with him. There were camels and donkeys and asses in profusion carrying or being led by turbaned men, veiled women, and everywhere squalid children. I had expected to be assailed by Arabs crying for baksheesh, but such was not the case, no doubt because of Colonel Gray's trim uniform and official manner. On the other side of the Nile donkeys awaited us, and we mounted them and set off in the direction of the three huge figures, triangular lighthouses rising from a sea of sand.

Gray must have supervised many such a visit and he had, in fact, mentioned the Prince of Wales's tour of Egypt.

Since I recalled that this took place in '62, he obviously had been on the scene a long time.

He had cautioned me about the heat and took pains to remind me of my weakened condition upon my arrival in Egypt. As a precaution I took my small medical kit with me. The black valise rode nicely in a saddle pouch on my donkey.

The monuments or tombs seemed but a stone's throw but proved to be considerably further. I suggested visiting the largest, that of Cheops. As we drew closer. I was amazed that the pyramid rising more than four hundred feet did not seem that tall, but the blazing sun, reflected from the stones in a dazzling manner, made an estimation difficult. At its base, I was imbued with the thought of climbing to the top, an idea that found little favor in Colonel Gray's eyes. However, it did not seem difficult since the pyramid resembled a huge staircase, if one can accept steps four feet high.

Gray decided to humor me, and close to half an hour later, sweaty and breathless, I was atop the oldest and largest of its kind. In former times it had been taller, but now its apex was a platform that extended thirty or more feet. Having Gray with me proved invaluable since he pointed out and named other pyramids, easily seen, along with various smaller tombs. From where I stood, the emerald green of the valley of the Nile was of breathless beauty. In contrast, the vast desert that was everywhere beyond the fruitful reach of the great river was awesome in its absolute desolation.

Gray's warnings about the midday heat were made in a genuinely concerned voice and I began to heed them, feeling as though I was in Neville's Turkish baths on Northumberland Avenue.

There was no shade, nor did there seem to be any at the base of the pyramid either, with the midday sun blazing on all four sides. Gray took me to the north side, saying that if we descended two-thirds of the way, we could gain the entrance to the tomb of Cheops and find refuge from the inferno. I agreed to this idea promptly. Gray cautioned me to step to the very edge of each of the great stones, a necessity if one wished to see the step below. Heights have

157

always bothered me but did not on this occasion, for all I could think of was relief from the desert sun and heat.

Our descent was really a succession of four-foot jumps from one tier to the next. Finally we made it into a dark corridor that pitched sharply downwards. It was airy and cool, thank heavens, or so it seemed in comparison to my ill-conceived climb, which I felt must have melted the superfluous fat from my frame. Gray offered to take me to the king's and queen's chambers, but since I understood there was little to see, I declined. I knew full well that the interior of Cheops was safe and constantly traversed by tourists, but I was aware of those tons of huge stones all round us and had an irrational fear of their moving inward and downward. When I was sure that my body temperature was sufficiently lowered, I was glad to vacate the entry to the colossus and descend to our donkeys.

In riding towards the Sphinx, we passed close by several large tents that I had noted from the top of the pyramid. Gray had explained that they indicated Arabs from the south and would be struck when the heat lessened and the Bedouins chose to continue, probably to Cairo. Some spanking horses were tethered by them, standing in the slight shade provided by these white, mobile shelters.

Gray was riding ahead of me as we drew abreast of the tents, probably computing the number of times his duties had involved escorting visiting idiots. It was then that a tall, bearded man emerged from the nearest tent. He was clad in flowing garments that to my untrained eyes seemed of excellent quality. Round his middle was a broad belt of interlocking silver links, and it supported an ornate scabbard that, judging from the hilt that protruded from it, contained a scimitar. His shoes were of a soft material, with much handiwork, and the toes were pointed. A desert dandy, I thought. Behind him came another man with an unkempt black beard. A curved scar ran from his left temple across his cheek towards his nose. The old wound had formed a puckered ridge in healing, which pulled the lower lid of his eye downward, lending a ghoulish expression to his face.

All this registered in a split second, for my attention was captured by the curved dagger the second man was pulling from a sash round his middle. My lips parted and as a shrill shout burst from them, my right hand grabbed at the saddle pouch of my donkey, plucking the medical kit from it. I threw it desperately and the object reached the assailant, catching him in the head as he lunged at the tall Arab who had whirled round at my cry.

I know not if my improvised weapon deflected the attacker's aim. The dagger plunged into the loose robe of the Arab, and there was a cry of pain from him as he kicked his attacker in the groin. Then there was the flash of the scimitar in the sun and a dull sound like a pole-axe striking home in a slaughter house. The assailant was on the ground, blood pouring from his neck, his head almost completely severed from his body.

I was off my donkey in a trice, every movement from memory and without planning or thought. As I raced across the sand to retrieve my medical container, I noted the Arab wipe his scimitar in a practiced fashion on the material of his garment and return it to its scabbard. But there was a growing redness in the vicinity of his ribs, and the blood was his.

Gray had reined round and was trying to grasp the situation. From the tent four or five forms emerged pell-mell, and as I opened my kit and noted that the contents were undamaged, it seemed that the group of desert men were about to annihilate me, for knives and guns appeared like magic. The wounded man spoke sharply in a foreign tongue that I assumed was Arabic, and the others drew up short. Then the dignified bearded man made as though to address me, but did not get the chance.

"I, sir, am John Watson, M.D. You are wounded, and I insist on tending your needs."

What I expected this to accomplish I do not know; I couldn't speak to the man in Arabic, not knowing a word. But this was no time to stand on ceremony, and I had his garment half open, exposing his chest on the right side and revealing a sizable though not fatal gash that was bleeding freely. As I touched him, there was a murmur from the Bedouins behind me, but another gesture from my patient subdued them. True to their instincts, they formed a half circle and watched intently. If an Arab cannot participate,

159

he makes a rapt audience. Gray had recovered his wits by now and his right hand was moving away from the army issue holstered at his side, realizing that the tenseness of the situation was relieved.

I grabbed one of the Bedouins who formed my audience and pressed him into service. With gestures, I managed to have him hold the bottle of antiseptic with a peroxide base that I had automatically secured from my limited supplies, while I fashioned a padding of cotton. The man's teeth were broken and his breath was so garlic-ridden that I could have used it as an antiseptic had I nothing better at hand. His eyes were wide with fright, like an unwilling volunteer in a magician's act. Poor beggar probably felt that he was just that, I thought, as I removed the bottle stopper and indicated for him to pour the contents onto the pad. A hand gesture stopped the flow of liquid, with which I then swabbed the wound. Since I had managed to clean off the blood, the considerable gash was revealed and the peroxide went to work with its customary fizzing sound and bubbling appearance.

There was a deep sign of wonder from my Arabian audience, though my patient seemed unconcerned and stoical. I now was able to wind a bandage round the man and, for a makeshift job, it seemed tidy enough. As I retrieved my kit from my Bedouin assistant, I was surprised to note that his broken teeth were actually chattering and his swarthy skin had adopted a pale cast. I realize now that to him and his companions as well, the action of the antiseptic had given the illusion that flesh was being created by my wizardry. The bearded leader's face was creased by a gentle smile of understanding.

"Some gesture of reassurance will work wonders," he prompted, in Oxonian English that startled me. It was as though we were an alliance of two in placating less sophisticated minds.

I returned my kit to the placid donkey, thinking furiously, and then retraced my steps to place both my palms on the turban of the shivering Arab and gazed skyward, fortunately towards the east, as I later learned from Gray.

"Dancer, Prancer, Donner, and Blitzen!" I intoned in a

sepulchral voice, and then removed my hands, clapped them once and smiled.

Jerk a toy from a baby and laugh and he will laugh with you, for it is a game. Jerk it away and scowl and he will cry, for he is being mistreated. It pays to know how to handle children.

My intent audience all chanted in Arabic and clustered round their comrade, clapping him on the back as though he had just won the French Legion of Honor.

My patient, showing no signs of indisposition from his bloodletting, seemed pleased.

"Aside from your medical expertise, Doctor, your alarm may have prevented my wound from being fatal. I trust our paths will cross again, for I am in your debt."

He turned to bark orders to his crew, a sinister-looking group really, and they set themselves to work striking the tents and dragging off the body of the late assailant. As I mounted my donkey, I found Gray regarding me suspiciously.

"Doctor, you were with Gordon, I presume?"

"No. Indian Army."*

"There are no Arabs in India."

"But a great many Mohammedans, Colonel. The Sikhs and Afghans among them."

Our journey back to Cairo was made in silence. I don't think Gray could make me out.

* Actually, Watson did not serve with the Indian Army. The Northumberland Fusilliers were of the British Army stationed in India during the Afghan war.

161

Chapter Fourteen

The Caesar Code

I had something to mull over myself: an Arabian sheik, for such he had to be, speaking impeccable English with an accent that made it odds-on that he was a university graduate. What was he doing in the shadow of the Sphinx leading a scurvy crew of land pirates? But then again, why not? Holmes had forecast a great meeting of Mohammedans in the Mosque of al-Ashar. No doubt my patient had come from some far-off oasis for just that gathering. I regretted that I had not questioned him regarding his social calendar but shoved that thought aside. Medical ethics, you know.

In our suite at Shepheard's, I was happy to find Holmes and Orloff alone. Their mood was a clue that their news was not reassuring, and such proved to be the case.

"Things have gone amiss, ol' chap. Chu's yacht arrived at Alexandria, but he is not aboard."

"Good heavens, Holmes!"

"They came by way of Rosetta. Obviously slipped Chu ashore there, and even now he is secreted aboard a native dhow making his way up the Nile Delta. Certain members of the secret service feel very chagrined, which helps us not a bit."

"But you are sure he's coming to Cairo?"

"There is going to be the great meeting we anticipated in the Mosque of al-Ashar in a week. That's what Chu is here for."

Orloff was seated upright in a chair, his weight balanced on the toes of his feet, his hands resting in his lap. The man's ability to remain completely motionless and relaxed was a source of wonderment to my medically trained mind. It was as though he saved every ounce of strength for those moments when it was needed. Possibly that was why he was able to move so fast when he had to. Now he spoke.

"Then there is the matter of the cable."

My eyes shot towards Holmes questioningly, and he seemed to wince.

"The Hishouri Kamu put in at Port Said. The coffin containing the corpse of Sidney Putz remained aboard, but a certain crate did not. Burlington Bertie and Tiny were not able to pursue the object, so we've lost that as well."

A horrible thought was crossing my mind.

"Look here, you are chiding yourselves for no reason. Chu suddenly altered his plans regarding himself and the sword. Might not my little foray last evening have been the reason? Certainly Loo Chan could have contacted the freighter, and I'll wager Chu's yacht has wireless equipment as well. The minute Chu learned we were in Cairo, he put an alternate plan into operation."

"It's possible, you know," said Orloff.

"There is an Arab expression," responded the sleuth, " 'All things are possible in the caravan of life.' Now let us see what is possible for us. We've had reports from the Intelligence people, the army, the civil authorities; all more chaff than wheat. Chu will be in Cairo. It is his plan that eludes me. I can't shake the idea that those tablets might have contained a secret of the past. You were at the pyramids today, Watson. How did they build them almost five thousand years ago with nothing more than the lever, the roller, and vast embankments?"

"Plus the flood waters of the Nile to float the stone," added Orloff, "and unlimited manpower."

"Wait!" Surprisingly, it was my voice that rang out. "Gray told me something interesting today. In the twelfth century, Saladin's son had the notion to demolish the pyramids. He started with the Red Pyramid of Mycerinus, which had a casing of Aswan granite. They had the wheel and tools the Egyptians never dreamed of. Civilization had advanced four thousand years."

"What is your point?" asked Orloff.

"They couldn't do it. The best they could manage was two blocks a day. Destruction is easier than construction, but they couldn't tear it down."

At this point there was a knock on our door, revealing Colonel Gray, whom I had just quoted.

"Mr. Holmes," he said respectfully, "there's a Chinaman, Loo Chan, who requests permission to speak with you."

I had prepared myself a small libation and now almost dropped the glass.

"He is alone, I assume," said Sherlock Holmes, getting a nod in response. "By all means have him come up . . . Wait!" The sleuth's added thought caught Colonel Gray at the door. "He may be a messenger, a role he has played in the past. If I see him to the door, have the Oriental followed. If Dr. Watson shows him out, don't bother."

Gray's face brightened. This was more to his taste. "I'll be standing by, sir."

Orloff was at the sitting room windows, checking the street below out of habit. Holmes's eyes, alight with interest, encountered mine.

"This may prove a dividend from your nighttime excursion, ol' chap."

When Loo Chan was ushered into the room, the habitual sheen on his face was no more noticeable than at other times I had seen him. With a short, courteous bow to each of us, he assumed a chair in a nerveless fashion, a picture of Oriental calm. But he did not indulge in flowery preambles, so often a trademark of his race. He did not question the presence of Orloff, who was standing, watching him closely.

"Mr. Holmes . . . I need. . . ." Loo Chan took a quick breath, his only sign of agitation, and began again. "I am in great need of something, and I have something of interest."

"The one for the other," was Holmes's rejoinder. My friend was seated with his legs crossed, leaning on one arm of his chair and regarding the visitor without antagonism or any other emotion for that matter. Loo Chan nodded, and Holmes continued.

"Then let us deal with your need first."

165

"There is an 'Orient Middle East' liner entering the Suez Canal, destination Macao. I would like to be on it."

Holmes's eyes narrowed. "You don't need me to buy you a ticket, I'm sure."

Loo Chan's heavy lids blinked rapidly. "I do need you to get me out of Egypt. Alexandria, Port Said, the canal are all . . . the expression is 'bottled up,' I believe. There is no warrant for me in England, but had I tried to book passage I would have been in custody in a minute. Something about my passport, no doubt."

Holmes shot a quick look at Orloff.

"He could be put aboard at Port Tewfik," said the security agent.

"What you ask can be done." Holmes let this hang in the air.

"I do not know, Mr. Holmes, Chu San Fu's plans regarding Egypt. I could tell you about the money he has spent of late in a number of Mid East countries, but I suspect you know more about that than I do."

"One thing. In Berlin. The Mannheim tablets?"

"I negotiated for them. Another of those rare items that Chu San Fu added to his collection."

"What happened?"

"He did not sell them when he disposed of his collection. They were stolen property, so he could not have put them on the market anyway. But he seemed to attach great importance to them."

The sleuth appeared disappointed. "You do have something?"

"I hope so." The Oriental shrugged. "As you know, part of my duties were associated with Chu San Fu's collection. There is a bit of guesswork involved in art objects. I developed the habit of attending estate sales and even disposal-of-property sales involving the belongings of unknowns. If their background was colorful."

Holmes exhibited interest as the Chinaman continued.

"I picked up the notebook of an explorer, Puzza, an Italian who had been with Giovanni Balzoni in Egypt. It had entries regarding certain escapades of the incredible Balzoni. One page contained letters without meaning that Chu San Fu found intriguing. Then, two years ago, he referred to it once as 'the gateway to the past.' The notebook has been by his side ever since."

"You have it?"

"No, but I have a copy of the strange message that my employer found so interesting."

"Which you will give me if you can flee Egypt for Macao."

Loo Chan indicated this was so. There was a lengthy pause, and the Oriental seemed to feel the need of some explanation.

"Last night, Doctor Watson used words that I had refused to consider. Now I agree with him." His slanting eyes turned towards me. "It's time to get out."

"Done," said Holmes.

Loo Chan removed a piece of paper from his inner pocket, passing it to the detective. After regarding it for a moment, Holmes gave a signal to Orloff, who took the Chinaman from the room and out of our lives. What the waiting Colonel Gray thought of that arrangement, I did not learn until later.

As the door closed, I voiced a thought tentatively.

"This could be bait of some sort?"

"No more than a ten percent possibility." Holmes was studying the message. "Loo Chan knows that if he has played us false, the Dutch authorities can pick him up in Macao. I'm inclined to consider this coded message as genuine. The timetable is right. It was two years ago that Chu's attention was caught by it. An idea could have been born in his mind at that time. One thing surprises me: the utter simplicity of the code."

Holmes rose and spread the paper on an end table, allowing me to view it by his side.

```
DW WKH IHHW RI WKH VLALWK UDPHVVHV
OLHV WKH ERB LQ HWHUQDO HKVV
XQNQRZQ WR NXUQD DQGDOPDPXQ
VRQ RI WKH KHUHWLF KHHYDGHGGRRP
```

"Simplicity, Holmes? You jest."

"This cipher might present problems but for the spacing, which is revealing. Consider the first line. There are seven combinations of letters. Six in the second line. We can assume they represent words."

"I don't see how that helps."

"Regard the same two lines, old fellow. There are three identical three-letter combinations. WKH. Surely that indicates the word 'the' to you. Three letters and oft-used. I can almost decipher this standing here, but let me hazard a guess. This associate of Balzoni——"

"Puzza was his name."

"Also an Italian. I assume this is a substitution cipher. One letter in place of another. Now if you were an Italian and were going to put something in code, playing a game with yourself perhaps, is it not reasonable that you should think of a Roman hero like the first Caesar?"

Not being able to interpret the thoughts of others with Holmes's facility, I didn't know what I would have done.

"I suppose that makes sense," I said.

"It is an historical fact that Julius Caesar encrypted his messages from Gaul by substituting letters three places farther on in the alphabet. D for A and E for B. Now let us test this with the three-letter combination of WKH. W becomes T and K is H. H represents the most used letter in the alphabet, which is E. The word is 'the' as we have already assumed. Just note the number of H letters in this message. We've solved it, Watson."

"We" had nothing to do with it, but if it made Holmes happy to put it that way, who was I to complain? When Wakefield Orloff returned to the room, the sleuth was seated, working on the cipher with a pen. It was so simple for him that he digested Orloff's report at the same time.

"Loo Chan will be on the train to Suez within the hour. I've arranged to have the train stop at a point along the Bitter Lakes. A boat will get him to the liner before it enters the Sweetwater Canal. No one will be the wiser, so we've kept our part of the bargain." The security agent regarded the silent Holmes thoughtfully. "Gray can bring a man from the code office if you wish."

Holmes waved one hand in an aimless gesture without meaning, and I took it from there.

"No need. Holmes has already deciphered it."

It is with joy that I report that Orloff's jaw dropped slightly.

"You do recall," I added with no little pride, "that Holmes's pamphlet on codes and secret writings is now required reading for the cipher division."

My moment of reflected glory was interrupted by the sleuth, who was regarding his handiwork with a frown.

"We may have broken one code and run into another. It would seem the late archeologist, Puzza, was of a whimsical nature."

Holmes allowed himself a small chuckle, and I suspected his humor was directed at himself.

"Our substitution key is correct, Watson, for the letters become words, but what we end up with is a rather clumsy rhyme. Let me read it to you:

"At the feet of the sixth Rameses
Lies the boy in eternal ease,
Unknown to Kurna and Al Mamun
Son of the heretic he evaded doom."

"The sixth Rameses I would assume is a pharaoh, but the rest means little to me."

Orloff offered no comment, so I made a suggestion.

"That Colonel Gray chap has been in Egypt for a devilishly long time and seems up on all these things."

"Capital idea, Watson!"

Orloff was already on his way to the hall and returned quickly with Gray.

"I didn't know what to do when you left with the Chinaman, Mr. Orloff, so I stayed at my post."

"Good thinking, Colonel," said Holmes. "Loo Chan is of no further concern to us, but another problem has arisen that requires your expertise. Can you make anything out of this?"

Gray read through the message Holmes handed him and then read through it again in the manner of the military. "Better say nothing than say it wrong" is an army byword. It produces accuracy, but has a stultifying effect on inventiveness.

"Well, sir," Gray finally said, stroking his moustache, "would this be in reference to a tomb, perhaps?"

"Very possibly. What prompted you to consider that?"

We were all clustered round the message on the table and Gray, quite delighted to be the center of attention, indicated certain words as he spoke.

"At the feet of the sixth Rameses could mean at the base of a statue of Rameses Sixth, of course. Thank God it isn't Rameses Second. There is no end to statues of him. The reference to 'boy' evades me, but Kurna and Al Mamun certainly indicate a tomb."

"Wait!" said Holmes. "Kurna." He turned to me. "Didn't Mycroft mention Kurna? A city of thieves?"

"Graverobbers," I stuttered.

"That's right, sir," said Gray. "Al Mamun refers to Caliph Al Mamun, who forced his way into the great pyramid in the ninth century in search of treasure. Bit of a disappointment, that, since it had been sacked centuries before."

"Then being unknown by Kurna and Al Mamun must mean an undiscovered grave. One unpillaged by graverobbers," I said.

"I'll accept that," said Holmes. "But look, does not 'son of the heretic' refer to the 'boy' in the second line?"

Gray's eyes lit up. "The heretic in Egyptian history would be Amenhotep Fourth."

"Pity," said Holmes. "I had hoped you would mention another name."

"Who?"

"Do you recall, Watson, that Rapp mentioned a pharaoh who espoused a one-god idea?"

"Ikhnaton," I said, and will never know how that name came to my mind.

"Same chap," was Gray's surprising reply. "Ikhnaton, Amenhotep, Akhenaten; all names for the same ruler. Took charge in 1379. Changed his capital from Thebes to Akhetaten. Wanted to do away with the other gods in favor of the sun god, Aton. Didn't make it stick, you see. Out of touch with his people and was not very prepossessing. When you are in the god business you have to have a bit of personality, to spread the faith, as 'twere."

Holmes's face had recovered it's enthusiasm. "Then this boy in the message must be the son of Ikhnaton."

Gray shook his head. "Ikhnaton or Akhenaten had no son. He was succeeded by Smenkmare. Brother, I believe. But wait a minute."

The Colonel studied the message again. "You have a cipher here, possibly written by an Egyptologist?" Holmes nodded. "When would he have been active?"

Holmes scratched his chin. "I read about Balzoni . . ."

"Oh, Balzoni." Gray was on familiar grounds. "Everyone out here knows about him."

"Actually, this was written by an associate of his."

"Balzoni left Egypt in 1819. I know because a year later he wrote a rather good book on his adventures. Point is that early in the century the tombs in Egypt were a bit of a new thing. At that time it was believed that Akhenaten was the father of Tutankhamen."

Holmes shook his head.

"You wouldn't know of him, sir. Minor eighteenth dynasty pharaoh. But he was very young when he became ruler of Egypt and died at an early age as well. Ruled for a mere nine years as I recall. I'm not so good on dates and numbers."

"I'd say you were doing quite well," commented Holmes with approval. He continued:

"All right, where are we? The message refers to a tomb. What would be important about that?"

"A tomb unknown to graverobbers, Mr. Holmes. That would be a rare bird indeed, for the pharaoh's possessions would be in it. The German expedition uncovered thirty graves of pharaohs and not a one of them that hadn't been looted."

"Then this Tutankhamen tomb would be valuable?"

"Unbelievably," was Gray's immediate response.

"And the reference to doom?"

"That can be read two ways. In a religious sense, the whole idea of the elaborate burials was to allow the pharaohs to make their trip to eternity in peace. Don't quote me, sir, but I've a thought that the despoiling of their graves would interrupt their progress to the hereafter."

"Seems logical," I commented.

"And the other meaning?" inquired Holmes.

"Political. After his death, Akhenaten the heretic was expunged from Egyptian history since his one-god theory was not accepted. Tutankhamen rejected the one-god idea, thereby avoiding the risk or doom of being removed."

"Well, the tomb seems to be of Tutankhamen, but where would it be? You mentioned the German expedition."

"That was Karl Richard Lepsius and his people."

"Where did he find so many graves?"

"Same place that was such a happy hunting ground for Balzoni. Wady Biban al-Maluk, the Arabs call it. The Valley of the Kings."

"Might not the boy pharaoh be there?"

Gray shook his head. "Lepsius's reputation as an archaeologist is enormous, and he felt that nothing was left in the valley. There's been no serious excavation work there since his time."

Holmes's eyes had that opaque look I recognized. "I read that book of Balzoni's you mentioned. As I recall, he stated more or less the same thing."

"That's right, Mr. Holmes."

"But that's it, you see. Puzza, an obscure follower of the Italian adventurer is dying. He cannot return to the Valley of the Kings, and he has no heirs. His possessions were disposed of at a public sale. He leaves an obscure rhyme. It was a jest, a bit of irony from a dying man, for he knew something that the great Balzoni did not, nor Lepsius either. He knew there was an undiscovered tomb."

Holmes's eyes sharpened, and he regarded Gray with that faint smile of triumph. "Might I guess that the tomb of Rameses Sixth is in the Valley of the Kings?"

There was a startled look on the Colonel's face.

"Dead on, sir!"

"At the feet of Rameses could mean beneath his crypt, I think."

Before Holmes even looked at him, Orloff was on his way out of the room.

As Gray and I exchanged a puzzled glance, Holmes chuckled.

"Mr. Orloff is a great believer in anticipation, a quality cherished by my brother."

Gray took a breath. "That would be Mr. Mycroft Holmes, sir?"

Holmes nodded.

"And the Rapp you mentioned is Sir Randolph Rapp?" Since the Colonel was looking at me, I agreed.

"If you'll pardon the thought, there're some heavy-weights involved in this matter."

Holmes was caught completely by surprise and chortled. "I follow your thought, Colonel, and you are more right than you know. However, the gentlemen in question are in London whereas you are here, and I am grateful that you are."

Colonel Gray's features grew redder yet, and he looked as though he had just received the Victoria Cross from Her Majesty. I'm sure he was thinking that it had all been worth it, even wet-nursing a seasick general practitioner who seemed fated to have unusual experiences.

Chapter Fifteen

The Sheik Reappears

Things happened fast after that. Orloff, with that uncanny ability to anticipate the plans of Sherlock Holmes, put official wheels in motion. I began to suspect that Mycroft had dispatched a covy of his operatives to Egypt to act as backup for his top agent in the field. It was arranged in short order that we were to leave Cairo and head up the Nile to Luxor by rail. Orloff was to remain in Cairo to keep his finger on the pulse of the people, but he informed my friend that a contingent of the Sutherland-Argyle Regiment were on maneuvers around Luxor prior to being shipped to India. I rather gathered that a detachment of the Scottish infantry would be available to Holmes if needed, and such proved to be the case.

It was obvious what had prompted Holmes's move. I had not forgotten the departed Cruthers or the fact that he had been investigating an archeological party in the Valley of the Kings prior to his return to England and death. Then there was that dagger he had concealed on his person, which my friend had identified as property of royalty. With the information that Loo Chan's cipher provided, it seemed realistic to assume that Chu San Fu had located an undiscovered tomb, though how this fitted in with his exciting Mohammedan unrest throughout the Middle East eluded me. Holmes wished to certify the possibility of a new discovery in the Valley of the Kings prior to the great Mohammedan conclave in Cairo. I found it somewhat alarming that there had been mention of members of the

Sutherland-Argyle Regiment in connection with this matter and wondered just what Holmes expected to find in the Valley of the Kings.

When we finally did reach Luxor, site of the ancient Thebes, it was evident that Orloff had made ample use of the cable. In the government buildings we were informed that the Scottish troopers were already over the river on the west bank awaiting Holmes's arrival. I was again wan and indisposed, for the swaying train had not benefitted my touchy stomach. Though nauseous, I was fascinated by the lush green of the fertile Nile plain, more evident because of the stark grimness and desolation beyond it rising gradually to towering cliffs. Small wonder that the Egyptians have through the centuries loved and cherished their narrow belt of incredibly fertile land, surrounded as it is by a nothingness of rock and sand. It was at the foot of the distant cliffs, the Theban hills, that the historic valley lay in which were entombed so many of the Nile's greatest rulers.

There was a look of sadness, almost apprehension, on Holmes's face as he conferred with me after Gray attended to details regarding the crossing of the river and the troops placed at the disposal of the detective.

"Now, ol' chap, we must come to a brief parting of the ways. I know our sea voyage did not sit well with you, nor the train trip either. Gray tells me this valley is a desolate and forbidding place indeed. Best you remain here until we reconnoitre the area and find out what's going on."

My mouth automatically began to form protests at the mere thought of being left behind when the case was coming to a head, but strangely it was Colonel Gray who weighed down the scales.

"Doctor Watson, you must come to my aid. I'm well aware that Mr. Holmes can take care of himself, but no matter how you cut it, I'm responsible. Not only for him but for those soldiers who are a bit new to this area and only have a vague idea of where they are save that this is a training area on the road to India. Let's put it this way: if every man isn't tip-top, we're at a disadvantage."

What could I say? As a medical man I well knew I was ill-equipped to trudge over rocky and hilly terrain trying to match steps with vigorous young Highlanders. Holmes's whipcord body and fencer's legs could manage it, but I saw in my mind's eye a middle-aged general practitioner gasping for breath and falling behind as the column surged forward. I nodded in agreement with Gray's words and tried to summon some esprit de corps to suit the situation.

"Well, it's a rum show, but—you chaps watch out for yourselves, will you?"

Holmes, for the first time that I could remember, avoided my eyes, but his hand rested briefly on my shoulder and there was a reassuring pressure from his long, tremendously strong fingers. Then he and Gray were gone.

A young lieutenant, but recently from Sandhurst I judged, who really hadn't the vaguest idea of what was going on, also had the good taste not to try to expand his knowledge of the situation. He took me and my belongings to the Luxor Hotel and volunteered to show me round the modern city that stood in the place of the former capital, Thebes. I declined his kind offer and, after a bath and change of clothes, made my way to the hotel bar for a stiff brandy and soda, which I willed to stay peaceably in my stomach. There is much to be said for assertive action, and after several growls of protest, my intestinal tract reflected a comforting warmth. Since success had favored my efforts, I repeated the dosage and decided to have a look round on my own. There were no claims on my time until Gray and Holmes returned with what information they could glean from the distant hills.

Luxor was now a modern city and a far cry from the river port that had flourished as the capital of so many pharoahs of the old civilization. As I left the hotel in an aimless fashion, I determined to try to detect what remnants of former grandeur had withstood civilization's onrush and were still in evidence. However, my sightseeing was fated to be of short duration. I was passing the entrance to a mosque when a tall figure left the citadel of religion, turning in my direction so that we were face to face, and an acknowledgment of coincidence was impossible to avoid. It was the desert chieftain whom I had encountered near the Sphinx.

I confess being taken aback at this unexpected meeting, but the Arabian exhibited no surprise. Rather, his greeting was accompanied by a shrug, a gesture of his acceptance of Kismet.

"Ah, the good Doctor Watson. Our paths cross again. What brings you south from Cairo?"

"I was about to ask you the same thing," I responded guardedly. Holmes chided me on occasion as being the most revealing of men, and I had grown more cautious through the years.

"My journey to Cairo was, as anticipated, a fruitless one. Another witless tale spewed from idle tongues in the bazaars." He sighed and shook his head. His bearded face and predatory, sharp features reminded me of a desert eagle owl, free and fierce.

"Men with idle hands and empty pockets do tend towards mischief. But come, Doctor, motivations are a subject you hear much of. Let us seek refuge from the fading sun, and I shall secure some coffee for you unless you prefer tea."

In a most casual manner, as though our meeting had been planned, the tall Arabian was ushering me to a table at a café nearby, and I admitted that the shade cast by its awning was welcome. Whoever my chance acquaintance was, he secured prompt, nay obsequious, service, and we were soon enjoying coffee served in the Turkish manner in small cups. It was viscous and thick, but strong with a sweetness my taste buds were unaccustomed to.

"We have now met twice, Doctor, and both times you were separated from your most illustrious companion. I trust that Mr. Holmes is in good health."

Well, I thought, this fellow is certainly well informed. My suspicions were aroused, of course.

"Holmes is, at the moment, on other business," I replied. Two can play the information game, and I decided to take a stab at it.

"Sheik, you are most familiar with me and my friend. Have we met at another time? In England, perhaps?"

The bearded face registered a negative. "As you easily deduced, I was educated in your native land. However, I did not meet Mr. Holmes there."

My nostrils quivered at this, and the scent was the

musky odor of doubt. Where would Holmes have met an Arabian sheik, pray tell? I had used that title as a quest for a name, but my companion had accepted it without comment. Then, of a sudden, my thoughts reversed. During the period that Holmes was thought dead, his wanderings had taken him to Khartoum, where he had visited with the Khalifa, a meeting that resulted in information communicated to the Foreign Office. I had always entertained private thoughts regarding his being in the Sudan at that particular time. My friend had never gone into detail regarding this part of his mysterious absence from England, though he had often spoken of his explorations during the same period when he passed himself off as the Norwegian "Sigerson."

"You are then of the Sudan?"

An affirmative nod joined forces with a smile.

"I see you have pieced some facts together, Doctor. I am from the south and do know Sherlock Holmes. I was able to be of some service to him at one time, and," he added with a candor unusual for those of these parts, "the reverse is also true. Do I detect some concern on your part for your friend's safety? This land is known to me and I am, if you recall, obliged to you."

This put matters in a different light, for I had heard that even the greatest rascals in Arabia were scrupulous regarding a debt of honor. I had an impulse to match his frankness and decided to give in to it.

"Holmes is with an expedition going to the Valley of the Kings."

"The Scottish soldiers," he said instantly. Conscious of the return of suspicion to my face, he explained. "My men are camped on the west bank awaiting my arrival. We noted the Highlanders there." He thought for a moment. "Now what would the king of sleuths wish to find in the gateway to Amenti?"

"Amenti?"

"An Egyptian word referring to the underworld. Though Wady Biban al-Maluk is certainly a place of mystery. Actually that desolate valley under the cliff at Deir al-Bahri was selected in a search for secrecy."

179

It was painfully obvious that I was following none of this, and the sheik poured me some more coffee.

"Forgive me, Doctor, but tales of the ancient land are endlessly told round campfires under the desert sky. It was the great king, Thutmose First of the Eighteenth Dynasty, who made the decision. The age of the pyramids was over, for their very size was a magnet to the graverobbers, and no secret doors or false passages could outwit them. So the great military pharaoh decided to construct a secret tomb wherein his mummy might remain, inviolate, for the after-life. He selected this valley beneath the cliff, which he could see from his capital, Thebes. His tomb, constructed by the architect Ineni was a hidden thing, and its secret was preserved until the nineteenth dynasty. How this was done but six miles from Thebes amazes me."

I had difficulty remaining in my seat. "Six miles! Why, I thought this Valley of the Kings was at least a day's march away!"

The sheik displayed his perspicacity. "Had you known it was so near, you would have attempted the journey?"

"Why—yes," I sputtered.

"Perhaps I've misled you, Doctor. The entrance to the valley is six miles from the west bank, but the place itself is sizable. Fully forty Egyptian monarchs were buried there, and some of the tombs are enormous. If I knew where Mr. Holmes was headed . . ."

"I don't think he knows himself."

"But you feel he may be in some peril?"

My memory stirred and I responded automatically. "All things are possible in the caravan of life. Holmes said that recently."

The man startled me with a burst of laughter, and he slapped a knee under his robe forcibly. "He has not forgotten. It was I who told him that." He seemed to reach a decision. "Come now, Doctor, you would be with your friend, if possible?"

"My dearest wish."

"Then it shall be fulfilled. Dearest wishes are the divining rods of destiny. The Scots are gone by now, for they would wish to reach the valley before dark, but even their ground-eating, in-cadence march cannot rival the swiftness of the finest Arabians on these plains. Let us depart, for we have an appointment with Anubis, the jackal god of the dead!"

Chapter Sixteen

The Charge of the Light-Horse Irregulars

In looking back on those later years of my association with the greatest detective the world has ever known, I cannot but wonder if madness had not become my lot. Here I stood on the west bank of the Nile but a few miles from stark and foreboding cliffs beyond which stretched the vast Sahara. I was better than three hundred miles from Cairo, and that city was, by design and style of life, a million miles from where I belonged. My habitat, by training and inclination, was Harley Street, where my conflicts should have been women with real or imaginary ailments and sniveling tots who needed to have their noses blown. Instead, I stood beside a scurvy-looking band of ruffians as sinister in appearance as their steeds were magnificent. What knew I of them or their leader either, despite his open and ingratiating manner? And yet there had been that moment in Luxor when he had spoken of Holmes and I had seen that flash in his eyes. A picture plucked from the scrapbook of time and projected like a magic lantern slide onto the mirror of his mind. I had seen that look before—in the green eyes of Wakefield Orloff and the brown ones of Von Shalloway of the German police—in the bland eyes of Slim Gilligan and the roguish ones of Burlington Bertie. I'd have staked my last shilling that the sheik belonged to that esoteric fraternity, the friends of Mr. Sherlock Holmes.

Upon our arrival at the Arab's camp, that grimy Bedouin who had assisted in my bandaging of the sheik descended upon me, all grins, and jabbering in Arabic.

"Mahoot is quite taken by you, Doctor Watson," said the chieftain. "He refers to you as the 'man of magic.' "

"I would have use for the arts of Cagliostro at this moment," I admitted, looking towards the towering cliff that seemed so near. "Nightfall is upon us. Can we make the valley now?"

For an answer, the sheik swung into the saddle of a superb Arabian stallion, signalling to his men as he did so. Mahoot, who seemed to derive a savage joy at the prospect of action, assisted me onto another Arabian, and in a trice the entire group were mounted and ready.

"Our horses are sure-footed, Doctor, and the rocky terrain we shall soon encounter holds no terrors for them. But be alert, for Arabians swerve quickly."

The sheik had no doubt noted the difficulty with which I had gained my seat. As we started out at a slow canter, which accelerated into a flowing gallop, I felt comforted that my saddle was much larger than the English type. There was but one rein, a curb undoubtedly, which made things easier for me, and I tried not to hold in my animal too tightly but let it take the lead, which it did, matching speed with the sheik's horse.

The set of tropicals that I wore featured large coat pockets, rather like a bush jacket. I transferred my trusty Smith-Webley, which I had with me, fortunately, shoving it into my belt where it would be more available. The band of fierce-looking Arabs that accompanied me made my firearm unnecessary in anything but a major crisis, especially since every one of my unusual companions was armed to the teeth. One's mind plays strange tricks. Here I was racing over flat and lush terrain, for all the world like my hero, General Gordon, surveying his defenses at Khartoum before that ill-fated and final battle. What was I thinking of? I blush to mention that I was wondering what the sedate members of the Bagatelle Club might think if they could see me now.

The graceful gallop of our steeds ate up distance, and in a short while the ground began to slant upwards. Fertile soil had faded away to sand, which was now replaced by rock, though the narrow road we followed was reasonably clear of obstacles and passable. Ahead of us loomed the stark cliffs of the Theban hills, and I knew that we were upon the entrance to the remote valley.

We curved to the right in the lee of the cliffs and our pace slackened to a fast trot as we followed a serpentine course. Then the valley was before us. But a short way back, the land was cultivated and there were date palms and greenery and the black, rich soil brought by Nile floods. Now all was limestone and flint with naught growing, a place of desolation. It was much larger than I had anticipated, though I sensed this rather than noted it visually since the sun was now gone and the last traces of it in the sky had disappeared. The moon was low and its light not revealing, and I wondered how the horses picked their way between boulders and outcroppings, but they did, for the desert was their element. Obviously this strange place was the result of violent flood waters that through eons of time had cut this crease in the cliffs that had become the place of the dead.

Then we heard it. There was no mistaking the sound. Gunfire! The entire party reined up, and we paused to consider the next move.

The sheik was gazing into the darkness, and he exchanged words with several of his followers before turning his bearded visage towards me.

"A rather brisk battle, Doctor, in the vicinity of a half-moon of graves almost due west."

With a small-scale war in progress, I did not feel that the withholding of information was practical.

"Holmes is in search of an undiscovered tomb of one of the pharaohs. Possibly he and the troopers found it."

"Only to discover that it was guarded, hence the gunfire. What now?"

I regarded him with a startled expression. "Why, we reconnoiter the situation."

"Well said," was his brief reply, and he whirled his horse and pressed forward at such a rate that I was hard pressed to keep up with him. Behind us the Bedouins formed a tight group, their eyes wide and their teeth flashing in the moonlight. Close by, Mahoot was sniffing at the air as if to catch the welcome smell of gunpowder. I recalled tales I had read of the American West. Was it not General Lou

Wallace who had described the Indians of the American frontier, such as the Sioux and the Cheyennes, as the finest light cavalry in the world? That may be, but it occurred to me that the horse was not indigenous to the Americans but came by way of the Spanish conquistadores, whereas I was with those who had ridden their mounts since the memory of man and, at the moment, would have matched my companions against any mounted irregulars in the world.

The sound of the firing was louder now, and the sheik slowed his horse to a walk and then reined in at the top of a crest. From his saddle bag he secured a very modern pair of binoculars with which he surveyed the scene ahead of us.

"The tombs of Seti First and Rameses Tenth lie there," he said, indicating a southerly direction. "The battle is, as you can see by the gun flashes, to the right."

"Near the tomb of Rameses Sixth," I said automatically, accepting the binoculars from him.

I noted that he gave me a surprised look. "Quite right, Doctor. How did—?"

"Something I heard," I explained quickly, viewing the night scene.

The moon had risen and visibility had improved. We were, I judged, in the western end of the valley, and ahead the desolate Eocene limestone and bedrock slanted upwards towards a projecting bastion of rock. Well up the slope were heaps of stone, removed no doubt from the numerous tombs of the area and interspersed with faults and fissures. The flashes of gunfire indicated that the Scottish soldiers and Holmes were shooting upwards towards the rocky escarpment that dominated the section. Well hidden behind large boulders just below the crest, another group was returning their fire.

Lowering the glasses, I noted that the sheik's head was shaking in a manner that registered disapproval of the scene before us.

"The Queen's soldiers are using their standard Einfield rifles."

"Of course," I muttered. To me a shot was a shot, but such was not the case with my experienced companion.

186

"The others have Winchester repeating carbines. The twelve-shot model, I'd say, along with some Martini rifles."

I just stared at him, amazed that he could deduce so much purely by sound. Then it passed through my mind that Holmes on several occasions had done the same thing relative to handguns.

"My point is, Doctor, that the troops can scarcely risk a rush up the slope towards their concealed adversaries. The Winchesters would chop them to pieces."

There was a heavier boom in the distance, and I surveyed the area of conflict again through the glasses.

"Why doesn't Gray pull his men back? They could regroup and attack from another angle."

Another, louder boom punctuated the sheik's reply.

"On top of one of those rocks is an elephant gun. Being long-range, it could make things costly if the British retreated."

"Then they are pinned down."

"And the moonlight is getting brighter every moment, which does not improve the situation."

I peered through the binoculars, my mind desperately searching for inspiration. What would General Sternways have thought if faced with a tactical problem such as this? The General had regaled Holmes and myself with stories of his quite illustrious career on several occasions after the sleuth had recovered his daughter's famous pendant of Ceylonese rubies. It was the geography I viewed that prompted a sudden rush of words.

"Sheik, could we not circle to the south and come upon that hillock from the rear? Whoever is up there is dug in below the crest, and if we charged over it, we'd certainly have them at a disadvantage."

"True," replied the desert chieftain with a quick smile of approval. "But consider, we could have them between two fires but would be exposed to two fires ourselves."

"That can be remedied," I said with confidence. From the side pocket of my jacket I extracted my notebook that was with me always. The pen with which I had written endless prescriptions was, of course, in my handkerchief pocket.

"Sheik, could not one of your men make his way upwards to the British with a note? At a signal, Holmes could have the troopers hold their fire as we attack from beyond the hill."

"The cry of the jackal," responded the Arabian promptly. "The gunfire has frightened them from the area, so there is no possibility of an error, and Mahoot is quite good at emulating the sound of the carrion beast."

As he spoke, I scrawled rapidly on a piece of notepaper, trying to summon the words that would explain our plan briefly. The sheik was rattling to one of his men and I caught the name, Holmes, repeated at least four times. The Bedouin dismounted, secured the message from my hands, and darted forward into the open, flitting from boulder to boulder and making use of every furrow cut by primeval floods in the rocky terrain to approach the Sutherland-Argyles undetected. Obviously our messenger was well aware of the menace of the long-range elephant gun and taking suitable precautions. The rest of our party had also dismounted now and were busy affixing pieces of leather to their horses' hooves, securing them with thongs of rawhide. As I vacated my saddle, Mahoot performed that feat for my steed. With a cunning bred of centuries of desert warfare, the Bedouins were muffling the hooves so that our progress over the bedrock of the area would not be revealed by sound. This sensible precaution prompted a sudden thought.

"Sheik," I stammered, indicating towards the soldiers, "your messenger! Will not the troopers mistake him for the enemy?"

"When he is close enough he will call out Holmes's name. Surely that will alert the British that he is friend not foe."

I was reassured. "Holmes will take care of it."

Now we remounted and were able to follow the crest that concealed us from the area of hostilities, in a southerly direction and at a good rate. The ground sloped away and kept us under cover as we rode in a half circle to approach, as planned, from the rear. Rifle fire, punctuated at infrequent intervals by the ominous boom of the elephant gun, continued. I imagined that Colonel Gray was keeping the opposition busy, hoping for a cloud over the now brilliant moon that would allow him to dispatch a man to secure reinforcements and extricate his party from the difficult situation in which they found themselves. Well, Colonel, I thought with some pride, the reinforcements are already on the scene, as you will learn shortly. I noted the riders around me checking their weapons and began to wonder just what I would do in the coming melée and also if this stratagem would work. General Sternways had stated more than once that the effectiveness of a cavalry charge was in part visual. The spectre of a wall of horsemen thundering towards a position was enough to strike terror in the stoutest defender's heart. But, he had added, mounted units were highly susceptible to ambush, and a sound knowledge of the terrain was essential. Dear me, all we knew was that we were to charge over a crest of stony outcropping, and what lay beyond this natural fortification and the boulders sheltering the snipers we knew not. At that moment, my morale was at a low ebb.

Suddenly, the sound of gunfire, now quite close, picked up its tempo. The messenger has arrived, I thought. Gray has his men pouring it on to cover our approach and capture the complete attention of the enemy. Had I been truly of the military, I would have considered a commendation for Colonel Gray.

My thoughts were cut short. The moment was upon us.

The sheik and his men were grouped at the base of an incline, and I thanked my stars that we had arrived undetected at our present position. The chieftain and his riders were regarding me quizzically, and suddenly it dawned on me that they were awaiting orders. I was in charge of this mad escapade. A physician, a man of peace, trained to save life and not to take it, was expected to head a group of desert nomads in a quasi-military maneuver in this remote, dried-out valley of death. My heart quailed.

Then a voice drummed in my ears. "This motley crew is here on your errand, ol' chap, and if the rush is blunted and the field is lost, it is you who must accept the consequences and blame. So on with it, you bag of aging bones!"

"Sheik," I whispered with more conviction than I felt, "we'll spread out and rush the top in a line, which will give us maximum firepower as we clear the ridge and, possibly, mislead the enemy as to our numbers as well. Have Mahoot give the cry of the jackal, then the British fire should cease and I'll give the signal."

Already the chieftain was relaying, in Arabic, soft words to his men to form a row of white steeds, which they did with alacrity. Bathed by the luminous moon, their white robes fanned by a faint wind, and seated on their steeds whose nostrils flared, they made an impressive sight pictured against the stark cliffs in the background. The moment produced an adrenalin flow into my blood, and for a wild second I imagined that this villainous-looking crew was transformed into the cream of chivalry and that we could charge inexorably to the gates of hell and back! I scarce knew what Holmes was up to, but the cause had to be right, and God supports the forces of light and those with the fastest guns.

Mahoot's evil-looking mouth opened and the howl of the jackal rose from his lips. In a moment there was a sudden cessation in the heavy firing, and I knew this was it. Seizing my trusty Webley in one hand, I rose in my stirrups, one arm aloft to lower and signal the charge. But my mount, feeling my weight shift forward, took this to be the moment and bolted for the top of the hill. I slammed back in my saddle and from my surprised mouth there came a cry that I'm told was a satisfactory blending of the rebel yell of Stuart's Confederate calvary with the ear-splitting cry of one of Chief Crazy Horse's mounted braves. I think the Arabs were as startled as I was, but they picked up the refrain and we cleared the crest for all the world like a mass of screaming centaurs infected with the madness of whirling dervishes.

My steed held his lead over the rest and we made the top in advance of the main body. I had cocked my weapon, an insane thing to do on horseback, and was bouncing like a rubber ball at every leap of my noble Arabian. As a result I lost both my stirrups and my Webley blasted off into the night, not aimed at anything. I shoved the weapon into my belt again, gripping the pommel of the saddle desperately but to no avail. I was thrown loose from my horse but still clung to the saddle with a grip fused by raw panic. Both feet hit the ground and I bounced with my heels flying upwards and was amazed when they came in contact with two Egyptians who must have been working their way back up the hill.

They were not alone, having two companions who at the moment were being run down by my horse, whose mouth was open and snapping at anything within range. The two I'd hit with my heels went rolling down the hill, and my steed's progress was impeded by the men in his path. Then my feet hit the ground again as my Arabian rose on his hind legs to stamp at those unfortunates before him. Nothing could shake my grip on the saddle since I felt it was my last link with sanity in a world gone mad. My body slid sideways and I was hanging by the pommel with my legs on the steed's vertically inclined rump. Then the Arabian's front legs came down and there was a cry of anguish from those beneath his devastating hooves, but the beast's impact with the ground snapped me forward and of a sudden I was back in the saddle, and my mount and I were plunging down the hillside towards the rear of the rocks that had been the snipers' lair. But there was no answering fire or men to shoot at or run down. Streaming from the rocks and down the incline was a band of turbaned rascals whose hands were raised or who were industriously throwing away their guns as they rushed towards the wall of bayonets that had come forth to intercept them. Casting frenzied looks over their shoulders, they made a dash for the Scottish soldiers as though their only hope of salvation was behind the thin red line.

By this time, lurching in my saddle like an inebriated man, I managed to slow down my mount, and Mahoot was beside me to seize the bridle. He peppered the air with a flow of Arabic liberally interspersed with the only word I could understand, which was "Allah."

Then the sheik was by my side.

"A memorable engagement. Your running down those men near the crest rescued us from a potential crossfire, and the enemy has been captured without the loss of a man."

No doubt I sputtered something, but I imagine it was unintelligible.

"My good Doctor, I read that you served with the Northumberland Fusilliers, but I misunderstood your function with that gallant regiment. I thought you were with the medical corps. An obvious error."

Before I could explain to the sheik that his original idea had been completely correct, Holmes had raced up towards us and was assisting me from the saddle.

"Dear Watson, I doubt if I shall ever carry firearms again. You outdid yourself as a marksman on this night."

I could only gaze at him dumbly as I fingered portions of my legs in hopes that they were still intact.

"Right after the signal of the jackal's howl, we ceased firing, of course, and then you came over the crest. Their sharpshooter, who had made life hellish for us with his long-range piece of ordinance, suddenly straightened up on the top of the rock that was his lair and looked backwards. Then I heard the bark of your Webley. You caught him right on, Watson, and he went tumbling from his perch. The others of your group were just appearing as you rode down and dispersed the four men who had gone back up the hill, for ammunition, no doubt. It was a chilling sight, with bodies falling right and left before your onslaught, and you were moving so fast you appeared half-man, half-beast."

Colonel Gray joined us during Holmes's words.

"It was a combination of things that did in those beggars for fair," he stated, indicating behind him where his troops were securing the thoroughly quailed enemy. "Half of them are shivering and muttering about Anubis and won't even look back up the hill. After the howl of the jackal and the doctor's appearance, and most unusual it was, they must have seized on the thought that 'twas the jackal god of the dead who was descending upon them. Took all the fight out of them, it did."

In a weary manner I began to inform the group of their host of misconceptions but was not allowed to. The results were important, and the execution of little interest now. It was Holmes, calm and assured as always, who took charge.

The great sleuth had made note of the sheik, and he acknowledged his presence now.

"It has been some time," he stated laconically.

"Indeed, Mr. Holmes. I trust Allah has smiled on your efforts during the interval."

"He smiled tonight. Your presence was most opportune."

"Doctor Watson, to whom I owe much, enlisted the aid of my band and myself."

My friend's keen eyes rested on me for a moment with surprise fighting a twinkle for supremacy. "I've said on occasion that you do amaze me, ol' chap, and this is no exception. But now, because of your triumph, fate has indeed lent us a hand, and we'd best move fast to take full advantage of it."

As the sheik and Colonel Gray regarded him intently, I could see my friend's machinelike mind sorting the pieces and placing them in order for presentation. His gaze centered on the Colonel.

"These Scottish troops, but recently from their homeland, have only a vague idea of where they are, I believe."

As the Colonel nodded, a smile of satisfaction touched Holmes's lips. "We shall keep it that way. When they return to their regiment and are dispatched to India, the story is that they had a brief skirmish with rebellious tribesmen, which was terminated by the arrival of a friendly band of Arabians. I think that sounds plausible enough."

The sheik contributed some information. "The men you have captured, they are from Kurna." He spat expressively on the rock. "The place of the graverobbers, which is close by to the south and east."

"I see," said Holmes. Then his attention shifted back to Gray. "Colonel, have your men keep close watch on the prisoners, for we can't have any escape."

"My men will gladly assist," said the sheik with a grim smile. "They have no love for the thieves of Kurna."

Holmes accepted this. "Then what is to be seen here shall be viewed by just the four of us," he said. "If you can secure torches, Colonel, we have some exploring to do."

It was shortly thereafter that we left the temporary camp set up by the Sutherland-Argyle and their unusual allies, the sheik's band. At Holmes's request, Colonel Gray, who was familiar with the valley, led us towards the tomb of Rameses Sixth which, according to the cipher of the Italian Puzza, was our marker in this strange rocky fastness.

What Holmes sought he found close to the entrance to the tomb of the Sixth Rameses. It was a narrow opening in the valley floor a short distance away, shielded by a low mound of rock that concealed it from the passing eye. It was certainly unprepossessing, but there was a stone step, unmistakably, and below it another. Holmes ignited one of the torches Gray had brought, descended a short distance, and then turned back towards the three of us with a strange look on his face.

"Sixteen steps downward I make it, right through solid rock. Now we shall learn what it is the Chinaman found."

He turned again towards the tomb, and we eagerly followed in his footsteps.

The sunken stairway descended steeply, I estimated at a forty-five-degree angle. At the bottom there had been a doorway, that was evident, but it had been removed, and the torch light revealed a passageway that slanted downward without steps.

We pressed down the passage and progressed about thirty feet when we found ourselves face to face with a door of stone blocks festooned by seals that, as Gray explained, were proof that the tomb had not been violated by plunderers. This remark promoted amazement within Holmes.

"Do you say that this doorway has not been opened?"

Colonel Gray shrugged. "I'm no Egyptologist, sir, but from the seals and the way the stones fit, I would think that it has been this way for thousands of years."

In the light of the torches, it was obvious that the sleuth was thinking intently.

"He came this far and no further. Not one unplundered tomb has been found in all of Egypt, and the Chinaman got this far and then stopped. I fear that tears it as far as my theory is concerned."

Holmes was speaking as though to himself, and it was the sheik who broke in on his thoughts.

"What did you expect to find?"

"That the Chinaman, for obviously this archeological

treasure was uncovered at his instigation, had opened this crypt untouched throughout the ages and found one or more of the golden tablets."

The desert chieftain's bearded face was expressive, and it was plain to see that Holmes's words struck no responsive chord with him.

"Actually," admitted the sleuth, "faced with the cold light of fact, my theory seems a bit far-fetched. And incorrect, if we are to believe Colonel Gray here. Therefore, let us backtrack, gentlemen. If Chu San Fu did not open the tomb, I see no reason why we should, and many reasons why we should not."

I confess it was with a sense of disappointment that I followed my friend back up the strange corridor hewn from solid rock and mounted the sixteen ageless steps towards the desert night sky. What secrets lay beyond that doorway that led to the past? Something about that thought had a familiar ring, but other plans were brewing, and my attention was distracted.

As we stood on the valley floor at the entrance to one tomb and surrounded by a multitude of others, Holmes was sunk in thought and seemed despondent. The sheik expressed a reasonable question, "What would you have us do?" at the same time that Colonel Gray inquired, "What now?"

Their simultaneous and same question drew a half-smile from Holmes and shook him from his mood of the moment.

"We are holding the tiger's tail, gentlemen. For the good of the Empire, it would be better if this tomb had not been found. What I would like to do is push back time and have it remain undiscovered. At least, until the present crisis is past."

I was incapable of following Holmes's reasoning, but the sheik found nothing unusual in his words.

"It can be done. Colonel Gray's British troops can seal off the valley using the excuse of military maneuvers. The Egyptians hired to guard the place can be pressed into service to refill the passageway and stairs, and in a short while the entrance will be no more. A simple job in this place where there has been so much excavation."

"What of the workers?" I asked, and then regretted it. For expediency I might better have not touched on the subject.

The sheik's wise smile served as a reminder that this was another part of the world to me, with customs and habits that I could never completely understand.

"My men and I will leave for the south and the campfires of our home. If we take others with us, it will not be the first time, and their lot will be no worse than it is now."

His words were reasonable and reassuring, but I sensed considerable elasticity in them as regards what would actually happen. However, Holmes did not seem disposed to inquire further, and I decided not to, either.

Our journey into the Valley of the Kings had been a bizarre affair, fraught, as it proved, with danger and complications, but its resolution was simple enough.

The following day, Holmes and I went with the Scottish soldiers and Gray to the entrance of the valley and, leaving the Colonel with the men, made our way back to Luxor. Prior to our departure, the sheik and Holmes had a private conversation that I would have given much to have been in on. The connection between the desert chieftain and the great detective puzzled me no end. Actually, I tried to lead conversations round to this matter on a number of occasions but got nowhere and remained ignorant of the situation until '96, when the reconquest of the Sudan began under Kitchener.

Holmes's mood of thoughtfulness, induced by the regrouping of facts, was supplanted by an air of impatience and activity. We wasted no time returning to the Nile and crossing it, where he made fast tracks for the Luxor army headquarters to dispatch cables. Then we gathered our belongings to return to Cairo. Gray was to follow on a later train.

En route, Holmes explained that he had persuaded the military to hasten orders for the Sutherland-Argyles' departure to India, and I could understand his concern regarding this. He wanted the troopers that had accompanied us on a transport before they could wander round Luxor and mention their singular engagement in a strange valley and its unusual conclusion. That Holmes wished all knowledge of the unknown tomb suppressed completely was most apparent, though his concern regarding this eluded me. Through the years he and I had played games regarding the progress of a case, and I must admit that he kept me on my toes with his varied moods and moments of loquacity followed by taciturn periods when he was so sunk in thought that he could barely summon a "good morning" and at times could not or would not do that. However, there is a limit to one's patience, and on the train back to the Egyptian capital, I determined to wrestle some sense from him regarding recent events and his apparent change of ideas. Much to my surprise, I found him not averse to discussing the case.

"After due consideration, good fellow, I must chide myself for being overly dramatic. This ancient land and its history is a never-ending mystery. But let us pass over that, for it has to be facts that are our sure tools. We know that Chu San Fu is a deep-seated rascal and a raving megalomaniac as well. Not an inappropriate mental state for a would-be empire-builder, I might add." This statement was accompanied by a thin smile. "He has caused a groundswell that has passed through the Mohammedan areas and will evidently reach its crest in Cairo at a meeting of the leaders of this widespread religion. Now the Chinaman cannot pass himself off as a true-blue follower of the prophet, for Mohammedanism has made no inroads in the Far East. Therefore he has some other scheme in mind, for it is his own aggrandizement that he is planning. Of that we can be sure. You recall that the hieroglyphics and the secret writings as well are recondite inasmuch as they reproduce visually not only words but ideas. The golden tablets matter has distracted me no end for they are, as of now, the only exhibits of the secret writings in any detail."

"Andrade being the one man who can translate them," I added as Holmes fell into a silence.

"Do not forget Memory Max, ol' fellow. I pictured this tool of Chu San Fu as capable of deciphering them, and I may still be right about that. Now don't laugh at me, but I did entertain the thought that these secret writings, until now undecipherable, might contain the key to some unknown power that would provide an explanation for the colossal monuments created by ancient Egypt, the construction of which we cannot as yet explain."

"Good Heavens, Holmes, you feared that some age-old force or process, possibly astronomical in source, might fall into the hands of a criminal madman?"

"It does sound like the awesome villainy from some transpontine piece, does it not? But the idea did occur, perhaps inspired by the unexplained mysteries on every hand in this strange land. I'm much relieved to be proved wrong."

"But how do you deduce that you are?"

"The tomb we found was unopened. Were Chu San Fu in pursuit of an ancient force, would he not have forced the door to that crypt in hopes of finding one or more additional golden tablets in the unpillaged tomb?"

Unable to detect a flaw in this reasoning, I nodded.

"So we must return to basics. Chu San Fu is here in Egypt to incite the Moslems to a religious crusade, another rising of the Crescent. Of that I am sure. His possession of the Sacred Sword is enough to gain, nay command, the attention of Mohammedans throughout the world. It is the Chinaman's ticket to the show, as 'twere. What have the golden tablets to do with his plan? In keeping with the parlance of those lurid American novels that you read, what is his secret weapon?"

"Well, Holmes—"

"And why would he, clued by Puzza's cipher, discover the tomb, dig to the very entrance, and then abandon the project? That makes no sense at all."

"Hmm. You did mention American stories. This entire matter of tombs is rather reminiscent of Western folklore relative to lost mines."

Holmes had been gazing out of the window of our car and suddenly turned to me. "In what way?"

"There's the matter of the Lost Dutchman mine in Arizona, you know. The prospector who discovered it is said to have brought in ore of an amazingly high grade. But he died or disappeared, and the mine has never been found. They are still looking for it, by the way. Then there's the Lost Englishman's mine. Rather the same story. A remittance man supposedly found the mother lode but then, at the death of his brother, was called back to his homeland to assume the family title and never returned."

"That I find unbelievable," said Holmes.

"And a bit too close to the Dutchman story. Personally, I think both tales were inspired by some glib confidence man in hopes of doing a salting job."

"Can we go over that last part again, Watson?"

A memory caused me to chuckle, and then I was prodded by the finger of guilt.

"See here, Holmes, the Empire faces a crisis, and I'm relating tall tales that may have no basis in truth."

"But stories have a root source, good chap, and sometimes it is of interest. Do inform me as to this 'salting' that you refer to."

"Well, it is a swindle scheme, pure and simple. An attempt to sell a worthless mine at an inflated price, though it backfired on one rascal. Happened in Colorado, you see. Chap called Tabor was an unsuccessful proprietor of a general store who grubstaked two miners."

"Grubstaked? You have picked up a most colorful vocabulary."

"Supplied two prospectors with goods for a share in their findings."

"Oh."

"Well, the two men that he extended credit to discovered the 'Little Pittsburgh' mine, which was the richest find in Colorado up to that point. Within a short time, Tabor bought out his partners and became a multimillionaire. But his sudden affluence did not increase his business acumen. He would buy anything, and soon became known as an easy mark."

"A what?"

"To put it bluntly, Holmes, a sucker. Some fellow in a far-off place called Leadville had a mine that had proved worthless, so he planted valuable ore in it, a process known as 'salting,' and then took Tabor to view the premises."

"Making sure that he found the 'salted' ore, I take it."

"Exactly. Tabor fell for the bait and purchased the mine. Paid better than one hundred thousand dollars for it, as I recall."

"I noted that this story promoted some humor in you, but it seems a sad tale of chicanery to me."

"It's not over, Holmes," I said somewhat smugly. "Tabor put a crew to work on the mine, and his foreman reported back to the tycoon that they had been had, that the mine was worthless. But Tabor was undaunted. 'Dig some more,' he said. 'I've a great name for it: the Matchless.' "

"Ever hopeful, I see."

"Possibly inspired. They dug ten feet down and discovered a vein that made the 'Little Pittsburgh' seem pale by comparison. The 'Matchless Mine' financed H.A.W. Tabor's honeymoon to Europe, during which he is rumored to have spent ten million dollars!"

Holmes's jaw actually dropped. "My dear Watson, the sum you mention is mind-boggling. I wonder what the man who salted the mine . . ."

He was in the process of lighting a cigarette and held the match for a long moment, its flickering light reflected in his keen eyes. Then he completed the operation slowly.

"Salted the mine. By godfrey, Watson, that's it! At the risk of being repetitious, may I say again that you do possess the innate ability to say the right thing at the right time. Now, I must think."

I could not get another word from him during our return trip to Cairo. He was in such a deep study that I did not dare try.

Chapter Seventeen

Holmes Seems Irrational

Following our active adventure in the Valley of the Kings, a long trip by rail was no antidote for my aches and pains, and the moment that Holmes and I returned to the welcome surroundings of our hotel, I found myself incapable of seriously thinking about the matter at hand, as critical as it was. A quick bath and I was between sheets and sunk in deep sleep. Night had fallen when I finally arose, considerably refreshed though stiff as a board. When I dressed and made my way to the sitting room of our suite, I was unprepared for the scene that greeted me.

Only Holmes was in evidence. Since he is tireless when on a case, I had not expected the sleuth to indulge in a siesta but rather a room crowded with colonial officialdom, discussing the next step in this most peculiar situation, which had strong overtones of international complications. There were evidences that Holmes had conferred with many, but to find him deserted when at the critical point of an investigation did bring me up short. I wondered if some new and unanticipated piece had been introduced to the complex chessboard that faced the great detective.

Holmes's pipe was going, emitting clouds of acrid smoke that served as evidence that his superb mind was toying with facts in search of a realistic pattern and a solution to the problems the pattern presented.

"Ah, Watson, you do appear much the better for your rest. Whilst you were so engaged, I've been able to resolve the necessary staff work attendant on the resolution of this sticky wicket we have chanced upon."

I stifled a yawn and my senses sharpened. Could it be that Holmes would map out his plan of action, a step that he had seldom taken in the past?

"You did indicate during our journey by rail that an idea had come to you."

"It has, prompted by your chance remark. Happily this inspiration has stood up before a searching analysis."

Holmes rose to his feet and began pacing the room as he had so often within the familiar confines of 221B Baker Street.

"The Government has seen fit to accept—endorse, sponsor, if you will—an unofficial investigation into the problem of an Arabian uprising. I don't believe we need to underscore again the far-reaching damage that this outbreak might cause. We can accept the inclusive phrase that 'the situation is fraught with peril.' Alas, I must place some of the blame on my shoulders."

"Oh, come now, Holmes, this madman's scheme, whatever it is, was not of your doing."

"But his ability to do it, is. In a previous case of ours* I swore that I would smash Chu San Fu. Had I but held true to that idea, we might not be in Egypt now."

"But Holmes, you broke Chu's hold on Limehouse and Soho."

"We closed him down. But he has, phoenixlike, risen again from the ashes of his defeat. The Chu San Fu's of our world, Watson, are like a deadly bacillus. They can be rendered impotent by isolation, but if allowed to break free, they are just as capable of epidemical infection and death as before. Extermination becomes the sole solution, as extreme a policy as that may be."

There was in Holmes's words a fatal conviction, and they produced a feeling of discomfort in me. His tone displayed an unusual fervor, alien to his normal cold and analytic manner.

"I have little reason to plead Chu's cause—"

"Nor I," said Holmes before I could elaborate on my

* The case of the Golden Bird.

thought. "The snake's fangs have to be removed. As I stated but a moment ago, this affair bears the name of an unofficial investigation, and after some thought I have decided to adhere to the title. We shall do what needs to be done, our way, my good chap. Can I interest you in dinner, prior to our departure for the native quarter of this strange city?"

Of course, I was dumbfounded. "Holmes, you jest. Chu San Fu in his intellectual dotage may have fallen prey to a Caesar complex, but he is not stupid."

"True, Watson. You are too old a hand to make the error of underestimating an opponent, and so am I."

"You reinforce my thoughts," I cried. "You are a marked man. The Chinaman knows that only you have the imagination and the ability to anticipate his moves and divert them. I would think, nay, I know, that right now his first thought is to stop Sherlock Holmes."

"Let us hope so, ol' chap. Dinner?"

From experience I knew that I had to bite back my remonstrances. Holmes had allowed the orchestra of his voice to play the overture, but I was going to have to wait for the first act of the opera of his composition.

What we had for dinner I cannot tell you. I was so consumed with worry that I ate without noticing the fare, certainly not according to my fashion. But one must admit that I had cause for concern. Holmes's tone when he discussed Chu San Fu and his second coming, as 'twere, had an ominous quality. That he would risk himself to stop the master criminal from instigating an uprising, I was sure. Therefore, it behooved me to stick to him like the proverbial plaster and to provide whatever assistance my trusty Webley and I could. Holmes was not impetuous or rash. He seldom made a move that was not well considered in advance, but I could not anticipate what scheme he had in mind to bring the Oriental to heel. For all I knew his meticulous mind had evolved a foolproof plan, but I could scarcely picture one that would not involve personal risk, and I promised myself that the danger would involve the both of us.

As for myself, the world would hardly recoil in horror if

mischance befell one John H. Watson, M.D. The picture of Her Royal Majesty being overcome with shock and grief did not come to my mind, nor did tremors spreading through the Empire. But all of these things I could envision should Holmes fall before a miscarriage of chance, and I vowed that if the bullet engraved with his name was fired and I was able to step between it and my friend, I would do so gladly. Because of him, I had lived a richer life to this moment than most are blessed with at their final hour. Surely I could say farewell to my existence with the heartening thought that it had all been worthwhile. Indeed, had I the ability to relive it, I would have it no other way than what chance, fate, or a divine blueprint had plotted for me.

Such thoughts, though grim in nature, did produce a heartening effect and lent starch to my manner and rigidity to my backbone. When Holmes and I strolled out on the veranda of the hotel, savoring our after-dinner cigars, I was a bit lightheaded and imbued with an air of fatalism and a spirit of being ready, come what may. My current of energy was somewhat short-circuited when I realized that I had felt much the same way on that well-remembered night when we waited in darkness and silence in Oberstein's house at 13 Caulfield Gardens to spring the trap on Colonel Valentine Walter. What was it Holmes had said prior to the conclusion of that case, certainly of vast importance to the Empire? Oh yes: "Martyrs on the altar of our country."

Suddenly I felt quite deflated as I recalled that on the evening in question Holmes had been wrong. Colonel Walter had not been the bird he planned to snare. Good heavens, suppose my friend had made a miscalculation regarding this matter?

"I say, ol' chap, you were standing rather like this when you saw the lawyer, Loo Chan, hastening down Sharia Kamel, were you not?"

"Quite, Holmes," I responded.

"In the direction of the Ezbekiyeh Gardens, I believe you said."

"Right. Do you suppose that he set himself up like a stalking horse to draw me into the net?"

"Doubtful," replied Holmes. "Rather fancy that he found you dogging his footsteps and decided to gather you in as a hostage. But your quick thinking regarding that matter turned the tables, did it not?"

"Come now, Holmes, that decision was forced on me. Would never have had the chance but for that flower pot or whatever it was that struck down the Manchurian who had grabbed me."

"I've given that a bit of thought, Watson. You do seem to operate under a lucky star, for which I am grateful. Let us try and retrace your steps when you were shadowing the lawyer. Possibly, the area of his hiding place may be revealing."

"Loo Chan is well on his way to Macao by now," I said, and then realized this was an inane remark.

"But Chu San Fu remains, and he may have gone to earth in the same area. The native quarter certainly seems like the section he would choose."

I fell in with Holmes's scheme, having little choice really. But I was not fooled. This was no spur-of-the-moment thought of his since he had mentioned such a trip prior to dinner. Had I planned on an investigation of the old town in search of the criminal hideout, I would have had a detachment of the local police with me, something that Holmes had the authority to do with the carte blanche conferred upon him by the foreign office. But then I recalled that, for reasons of his own, he had decided to go it alone without the benefit of the local establishment.

My nighttime excursion into the byways of Cairo was of recent vintage and I had little trouble following my previous path. Again, in a remarkably short time, the lights and sounds of the small European quarter were behind us and we were into the ancient city, much of it as it had been when it was called "Babylon-in-Egypt," and just as crowded, huddled, and secret as when first erected by Chaldean workmen. I recounted to my friend my actions when following the Oriental lawyer, though I did not mention my thoughts regarding what I hoped to do or my considerable doubts as to my ability to do anything. Holmes's keen eyes were darting everywhere, and that peculiar sixth sense of his regarding directions was, I sensed, associating our progress with whatever knowledge he had of the local geography.

Finally we arrived at the alley-mouth down which Loo Chan had disappeared and into which I had ventured from a different direction. Holmes surveyed the scene, his aquiline nose held in such a manner that had its shape been different, I would have sworn he was sniffing the breeze to scent the spoor of his dedicated enemy.

"Come, ol' chap," he said suddenly, "we shall backtrack. The next street over, if I read the signs right, would eventually lead us to the vicinity of the Mosque of al-Ashar, which is our one clue in this muddled mess. Chu San Fu intends to go there if I am correct as to his plan. So let us reconnoiter in that direction."

We reversed ourselves and went back another block before making a right-angle turn on a fairly sizable side street. The squat and squallid dwellings were reproductions of each other for a block and then, for half of another. Then Holmes drew me to a stop in the shadow of a one-story building, indicating the other side of the street.

"Really, the only edifice of any size that we've seen for some time, Watson."

It was that. Contrary to its neighbors, it was set back from the street and rose four stories. The ground floor was not visible, being shielded by an imposing wall, the top of which was armed with shards of glass set in cement. There was no gleam of light from its windows, and the whole structure had an abandoned and dilapidated appearance.

"Surely not a residence, Holmes, in this or former times."

"I suspect it served, during part of its history, as what our American cousins would call a 'pokey.' Are those not bars on some of the upper windows?"

There was moonlight to aid our investigation but I could not make out the ironwork that Holmes referred to. Small wonder, since his night vision was of the keenest whilst mine did not exist. The aged edifice had certainly caught Holmes's attention, and after a half-minute or so during which he subjected it to the closest scrutiny, he motioned to me and we continued our way down the dingy street but paused again after a dozen or so steps.

"Hmm, this is opportune, Watson. An alleyway running on the far side of the establishment. That will provide us with the opportunity of viewing it from another angle."

I was about to remonstrate but instead was forced to follow my friend's long strides, which took him to the end of the block where we crossed the street and came back upon the place that so intrigued him. Again Holmes took refuge in the shadows of a doorway close by the alleyway.

"See here," I said, puffing a little, for our pace had been swift. "Doesn't this strike you as a bit too easy? Not a soul about. Not even the howl of a mongrel to disturb the silence."

"No mystery there, Watson, for the native population are long abed."

"But we haven't the foggiest about what may be within this former jail or whatever it was."

"Perhaps nothing at all, but we are duty-bound to find out, are we not?"

Guiding me with his hand, for the alleyway was dark, Holmes directed our footsteps within it. On our right was a continuation of the wall that fronted the house, and I noted that its crest was also guarded by broken glass, which would have made it difficult indeed for anyone trying to climb over it. My heart sank, for this had all the elements of a trap into which Holmes was marching with purpose and propelling me as well. Somehow my earlier heroic thoughts seemed dim though the passage of time had been a short one. Then it crossed my mind that if this strange building was so well designed to resist outsiders, it could hardly serve as an effective device to lure us within.

That comforting thought was promptly dissipated when Holmes came to a halt but a moment later.

"Here we have it, Watson. A gate through the wall, which in times past and perhaps even now serves as an entryway to the alley."

"Now listen, Holmes, if that gate happens to be unlocked I'm not taking another step. This whole matter bears too close a resemblance to that Watney Gas Chamber adventure."

The faint luminosity of the night sky allowed me to catch the flash of Holmes's teeth as they were revealed in a broad smile, not at all in keeping with the peril of the situation facing us.

"My dear chap, excitement has caused you to mix fact and fantasy. You know full well that my exploits in the Watney Gas Chamber, as heroic as they seemed to countless theatre-goers, were but reflections of the ample imagination of that American dramatist."

"And besides," he added, "the gate is locked, which may allay your fears though I find it inconvenient."

As he searched in his pocket, I felt another stab of fear. Of course, Holmes had with him one of those efficient devices, possibly designed by Slim Gilligan, that would make short work of the lock facing us. But my friend's actions seemed to follow an irrational path. A mysterious building by its very dimensions certain to stand apart from its fellows, an area wherein Holmes's enemies were known to have been—the whole matter shrieked "Ambush!" Here was the master of deduction blithely being taken in by a deception like a youthful Inspector Hopkins rushing down a false trail. It just didn't make sense.

Holmes had a thin piece of steel in one hand and had already inserted it in the large keyhole of the door facing us.

"The lock is an old one, Watson, but I think we can force its secret from it."

"Without a doubt, Holmes, but is this not madness? The street entrance is an impossibility without a scaling ladder, but here we have a convenient alley gate dangling before our eyes like the enticing lure on a fisherman's line. Does it not strike you that we are about to be reeled in?"

"Come now, we must not overdramatize. Ah, I think I have it!"

There was a long, regretful-sounding click, and Holmes withdrew his pick-lock and tested the handle of the door, which turned, and I heard the creak of hinges. Then another sound intruded itself upon my ears. Footsteps at the far end of the alley. I moved closer to Holmes, in the protective shadow of the wall, and my anxious eyes searched the dim passage ahead of us. There were two ominous silhouettes in the distance, and the distance was not as far as I would have wished it to be.

"Good heavens, Holmes, it is those two giant Manchurians."

The sleuth's thin face was cocked to one side. He had already spotted the shapes that were closing in on us and was registering on something else. There was the sound of stealthy footfalls behind us as well.

"Holmes, we've been lured here and now, like game-beaters, they are flushing us into the trap."

"Well, Watson, we have no alternative at the moment."

He had the gate open in a trice and we flitted through it with the haste of desperation. As Holmes closed the portal, I leaned my considerable weight against it and he worked his pick-lock feverishly. The sweetest sound I could imagine was the click that signalled that the door was secure, for a moment at least.

"Come, ol' fellow, if we have bought ourselves a bit of time, let us make use of it."

I followed on his coattails, for it was infernally dark within the grounds of this ancient place and I could but depend on Holmes's ability to operate with proven efficiency while under the blanket of night.

His half-trot took us in the direction of the building, which now loomed before us with all the ghostly charm of the House of Usher! Evidently he spied no exit from the grounds, and I of course could see little at all. As we circled round the building, I did note that the front was devoid of a veranda or porch, consistent with the architecture of the area. On the far side of the building there was a section where the darkness seemed deeper, and Holmes made for it. It was a recessed door, and again he resorted to his burglar tool. Now I heard sounds in the distance and assumed that the Manchurians and whoever else was with them had gained access to the yard area. If Holmes could open the door to the building, perhaps we could secrete ourselves within and avoid capture. This time there was no tell-tale sound of tumblers, but of a sudden the door came ajar and I thanked fate for the time Holmes had spent studying the techniques of various robbers, many of whom he had brought to justice.

We slipped into the completely black interior of this deserted pile that had led to our undoing. But the last card was not played, and Holmes and I had been in a few other fixes that were just as desperate. His long fingers were on my wrist guiding me forward when there was a sudden burst of blinding light. Then I heard a sibilant voice that was easy to identify.

"Good evening, gentlemen. How pleased I am that you chose to drop in."

Suddenly a weight struck me from above and I was borne helplessly to the ground, threshing as I fell but to no avail. It was not human hands that had seized me but a netlike object, which I judged to be of some sort of metal. Its weight alone kept me pinned to the ground, and the shock of its impact certainly dulled my senses. But not so much that I was unable to screw my head round and, through the blaze of lights, I saw the wizened and yellow face of Chu San Fu standing above me. In his hand was a glass container that he emptied with a smile that was more contemptuous than humorous. From its narrow mouth came a flow of crystals that seemed to explode as they fell round me. Then there was a faint mist and a peculiar scent in my nostrils, and I lost consciousness.

Chapter Eighteen

Shadow on the Walls

My first thought was that my eyelids had been glued. I tried to open them but they resisted me. Then I accepted the fact that my lids were just too heavy. It was all too much of an effort. One's mind does exhibit strange quirks. I knew not where I was or how long I was slated to be anywhere, and at this low point of my existence I suddenly as though guided by a mystical power found myself following the path of logic. It was all wrong. Everything was wrong, and it had been from the beginning. Not our being taken by Chu San Fu, but before that.

The coming of the now-dead agent, Cruthers, to our chambers had been the beginning, of course, and his mention of the name of our arch-enemy had been the first alert. The additional information supplied by Mycroft Holmes had sketched the outlines on the canvas of the case, and then Deets's appearance at our door had added revealing brush strokes. Holmes, with his usual brilliance, had joined the two cases into one, but from that point it was as though we had been led by the noses. He had anticipated the taking of the Sacred Sword but, to my astonishment, had allowed the theft to be committed, and now this religious relic was in the hands of the enemy.

We had preceded Chu San Fu to Venice but had allowed him to depart from the Jewel of the Adriatic with his accomplice, Memory Max, whilst we followed a will-of-the-wisp to Berlin. Holmes had outdone himself again by deducing the unknown grave in the Valley of the Kings, and we had routed Chu's henchmen guarding the place. But again we had vacated the field, none the better, as far as I could see, for our triumph. Holmes had indicated on the train back from Luxor that he had finally secured whatever information he had been seeking but, upon our return, had not availed himself of the considerable forces at his beck and call but had instead taken off with none but me at his side, walking full tilt into a trap. Was this the work of he who was hailed as the finest mind in England?

The Anglo-Saxon has been accused of insatiable curiosity and sometimes of flights of fancy, but at this moment it was the practicality inherited from my staunch forebearers that intruded itself forcibly on my thoughts.

Watson, I thought, you are naught but Boobus Brittanicus. For years, your claim to fame has been that of biographer, and has your inimitable friend ever let you down? It is he who is the master of logic, not you. If, as Holmes has generously stated, it has been your faith that has spurred him on then stand fast. Remember Wellington's men at Waterloo. What of Nelson's sailors at Trafalgar? Did they lack faith as that immortal sea-dog got himself shot to ribbons on the road to glory? Stand fast!

My eyes opened in more ways than one. I was lying on a pallet and looking at the slats of what was evidently a bed above me. It was a double bunk, singularly an arrangement much-used on a man-of-war. Aside from a slight giddiness, my principal feeling was that of guilt at the path my thoughts had been following. Logic, indeed! I had been drugged in some manner and had been suffering mental aberrations as an aftereffect. Any doctor could diagnose that.

With a groan I swung my feet to the floor and assumed a sitting position.

"Ah, Watson, you have rejoined the land of the living."

How welcome were the familiar tones of my friend, and my bleary eyes located him beside a barred window that, along with a door mounted on metal hasps, seemed the only openings to the limited area that surrounded us.

"Where are we, Holmes?"

"In a cell, considerably removed from the ground level."

As he spoke, Holmes was actively engaged in some manner at the window, and I stumbled to my feet to lend what assistance I could.

"Rest easy, ol' friend, until you regain your equilibrium," said the sleuth.

He had a piece of timber between two of the bars and was using it as a lever. There was a strained sound to his voice, and the muscles of his arms and shoulders were tight under his jacket. I well recalled that day in '83 when my friend had straightened out the steel poker, bent into a curve by the villainous Grimesby Roylott, with one sudden effort. I knew the strength he was exerting. Suddenly, he relaxed with a smile.

"This is an ancient structure and I sense that I'm making some progress with these bars. But a moment, Watson, and we shall try together."

"Where did you—?"

"One of the slats on the bed," he replied, anticipating my question and gesturing with the wooden piece in his hand. "Whereas the passage of years decreases the strength of masonry, seasoning increases that of wood. I judge this slat has supported the backs of many prisoners in years long gone."

I was looking out of the window now and could see that we were four stories up, at the top of the building. I noted Holmes's scarf attached to one of the bars and saw that it fluttered limply in the occasional wind that fanned our place of captivity. Suddenly my eyes blurred, and I had to rub them for a moment and shake my head before they came back into focus.

"When I saw Chu San Fu and his infernal phial of crystals, I was able to gasp some untainted air and did not receive the full shock of the gas he subjected us to," explained Holmes.

"What did the beggar use?"

"Haven't the faintest. The Chinese are an ancient race, and I imagine they have a few tricks that our pharmacies, for all their modern developments, might find of interest. Our laboratories as well."

Holmes was rubbing his thin, amazingly strong arms,

and his manner, to anyone not used to his calm acceptance of adversity, would have been infuriating. I found it reassuring.

"Look here, if you think we can budge one of those bars, I'm ready for action. But considering our height from the ground, it seems like labor lost."

"A possible exit of any kind could be helpful. Here, ol' chap, let us give it a go."

I was able to position my hands over Holmes's and we put our backs to it. I could feel the iron bar shifting slightly. Then the veins in my friend's forehead stood out for a brief moment, and there was a grating sound.

"Enough, Watson. We have it!"

I was puffing and gasping, but the lower part of one bar was disengaged from its long resting place and was free. A moment more and Holmes had the top of the round metal piece loose as well and was hefting it in his hand.

"Iron is a formidable weapon. The age of copper and brass was the golden one for Egypt. When the Hittites appeared with iron weapons, the great decline set in."

"You have some plan for our escape?"

"At the moment, no. Our incarceration came as a surprise. I was counting on Chu San Fu's overweening ego to keep us on the scene if only to tell us how clever he is."

"Then you expected to be captured?"

"Always a possibility, Watson. One that occurred to you as well, but you followed my misguided footsteps nonetheless. Dear, loyal friend."

For a brief moment Holmes regarded me with that half-smile that in others might have seemed supercilious, but I divined his thoughts and was deeply touched by them.

"Well," I said with buoyed spirits, "if we can remove one bar, two should not be beyond our capabilities."

But it took us another five minutes, and hard labor it was before we had the second bar out of the window.

"What now?" I asked, taking in deep breaths of air.

"We would need wings to go out the window, so we have little choice but to await what fate has in store for us. However, it is not such a terrible situation. Obviously, Chu had us removed to this cell because other matters claimed his undivided attention. I suspect that sooner or later he

214

will order us brought to his presence to gloat a bit before he gives his henchmen the high sign to do us in. The Chinaman has all the instincts of an Oriental despot and, if born in another time, would wish himself to be no less than a Mandarin."

Holmes indicated the door to our cubicle. "You will note the barred grate, Watson. I tested that while you were still unconscious. Should a guard drop by to check on our behaviour, I've a thought in mind. You might be attempting to maneuver your way through the window. If he were to enter to prevent an escape and I were behind the door, I could certainly cosh him with one of these iron bars."

I was gazing at him in astonishment, entranced by the ingenious escape plan that he had rattled off in his matter-of-fact manner. Then he shook his head.

"It's a thin reed, Watson, forced on me by the chill wind of desperation."

"But why? Sounds like a capital idea to me."

"If the man or men have any sense, they will not enter this cell without both of us plainly visible. Possibly Chu San Fu is served by idiots, but I doubt it. Like calls to like."

"That went past me, Holmes."

"The Chinaman has rallied the remnants of his once considerable underworld empire in this last-ditch effort. He must be using a considerable amount of what we might call 'local talent.' I'll wager that from the bazaars and low haunts of Cairo he has secured the most accomplished of the scoundrels at hand. Possibly my scheme should be abandoned in the hopes that we will be taken to Chu and can wreak some havoc in the ranks of the ungodly then."

As my friend mused, I had crossed to the door and was peering out of the narrow grating into the dark corridor beyond. I never did learn if Holmes decided to try his scheme or not, for suddenly there was a voice. It was close; it did not come from the corridor; and I wheeled round as though I had received an arrow in my posterior, half expecting to find some form that had materialized in our cell. But there was only Holmes, and I must say he looked as amazed as I felt.

"Holmes . . . you iss in der? *Nicht war?*" The voice

was low in tone, almost a whisper, but its timbre gave it a carrying quality. Wildly, I looked round the cell for some flue or vent but could locate none.

"Come *verrunter* und help me get into dis here place."

My friend had sprung to his feet and rushed to the window. As I followed in his wake, he cautioned me back.

"Watch the door, Watson. An intrusion at this time would be inconvenient."

I obeyed him promptly, my mind in a whirl. The voice came from outside the window. Holmes had said we couldn't get out of there without wings. How then could anyone get in? I stole a quick glance from my station at the grate and saw Holmes pulling a thin, wiry form through the opening. There was something strange about his appearance, and for the moment I could not divine what it was. But help was at hand, and with considerable effort I forced myself to gaze into the corridor and listen intently so that I could warn Holmes if anyone approached.

"How is it without, Watson?"

"No sign of light. No sound either."

"Then I guess we're safe for the moment."

Whether Holmes meant that I could abandon my post or not I did not know, but I could not help returning to the center of the room, such was my curiosity regarding this most unusual happening.

Our visitor was removing strange-looking, rubberized objects that were attached to his hands with a glove arrangement. I noted that there were similar devices on both knees and on his feet as well.

"Who are you, sir?" I stammered.

"Zo, who else could climb up here—four flights and flat as a *fancuchen*! Pretty goot job if I zay zo myself."

"Shadow Schadie," exclaimed Holmes, and his smile was half mirth and half admiration. "The only man who can walk up walls."

"Vell, maybe not der only vun, but der only vun in Cairo."

"But what are you doing in Egypt?" I heard the words but didn't realize I was saying them, I was so amazed.

"It's der payoff," was Schadie's reply as though he were discussing the price of a mutton chop. "You go to der

216

clinker und you see mine son und I don't know vat you say to him but der vord iss oudt. He iss gonna be all right up here in der noggin."

The famous thief was tapping his forehead and there was the light of excitement in his deepset brown eyes.

"Dey iss stickin' him in der booby hatch because he ain't got all his stuff upstairs put now he iss makin' big recovery. Dose doctors, dey don't know vat to dink, but dey iss lettin' him oudt from der nut farm."

"I wondered about that," said Holmes. "Then Heinrich Hublein is your son."

"Vot kinda detectiff iss you? You should haf known dat right along. Shadow Schadie is der only man vot can valk up valls. Zo you dink some clunker iss comin' along vat can do it? Nein, he iss mine son. It's in der genes. Dot's how he done it."

Such was the conviction and intensity of the thief's words that he did set me back on my heels, but then he paused for a moment and continued in a more reasonable tone.

"But I vill tell you diss. Vork hard he must haf to master der technique. Dis kinda t'ing, it iss not zimple."

"Well," said Holmes, and his calm acceptance of this strange story did grate on my nerves a bit. "I'm delighted to learn that your son has regained his sanity, but that still doesn't explain your opportune presence in Cairo."

Schadie regarded him suspiciously. "You iss Sherlock Holmes, no?"

The sleuth's upraised palm halted more words from the German. "Wait! You told me—the payoff. Inasmuch as young Heinrich is now sane, you feel an obligation to Doctor Watson and myself and followed us to Cairo."

"Now dat's der kind off deductions vot I'm expecting from you." There was a glint of humor in the second-story man's eyes.

"Then I'll attempt one more. It was you who followed Doctor Watson when he visited the native quarter before. In a dark alley, not far removed from this place, you sandbagged a giant Manchurian who had captured him."

"About Manchurians I don't know. But he vas a big fellow undt he vas a Chink."

217

"Holmes, how did you ever figure that out?" I blurted.

"Oh, come now, Watson. Who ever heard of flower pots in Cairo? You know we can carry this lucky star thing of yours just so far."

I did bridle a bit, I must confess. "That's all very well, Holmes, and we've had a nice discussion, but how are we going to get out of here? Mr. Schadie may be able to walk up walls, but I don't think he can walk through that door there."

"Dot's a fact," admitted the German.

"Now there is good reason to feel the plan we discussed will work, Watson. The advent of our welcome ally here will allow both of us to be in view and seemingly harmless."

Suddenly the sleuth tensed and his head cocked to one side in the familiar manner that indicated his abnormally acute sense of hearing was at work.

"Quick," he whispered, "over by the window, Watson."

I understood his intent immediately. From the window I would be in full view of anyone looking in through the grate in the door. Also, my form would conceal the fact that the bars had been removed. As I crossed to the aperture, Holmes handed one of the iron bars to Shadow Schadie and indicated, in dumb show, for the German to stand where the open door would conceal him. Evidently he did not have to signal Schadie what to do with the bar at his disposal.

In another moment, Holmes had joined me by the window.

"Rather glad I fastened this neckpiece since it signalled our cell to Schadie," he said in a calm voice, his dexterous fingers unknotting the material, which he placed in a coat pocket. I could hear the footsteps that had alerted Holmes plainly, and then a face peered through the grate. Whoever it was played a lantern through the opening and into the room, and its rays rapidly found the both of us by the window. There was an exchange of Arabic from without, and then the sound of a key in the lock. The lantern remained trained on us unwaveringly. The door was opened with confidence, and the man with the lantern entered first.

After him came another Arabian with an ominous-looking Mauser automatic that he held with a familiar air.

I was surprised to see one of his race with a handgun since cold steel is their most natural weapon, but Holmes had said that Chu would have recruited the most proficient of the ruffians available.

As the man with the gun gestured towards us, Holmes stepped forward as though to speak, and suddenly his right foot came up. The toe of his shoe caught the wrist of the Arab, and the Mauser spun into the air. There was a clunk in the background, and the lamp fell to the floor followed by a body. The gunman's mouth opened, but before he could utter a cry of pain or alarm, there was another soft clunk and his eyes rolled as he fell like a wet sack of grain, joining his comrade on the hard floor.

It had been but the work of a moment and the resultant sounds had been inconsequential. The door was open, our guards were unconscious, and we were free.

Holmes retrieved the lamp from the floor with a sweep of his arm, and then he had the Mauser as well.

"We're going down, Schadie. This place is crawling with Chu San Fu's people. I think we can consider your payoff as made in full, so if you want to leave the way you came, why not?"

"I could do dot," replied Schadie. "But dot dere iss a Cherman gun vot you got, undt I know how to use it."

Holmes tossed the Mauser to the thief, who caught it effortlessly. "You are so good at following people, best to lag behind. If Watson and I are apprehended, they won't be looking for a third man."

"Zo—I'm der ace up der hole. Vell, ve giff it a try."

Chapter Nineteen

The Clash of Two Minds

One has to become acclimated to rapidly changing situations when associated with the world's greatest detective. While I accompanied Holmes down the dark corridor outside our former cell, my brain spinning like a child's top, I was able to retain a grip on reality by virtue of the fact that positions had been switched in a similar manner in past cases as well. Only a few moments before, we had been the imprisoned ones, and now it seemed we were cast in the role of the stalkers.

Holmes had kept the lamp, and its illumination guided us to a flight of stairs leading downward. Nowhere were there light fixtures or furnishings, and the building was but a deserted shell that housed the apparatus of Chu San Fu.

"What exactly are we doing, Holmes?" I queried in a soft whisper not only inspired by a desire for secrecy but by our stark surroundings as well.

"Searching for confirmation. Since a metalworker requires heat, I feel that will be available in the furnace area of this extensive ruin."

Holmes did not elaborate on this thought and as we progressed downward, our ears attuned to any sound, it hardly seemed the time to badger him. The myriad questions that fluttered through my mind like aimless butterflies could remain unanswered for the moment. My principal concern was some means of removing ourselves from the crumbling walls of masonry that surrounded us, pro-

221

ducing much the same depressing sensation that I had suffered through within the great pyramid.

Shadow Schadie must have been following in our wake, though no sight or sound served as a clue to his presence.

It occurred to me that if this ruin was teeming with the followers of the Oriental master-criminal, we were marching round in a most free and open manner. As though to confirm this thought, when we rounded a corner leading to the second landing, Holmes and I found ourselves face to face with a pair of villainous-looking Arabians.

Holmes immediately began speaking, quite loudly, in the fluent German that, along with other languages, he had mastered during his boyhood travels on the Continent: "These words are for your ears, Schadie. We are facing two more Arabs, no doubt looking for the other two in the cell. Delay them by all means, ol' chap."

With a half-gesture, Holmes acknowledged the presence of the Arabs who were gazing at us in surprise and then shouldered past them, leading me by the elbow.

I noted one of the Arabians shrug at the other, and then they continued up the stairs we had just vacated. As they disappeared, I let out a deep sigh.

"What, by all that is holy, did you do, Holmes? Hypnotize them?"

"Merely assumed that this is a multilingual establishment, Watson. A potpourri of dissidents, opportunists, and mercenaries of crime, not all known to each other. Those Arabs are looking for our two guards who have not returned, and I instructed Schadie to dispose of them."

"Rather imagine he will. Seems like an efficient chap though he was critical of your methods, Holmes."

"We shall not take umbrage at Mr. Schadie's manner, Watson. After all, he can walk up walls and did so in our behalf."

There were now sounds, previously inaudible, in this rambling wreck of a place. They were not distinguishable but merely joined forces with the feel of people present somewhere. One in particular remained constant, and it was towards this that Holmes directed our footsteps.

"Internal combustion engine of some sort, Watson. From the narrow stairwell and the lack of traffic, I would say we are descending the back stairs, which should lead to the area that we seek."

It did so somewhat faster than I anticipated, though we did not encounter any more stray members of the criminal conspiracy that we were in the middle of, and unarmed at that. With the thought that Schadie might be occupied elsewhere with the disposal of the two ruffians we had met on the stairs, I felt the lack of a backup person in this mad adventure. I was casting a worried glance over my shoulder when I felt Holmes tense at my side. In front of us loomed a door, and there was a definite indication of light on the far side. Holmes extinguished the lamp that had guided us, and we made for the portal.

It proved unlocked. Holmes eased the door open, and the first thing I saw was an iron railing. Peering over the sleuth's shoulder, I could see a large room with its floor at a lower level. Now the cyclical sound of an engine was quite apparent. This had to be the boiler room of the building, and the door through which we peered opened on a narrow catwalk running its length. I assumed that further on there was a flight of iron stairs leading to the basement level. What captured my eyes was a number of men busily engaged in some process, the purpose of which I could not divine.

In the center of the sizable area was a table, much like that of a draftsman, and seated by it on a high stool was a tall man of advanced years. He was peering with a hand glass at a gleaming object that I estimated was four feet in length and at least two and a half feet wide. The basement chamber was brightly lit and the tablet, for such it was, glistened. Its reflected light was that which, through the centuries, has driven men to prodigious efforts and to deeds that promote a shudder. It was the yellow gleam of gold that has fired the furnaces of greed throughout history. But the tablet, whose worth in rare metal must have been enormous, seemed of no concern to the man at the table. He was studying the inscriptions that covered it and referring to a number of photographs spread out on the table along with several lithographs.

"Memory Max," whispered Holmes. "Possibly it was his name that led me down the wrong trail. I recalled his fame as one of those rare photographic-memory types and did not consider relevant that he was also a master forger."

Holmes's words would not have been audible five feet from where we were standing. Perhaps it was a subconscious recognition of the fact that his name had been used that caused the man at the table in the basement to suddenly raise his head, and then, to my horror, he turned and was looking straight at us. The light of the large room penetrated through the half-open door that was our observation post, and I saw Memory Max suddenly spring to his feet in alarm, his mouth opening to sound a warning.

Holmes closed the door quickly, seizing me by the arm and propelling me back along the corridor that we had traversed.

"We were spotted, Watson, worse luck. But all is not lost. Let us strategically make ourselves known of our own volition."

We were rushing towards the front of the building. Then it dawned on me what Holmes intended to do.

"Good Lord, you are not just going to brazenly burst in on Chu, are you? Let us take to our heels, Holmes."

"We're outnumbered and surrounded, ol' fellow. When all is lost, attack! A theory that you used quite effectively in your adventure with Loo Chan, if you will recall."

Holmes had me there. I had blundered in on the Chinese lawyer and created enough surprise and consternation to bluff myself out of a messy corner. Possibly it would work again, though I sensed that Holmes was motivated by another and deeper purpose.

We were in a wide hall now that seemed to run the length of the building, and through open doors several men registered on our pell-mell rush past them. I did not take time to note their appearance or nationality.

Then we were in the main room of what had to have once been a government building. It was two stories in height and seemed too imposing for a common jail, but perhaps that was a function assumed by the edifice later in its varied history. It was brightly lit. The tall windows that stretched along the front wall of the building were all cunningly covered by a feltlike material that provided an effective blackout. In direct contrast to the building's abandoned appearance, this place seemed as populated as St. Pancreas or Waterloo Station. The whole busy scene was dominated by a huge chair on an upraised section of the floor in which sat the bewhiskered Chu San Fu.

"Well," I thought, "he's come as close to a throne as he could. Or would," was my second thought, for I was betting on Sherlock Holmes.

Our sudden entrance caused a universal cessation of activity, and this core of Chu's criminal conspiracy became as silent as a pharaoh's ancient tomb.

"We are delighted to drop in on you again, Chu San Fu," said Holmes in his most casual manner.

As he advanced towards the several steps leading up to the Chinaman's elevated position, I could do naught but follow and hope that I seemed as unconcerned as my friend did.

The Oriental's amber eyes shifted quickly to the door through which we had come.

"Where are your guards?" said Chu San Fu. There was a flicker of worry in his eyes.

"Disposed of, but let's not dwell on that. We had to come face to face. That was your intent all along so that you could inform me that, at the last cast of the dice, it was you who had scored the winning point. Well, I am the bearer of sad tidings. It is all over. It's not going to work at all."

I am sure that better than half the men in the room didn't understand a word Holmes was saying and the rest couldn't divine what he was getting at. But such was the conviction of his manner, so bright was the triumphant light in his commanding eyes, that they remained motionless, transfixed, as was I for that matter. A room populated by the dregs of the underworlds of half a dozen nations was suddenly dominated by two personalities. The rest of us might as well have been pieces of furniture. The resolution of this monstrous matter now rested in the clash of two minds, and every man jack of us knew it. The whole affair was reduced to its basic elements. The evil genius of the crime czar, Chu San Fu, and the brilliance of my friend, Sherlock Holmes.

Chu's frail and aged form seemed to have shrunk within

the ornamental Chinese robe that he wore, but this was but the reaction of a moment. Then his lips twisted in an evil smile as he realized again his position of strength.

"You speak bold words, Holmes, for a man in the clutches of his sworn enemy."

"You know me well enough to realize they are not idle ones. I'll give you high marks, Chu, for not fearing the devil himself. Had I, some time back, outlined your plan and its scope, I would have been laughed out of Whitehall and Scotland Yard as well. The very grandiosity of your scheme lent it a protective cover, for it savored of the dreams of a madman."

"There have been other so-called madmen," replied the Oriental stroking his long white chin whiskers, separated into two strands as was his custom. Holmes dismissed his words with an imperious wave of his hand.

"Spare us the recitation of conquerors like Genghis Khan and Napoleon, for that monologue has been oft-used. You are making ready for your revelation at the Mosque of al-Ashar."

I had been waiting for it and rejoiced in the viewing. It came as I knew it would. That sudden stab of fear in the closely guarded eyes of the Oriental.

"You know of that?" he asked, and there was a quaver in his voice.

"I know of it all. The tomb is now covered, and the entrance to the Valley of the Kings is guarded by an army detachment."

Chu San Fu sprang to his feet instinctively and then sank back into his imposing chair, steeling himself to recover his control and his dignity. Holmes had often said that the grip of a criminal on his underlings was in large part psychological, and the Chinaman was aware of this as well.

"How did you find the tomb?" he asked in a flat tone.

"Followed the trail that led you to it," was Holmes's glib response. "No difficulty there, but I will admit that the golden tablets and the great store you placed in them threw me off a bit. However, a remark by my associate, Watson, brought me back on target."

"How much do you actually know?" Chu's query was

delivered without any show of emotion. Centuries of Oriental stoicism had taken charge, and his face was now as impassive as a sheet of burnished bronze. I also suspected that for the first time he was actually considering the possibility of defeat.

"I don't know," said Holmes, "how long you have nurtured this scheme, nor is it important. You took a series of facts and had the imagination to fuse them into a unity—your plan being to rewrite history. Events dealt you a nice set of cards. First, you had a basic truth. This Nile Valley is the origin of recorded history, and no one will deny it. There are myths and folklore about other civilizations, but they left no mark of their passage nor monuments of their greatness that can predate this birthplace of civilization. All that comes from ancient Egypt is marked first in the book of man. That was the base of the power pyramid that you strove to create."

"The next fact you seized upon was the pharaoh Akhenaten's attempt to establish a utopia at Tell el-Amarna built round a one-god religion, long before Christianity, of course. Possibly that is what sparked the idea in your mind."

Chu San Fu gave no indication one way or another but simply gestured for Holmes to continue. I could not decipher his emotions at this point.

"Many knew or suspected that the Sacred Sword had been placed in the hands of Captain Spaulding as a safeguard against a fanatical religious uprising, and you decided to secure it as your opening gun. By spreading the word throughout the Mohammedan world that you will appear with the fabled sword, you have drawn an audience of religious leaders, but the sword is only the beginning.

"It was the decoding of the secret writings by Howard Andrade that opened the road to authenticity. It gave you the cloak to conceal the mark of the charlatan. No one but Andrade has been able to decipher those obscure symbols. You have two of the golden tablets, and it is known that they provide examples of the writings, another fact that you planned to use to your advantage.

"You planted Memory Max with the Englishman, depending on his photographic memory to record the key to

227

Andrade's discovery. Then you spirited Max here with the tablets to remove the original hieroglyphics and forge a new message upon them. Little is known of the pharaoh Akhenaten. The Egyptians attempted to obliterate him from their written history. But you plan to write that history to suit your purpose. In your version, duly forged on the golden tablets, the god Aton, espoused by Akhenaten, will bear a striking resemblance to the Allah of Mohammed. Akhenaten will be recorded as the first prophet, making Mohammed the second, and it will be foretold that the third prophet will come from the east, bearing the sword of he who preceded him.

"You hope to shake a widespread religion to its core. Especially since the golden tablets will be found within the only unrifled tomb of a pharaoh as yet discovered. Your thought was to plant them within the tomb, of course, then have the royal grave covered and its location revealed by you in a vision before the gathering of Moslems in the mosque. Once the tomb is found and the tablets discovered, the world of archaeology will see to it that Andrade is summoned to translate them, which he will eagerly do, being an unsuspecting tool. The whole fabrication will defy doubt—the tablets being genuine, the tomb as well, and the message of the coming of the third prophet being revealed by an unimpeachable source. Really, the detail of the plot is admirable. However, it won't work now."

Chu San Fu had been watching Holmes with unmoving eyes. Several times there had been a restless shifting among his followers, who formed the mute audience for Holmes's re-creation, but the Oriental had halted them with a slight gesture of one of his thin and bony hands. Now he replied in a businesslike voice, much more chilling to me than an emotional outburst, since it indicated that his first-class brain was still working efficiently and had not given way to panic or frustration.

"You have blunted my capabilities, Holmes, but not destroyed them. The tomb idea was a major part of my plan, but it can be abandoned. The golden tablets can be discovered in some other manner, though not as convincingly, that I'll admit."

Holmes was shaking his head. "Come now, you intend

to appear as the rumored messiah. You cannot pass your-self off as anything but Chinese. Mohammedanism spread as far as India but no further east, so that is one mark against you immediately."

"Holmes, you are thinking hopefully, not rationally. Prophets spring from faith, not countries. The man who has the Sacred Sword is the one who will grasp their attention. When I appear and it is verified that I have the authentic sword of Mohammed, then all the various sects of the Islamic religion will be prepared to listen and to accept."

"I must agree," was Holmes's surprising response. "I suspected some time ago that the sword was vital to your plans, though I had but a dim idea of what you were up to. Therefore, Watson and I were observers the night your men stole it from the Mayswood farm."

Chu San Fu's restored confidence received a jarring blow from this revelation.

"Doctor Watson was within the house, that I know, but you were not there."

"Correction. I was. You used four men. They came in over the balcony to the secret room they already knew about. They placed the sword aboard the early freight to London and from there it was taken to the hold of the Hishouri Kamu to be transported here."

Each statement from Holmes was like a body blow to the Oriental. His calmness was a departed thing, and his jaw hung loosely.

"If you knew all that—"

"Now it is beginning to dawn, is it not? Do you think I would have let you take that sword and the commanding position that it would bring to you? Two nights before you raided the Mayswood Farm, my men performed the same function. They took the real relic and left a duplicate in its place."

I believe I was as astonished as the Chinaman. Chu sprang to his feet, crossing to a small table adjacent to his chair on which was a teak case fully five feet long. As he feverishly opened it, I realized why Slim Gilligan and Slippery Styles had been down country before my arrival. Holmes had been one step ahead of his adversary all along.

It was Chu San Fu who had been led by the nose and down the path of deception.

Chu was removing a curved weapon, more of a scimitar I would have said, from the teak case. Its hilt was festooned with shiny stones, and it certainly was an impressive object.

"Regard the jewels in the handle," suggested Holmes. "It's a nice job, for three deft but dishonest men worked better than twenty-four hours without stop to create it. But the jewels are glass, Chu. The Mohammedans who will inspect that relic are not without knowledge, and they will label it as spurious in short order."

"No!" cried Chu San Fu, and in his voice was the anguish of a thousand tears. "It cannot be!"

"Your eye tells you that it is, but your mind refuses to accept it."

Holmes's voice had that whiplash quality that I remembered from other times. His inexorable flow of facts, one hard on the heels of the other, had worn down his adversary, and it was now the man from Baker Street who held the upper hand.

"Your dreams of a unified Islam stretching from India to the Atlantic with you as its spiritual leader have, like the murky visions induced by an opium pipe, faded into nothingness. But you recoil and demand proof, so I will give it to you. The night is long upon us, but by now a special edition of the newspaper *Al-Ahram* is on the streets. It has picked up, from the Reuters' wire, a story already well circulated in England and elsewhere. The Sacred Sword of the prophet Mohammed was recently stolen from its hiding place but has been recovered through the efforts of a consulting detective named Sherlock Holmes and is in the hands of the British Government for safekeeping. Right now the story is spreading like wildfire throughout Cairo, and those religious leaders who responded to your siren song are making ready to return to their own lands. The show is over. The theatre is empty, and your drama has failed."

There was a nervous tick that evidenced itself on one side of Chu San Fu's mouth, and his eyes had a wild and frantic look about them that sent tingles down the short hairs on the back of my neck. Evidently Holmes noticed it too, for his next words were delivered in a calmer manner.

"You know I am right, but you still won't accept it. So be it. Just have one of your men secure a copy of the special edition and you will have proof."

Chu San Fu was breathing deeply, and by what means he signalled his wishes I could not see, but suddenly Holmes and I were seized by the men surrounding us and placed in two chairs. A dirty-looking Lascar proceeded to tie my hands and lash me to the chair, and I noted that one of the giant Manchurians was doing the same thing to Holmes. Another signal from Chu, and a ferret-faced half-breed made for the door.

By the main entrance was an obese Chinese who swung up a wooden bar that had nestled in two large metal "L" shapes firmly secured to the stout door. Peering through a peephole, the fat Oriental then unlocked it and the half-breed slipped through in search of a newspaper as suggested by Holmes. The round guardian of the gate then relocked the door and placed the wooden bar across it again. I judged that it would take an explosion to break that bar, and this thought was of little comfort. When Holmes's story was confirmed, what was our fate to be? Or had Chu already, in the back of his mind, thrown in the sponge? Possibly he was planning our end with considerable gusto even now. I cast a quick glance in the direction of the crime overlord but the Chinaman was back in his chair, his chin resting on a knotted fist, staring into space with unseeing eyes as though in deathly fear of what was to come. The other men in the room were exchanging information in soft tones and in a variety of tongues, and there was an aura of confusion as the whole group waited for the proof that Holmes had promised.

It seemed no time at all before there was a nervous tattoo on the outer door. The rotund Chinaman swung the bar from its sockets and began to unlock the door when inbred caution caused him to glance through the peephold. Suddenly he twisted the key back to the lock position just as the brass-studded wooden barrier swayed from a thunderous blow that sent the Chinaman reeling. He lunged forward again when there was another tremendous crash

231

and the door was sprung from its hinges and propelled vertically back into the room, taking its guardian right along with it. Behind the wall of wood was Tiny with his perennial grin and baby face, and a welcome sight he was. Close by the squat colossus was Burlington Bertie with a short billy club swinging from his right hand.

Still holding the door, which must have weighed better than seven stone, Tiny extended his arms and the fat Chinaman flew to one side, hitting the wall with a resounding crash. Then the door was over Tiny's head and he launched it into the crowd of men in the room like a projectile. There were screams as the object felled at least three, possibly more. The two giant Manchurians, unlike the rest of the ruffians, were not frozen in their tracks, for they were bred for conflict.

The first one was headed for Tiny in a trice, aiming a massive blow at the boy's head. Tiny's open palm caught the Manchurian's fist in midair, and then his hand closed and there was a crunch of broken bone as Tiny's other hand caught the wrestler under his chin. Suddenly the Oriental strong man was in the air, and Tiny swung in a full circle and let go, allowing a tangle of arms and legs to spin through the air before crashing to the floor and taking two other scoundrels with it. The Manchurian's brother had rushed Burlington Bertie but never reached him for the Cockney tangled up his legs with an artful foot. As the second bodyguard collided with the floor, Bertie's billy club swung in a short arc and there was a sound like an axe making contact with a ripe melon and the second Manchurian was skidding towards the now open door with blood pouring from his mouth.

The attack had been so sudden and violent that I could not keep track of events. The room was a frenzy of screams and groans, with some trying to retreat before the onslaught of the lads from London. Chu San Fu had been petrified, like the others, for a moment. Now he was on his feet. The wild look in his eyes was akin to that of a drug-inflamed dervish as he scrambled to the teak box to secure the sword that he had considered his passport to a life of greatness.

I was trying to gain my feet, a difficult task when tied to

a chair. I noted that Holmes's chair had been tipped over in the melée and my friend was attempting to bring himself upright on his knees. By now, Chu San Fu had the sword in his hands. I knew that he intended to take the cause of his downfall with him in this final conflict. Out of the corner of my eye I saw one of the felt curtains that shrouded a great window fall of a sudden into the room. There was a crash of glass, and then a body was fighting itself clear of the blackout material. Chu was headed for Holmes, the sword swinging from his scrawny arms, when there was a blast of sound. I felt the wind of a high-velocity bullet that flashed past my face. Suddenly the sword in Chu San Fu's hand disappeared and I realized that the Mauser bullet had caught the weapon at its broadest part and shattered the blade. Chu staggered back, still holding the ornamental hilt. There was a thin sliver of steel left, a mere fragment of the former weapon but still deadly. The wild-eyed Oriental recognized this fact and made for my hapless friend as I screamed a warning and tried to push myself in his path. Then, out from the tangle of blackout material sprang Wakefield Orloff, that deadly steel-rimmed hat in his hand. His quick eyes and uncanny reflexes seized the situation at a glance. One amazing wrist flipped in what seemed almost a casual gesture, and his hat was spinning through the air. The rigid brim caught Chu San Fu on the back of the head, causing a crunching sound. The Oriental's body was toppled by the impact, and he fell right on top of what was left of the counterfeit sword. There was a grunt, then a convulsive shudder, and a sliver of steel slid up through the back of the now late criminal mastermind. The sword had proven to be his passport to another world.

The charge of Tiny and Burlington Bertie, augmented by Orloff, was too much for those left standing, and men were fighting each other in their attempts to escape towards the rear of the house—anything to remove themselves from those awesome instruments of vengeance that had descended upon them. Orloff was beside Holmes, his throwing knife severing the bounds that secured the great detective, and a moment later he had me freed as well. Then there came a back-up of thoroughly cowed criminals who had run headlong into a police squad that had entered through the rear of the building. I saw more uniforms at the front door and realized that the battle was over and the field was ours.

In the confusion of captured criminals, police, and elements of the army, I searched vainly for Shadow Schadie, for I had not forgotten the Mauser bullet that had nearly creased me but had stopped Chu San Fu's fatal mission for that magic moment before Orloff went into action. But Schadie had simply disappeared, not so strange for one who could walk up a wall.

Chapter Twenty

Aftermath

Dawn was not far removed when we were finally able to enjoy a quiet moment back in our suite at Shepheard's Hotel. The remnants of Chu San Fu's organization were incarcerated, and certain cables had been dispatched to London. Colonel Gray, at Holmes's orders, had been placed in charge of the windup of the affair and had shielded us from numerous congratulations from the army and civilian authorities. It was generally accepted that the crisis was over, and we had been able to drag ourselves from the area of decision making.

Tiny and Burlington Bertie were snoring lustily in an adjacent room as Orloff joined Holmes and myself for a libation. Though I usually did the honors, on this occasion it was the sleuth who presided over the bottles. It was mighty comforting to sit at peace with the world for a change with a brandy and soda in my hand.

Holmes and I had carefully refrained from making mention of Orloff's crashing through the window of Chu's headquarters and his split-second rescue of my friend and possibly myself as well. This would have but embarrassed him. There were still matters of policy, and Orloff posed them promptly.

"What of the tomb in the Valley of the Kings?"

"That whole matter is best suppressed," stated Holmes quickly. "The boiling pot has subsided, and if we wish to keep it that way, let us have no sensational discoveries or anything else to draw attention to this area for the moment."

Orloff nodded. "Gray's men circulated the rumor of the false prophet quite well, and now that Chu San Fu will just disappear, the whole furor will die down."

"Well, of course," I interjected, "the story in the newspaper should have disposed of it already. The sword being in England and—"

I allowed my voice to dwindle to a stop, for both of my companions were regarding me strangely and possibly with a suggestion of mirth.

"Good fellow," said Sherlock Holmes, "do always believe me. However, I must confess that there was no story in the *Al-Ahram* or any other paper. As far as we are concerned there is no Sacred Sword. My tall tale was simply a ruse to have Chu dispatch one of his men outside the building. This was the prearranged signal for Tiny and Bertie and Orloff here to hit the place, backed up by the locals. I realized that we might be in a tight spot and wanted our lads on the scene first should a rescue be required. A good thing I did."

The truth was finally seeping through my lethargic brain. "We were followed from the hotel then."

Holmes nodded. "And not just by Shadow Schadie. It was, to use the jargon of the American underworld, 'a loose tail.' We made ourselves available in the area where I suspected that Chu San Fu was hidden and let whatever was to happen, happen. Once Orloff knew where we had ended up, he moved in with the reinforcements."

"And waited for the appearance of one of Chu's men before rushing the building."

"Exactly. There were holes in the plan, but it was the best I could come up with. Obviously, you felt I was courting capture, Watson, and you were right. Chu had to be disposed of in some manner. That he went by his own hand proved convenient."

I did not choose to comment on this. The Oriental had fallen on the remnants of the sword and had been skewed by it, but I had heard the sound of Orloff's reinforced hat when it hit the man. Possibly he was dead before he reached the floor. But such conjecture served no purpose, and I dismissed it from my mind.

"Then it's back to London?" asked Orloff.

"By way of Berlin," replied Holmes, to my astonishment. "I have a little duty to perform there, and Gray is giving me a hand."

Holmes had risen from his chair and was looking out the window towards the street and the star-studded Egyptian sky just now tinted with the first rosy hue of the coming day.

While I was digesting this new idea, Orloff returned to a subject he had mentioned previously.

"There's liable to be another offer of knighthood. Will you accept this time?"

"Little chance. I rather fancy I ruffled some feelings with my first refusal. In any case, I have already been amply rewarded for this singular adventure."

I was about to question Holmes regarding this when he turned towards Orloff and me suddenly.

"You know, it was the scheme of a Mad Hatter, but it would have worked."

"Oh come now, Holmes," I remonstrated automatically.

"You have been too close to it, ol' fellow. Never mind your thoughts. What of the dockworker in London, the tailor in Paris, the German baker and their cousins everywhere? They read of the discovery of an unknown tomb, the first of its kind ever revealed to the eyes of modern man. The seals on the inner door are as they were when the crypt was closed over three thousand years ago, and inside are the golden tablets with a new concept of the first prophet of Allah."

"How would Chu have worked that?" asked Orloff shrewdly.

"The inner door was of stone. Chu could have effected an opening and slid the tablets through into the interior of the tomb. I imagine that such an opening, not large enough for a man, could have been concealed readily enough. I tell you it would have shaken the foundations of more religions than that of Islam. You forget the spell that this strange land can weave. What of the man you mentioned, Watson,

Charles Piazzi Smythe of our century, not without impressive credentials? He was Astronomer Royal of Scotland, you know, and was absolutely convinced, and convinced untold others, that the measurements of the inside of the Great Pyramid foretold the entire history of the human race."

I suppressed a yawn and rose to my feet.

"Come now, Holmes, you've solved this problem, so let us not spend good time on might-have-beens. This adventure is over."

A Retrospection

I was wrong, for Holmes's adventures seldom end swiftly. Conclusions take a while, as they did in the tragic Birlstone matter and others that I could mention. Holmes and I did return to Baker Street by way of Berlin. In the German capital, the sleuth returned the two golden tablets to their legal owner, Herr Mannheim, the great collector. The industrialist got them back in their original form since Holmes, aided by Gray, had convinced Memory Max that he had best obliterate his forgeries and return the original secret writings to their surface. Holmes can be very persuasive when he's of a mind. Herr Mannheim decided to drop his charges against the misguided Heinrich Hublein and some six months later, due to the great influence of the steel tycoon, young Hublein was released from jail. As to whether he became reconciled with his father, Shadow Schadie, I do not know. Sometimes, in the dark of night, I shudder at the thought that Holmes and I might have loosed two men who could walk up walls on an unsuspecting public. But it did seem like the sporting thing to do at the time.

The final resolution to the case came round the time of Hublein's release. I was looking for our checkbook and, without thinking, opened the upper-left-hand drawer of the desk, which was usually locked for Holmes kept private papers within.

Right on the top was a sheet of notepaper carefully mounted between two pieces of glass. I observed that it was resting on what I assumed was the letter from Irene Adler. I had no intention of viewing Holmes's confidential mementoes, but I could not fail to recognize the paper and the ink-scrawled words upon it, for I knew them by heart.

Holmes: At the cry of the jackal, I shall attack from the rear with a detachment of light horse.

Yours for victory,
Watson.

Now I knew what Holmes meant when he said he had been amply rewarded for our singular adventure.

MORE BEST-SELLING MYSTERY AND SUSPENSE FROM PINNACLE

More Best-Selling Fiction from Pinnacle